The Cabin

JASINDA WILDER

The Cabin

Part One

An Icarus Love

One

NDA

"ALL RIGHT, MR. BELL. YOU'RE ALL SET HERE, I THINK." The nurse is that peculiar, unique brand of brusque efficiency and Zen-like kindness you only find in an oncology department. She fiddles with the IV line puncturing my left arm, the off-white, veiny medical tape securing it to my forearm. Her eyes are brown, the exact shade of a chocolate Labrador's fur. She is warm, and caring, but lurking beneath that veneer of caregiver kindness is the detached iciness of someone whose job it is to watch people die.

"It will take a couple hours for this to drip through, and then we have to monitor you for—"

"I know," I interrupt. I open the lid of my laptop. "I've been through this a few times."

She smiles. "Of course, Mr. Bell. If you need anything, just press the call button."

I hesitate a few seconds and then say, "There is something." Then I glance at the curtain which is not quite pulled shut.

She catches my meaning and brings the two ends of the curtain together, the metal rings rasping with a rattling ring. "What can I do for you, Mr. Bell?"

I reach into my messenger bag, sitting on the floor next to this monstrosity of a chair—a freakish, Frankensteinian thing, not quite a lounger and not quite a clinical, medical device, but something in between. It's made from a rubbery plastic or vinyl material that squeaks at every slight movement, and is too hard and too upright to be truly comfortable, but when you kick back in it and lift the footrest, it forces you into a near-horizontal recline in an unnatural defiance of gravity.

The chair is distracting, and I hate the chair almost as much as I hate the ward, the IV, and the whole damned morbid circus.

In my bag is a thin manila folder. On the label I've written three letters in neat block handwriting, in black Sharpie: NDA. I withdraw a single sheet of paper, on which are two and a half paragraphs, single-spaced. It's in tight, clear legalese, drawn up by my attorney, printed on formal, intimidating letterhead. I hand it to the nurse whose nametag, clipped to her pale green sleeve, announces her as Tiffany Snell, R.N, O.C.N.

"This is an NDA, a nondisclosure agreement."

She allows a frown, briefly. "Okay?"

I keep my voice low, not whispering, but pitched for her ears only. "I'm here alone, as I'm sure you've noticed."

"Yes. Which is why your observation period has to be so long."

"I know."

I reach into my bag and pull out a pen—it's a nice pen, hefty, metal, with a satisfying clicker, and on the side is my name: Adrian Bell, and my logo, a coat of arms with my monogram. It's recognizable to most people, that logo; you see it on the title page of my books, on my website, and expensively animated as a production company logo during the title sequences when you watch movies made from my books. I hand her the pen, tap the NDA with it.

"This says you will not disclose to *anyone* that I was here at all, let alone why. I'm paying for this with cash, so there's no insurance paperwork trail."

She frowns again as she reads. "Why is it a secret, may I ask?"

"I have my reasons," I say. "Whatever else must be done in the process of this infusion, I would like *you* to do, including observation and my eventual discharge. All right? This means that just one person has to sign this little item." I tap the NDA again.

"And if I don't sign it?" It's not meant belligerently, just…a simple question.

I smile. "Tiffany—Miss Snell. Do I really need to spell this out? You know who I am. I don't want this getting out. That's all. I'm protecting my privacy."

She breathes out gently—it's not a sigh, more of a

thoughtful breath. "What about your wife? Why isn't she here?"

It takes all I have to not wince at the question. "I'm going to have to decline to answer that, Miss Snell. Can you please just sign? It just means you don't tell anyone I was here. If coworkers ask, you simply say you can't talk about it. Don't make a big deal about it, just that—I can't talk about it. That's all." I pause, smile again. "Would it help you to know I'm a yearly donor to this facility?"

She rolls a shoulder. "Not really. I'm just a nurse." Another of those thoughtful out-breaths. "Mr. Bell, I'll sign your NDA. But I have to register my thoughts with you. Hiding this is not fair." Her warm brown eyes momentarily reveal the sadness she normally keeps hidden. "I've seen your file, obviously. What you're dealing with, it's…it's not…"

"It doesn't have a stellar survival rate," I finish. "I know."

"Hiding it from your wife, Mr. Bell—"

"Adrian."

"It's really, really not fair of you, Adrian. You're not doing her any favors. I obviously don't know a thing about your marriage, but if she loves you—"

I let out a shaky breath, cut her off. "She does, Tiffany. More than I deserve. More than…More than is, perhaps, healthy."

"So why—"

"I have my reasons," I say again. Now I do not smile. I frown in a way that says this conversation has to be over. "It's not fair of me, I know. Believe me, I know. But it's not fair that I have this. That I'm here. It's not fair that I'm paying as much for this treatment as I am. What in your life can you list as unfair, Tiffany? A lot, I'm sure. Fair is a myth. Fair does not exist."

She gazes at me evenly, steadily and then takes the pen from me. Signs the NDA in a nurse's hasty scrawl. Dates it. Hands me the pen.

"Keep it."

She lets a small smile cross her lips. "I've read all your books, you know. I enjoy them. They make me feel like I can believe in love again." She gestures with the pen. "Thank you."

"If you happen to have a copy with you, I'll sign it for you."

She bites a lip. "I do, actually."

"Bring it when you come to check on me."

She nods, hooks the pen by the clip at an angle in the V of her scrub top. Smiles at me again, and leaves.

You catch more flies with honey than vinegar, my mother used to tell me.

I enter the passcode on my laptop; there's Wi-Fi here, so I could check email, but I don't. In fact, I turn Wi-Fi off, so I won't be distracted by the siren song of email, pull my wireless earbuds from my bag, and turn on Rostropovich via my phone.

I open my manuscript. Close my eyes, take a deep breath, hold it, and let it out slowly. Repeat four times. Pushing away, mentally, the fog of the chemo, the pinch of the IV, the continual beeping of IV machines indicating a bag is finished, the occasional static PA announcements, the squeak of sensible sneakers, and the murmur of quiet conversations.

Push it all away. Find my flow.

It's there, under the surface. It's always there; it's always been there. Like Louis L'Amour said, I could sit in the middle of Sunset Boulevard with a typewriter on my knees, and once I'm in the flow, I wouldn't notice a thing but the words on the page.

With this story I'm working on now, though, it's harder, and it takes more effort to sink down into it, more mental gymnastics to get into the flow. I need to find the right balance, tap into the necessary emotions, while still remaining the objective storyteller.

This one is personal. More than all the other books I've written over my career, this one...this one requires more of me.

And I have to get it right.

I'm writing it for an audience of one. Well, two. But really, just one. Her.

My love. My Nadia.

Two

ICU

"LET'S PUSH EPINEPHRINE…WHAT'S HIS BLOOD pressure?"

"Eighty over fifty and dropping."

"Medications?"

"Paramedics say the family didn't speak English, and he has no file on record anywhere we could find, so medications unknown." I check the chart again, but there's nothing there that can help us.

The patient is a male, forties—Luis Hermano—admitted to the ER earlier in the week for a heart attack, from which he was recovering in the ICU where I work…and is now suffering an unexpected anaphylactic shock. Non-English speaker, uninsured, no medical history available…unconscious and unresponsive.

The attending physician, Dr. Wilson, and two other nurses—Lydia and Sally—are in the room, and we go through the process of keeping the patient alive. He stabilizes somewhat, and now we just have to figure what caused it—we go through medications used during surgery, during recovery, try to determine if he could be on any medication that would cause the anaphylaxis...and by the time that's done Dr. Wilson is being paged to another room, and my watch is going off because it's time to check on Mr. Renfro in 213, who's supposed to be up and walking every hour or two, and then Mrs. Lasseter in 215 will need another dose of painkillers to keep her comfortable...and by the time I've made my rounds and administered medication and turned patients and checked vitals and crossed items off my checklists, I'm supposed to have been off duty for an hour and I still have another hour's worth of wrap-up to do and I've been on since six this morning, never ate dinner because of Mr. Hermano going anaphylactic and then the John Doe with the coma in 219 woke up screaming while I was with Renfro...

Finally I clock out, shrug into my hoodie, shoulder my purse, wave goodbye to Dr. Wilson and Sally and the others, and head for the elevator. I'm waiting for the elevator when I hear Dr. Wilson's shoes behind me.

"Nadia."

The elevator arrives, but I hear the news in Dr. Wilson's voice before I even turn around. I don't want to turn around. I just don't. But I do. Wilson's face is tight, hard, pinched.

"Mr. Hermano?"

He nods, and I wonder if his goatee is whiter right

now than it was this morning. "He coded while you were with Mrs. Lasseter."

"You didn't page me?"

"There wasn't time. I don't think the stent took. I dunno. He was gone by the time I got there myself. I just thought you should know."

"Thanks."

"Good work today, Nadia." He hesitates.

"What?" I ask.

"You worked a double today."

"Yeah."

"And yesterday."

"Yeah."

"And you're on the schedule for another one tomorrow."

"Adrian is out of town." I shrug. "I'd rather be working than at home alone."

"I get that, I do. But…I need you on your A-game. You're my best nurse, and if you burn out, I'm screwed. Who's gonna take your place? Lydia? Sally?"

We both know neither Lydia nor Sally are cut out for the ICU, not long term anyway. They're both great nurses, but Lydia belongs somewhere like the L&D floor, and Sally is just too sweet and innocent for this work. The ICU is brutal. You have to care, and deeply, but you also have to keep a certain part of yourself walled off from it all. You have to be able to leave it all here when you clock out. Sally takes it home with her, I can tell.

"I'm not going to burn out. I promise."

He just sighs. "Still. I'm going to have Lacey get the second half of your shift tomorrow covered. I'm not going to have my best nurse work three doubles in a row when we're not short-staffed."

"Alan—"

"No." His pager, hanging inside the hip pocket of his scrub bottoms, buzzes, and he tilts it to check. "You work the morning shift, and then you go home and you have a glass of wine with lunch and you…I don't know. Go for a walk. Binge Netflix. Whatever. Just take a few hours to breathe, Nadia. See you Thursday. I have to go."

I hate time off.

I get antsy. Bored. Especially when Adrian is traveling.

I've worked crazy hours since I was a teenager, working full time after school and a second job on the weekends, so I could save up for my first car. Then I worked full time and went to nursing school, and then once I was a registered nurse I was working at least sixty hours a week supporting Adrian as he got his writing career off the ground. And now it's just… habit. A lifestyle.

I call the elevator again and get on. The ride down to the parking garage is short, and the walk to my car long. It's after midnight, and my eyes burn. I'm the kind of tired that leaves streaks at the edges of your vision, where time seems slow, syrupy and then way too fast, where it seems to take ten minutes to get into my A5, set my purse on the passenger seat, start the engine, and buckle up—and then I blink and I'm half-way home with zero memory of the drive. Then I'm waiting at a red light for an eternity, sitting at an empty intersection where the shops are closed and dark and the streets damp after a brief rain shower, making the traffic lights glint off the blacktop in a smear of red and green.

The radio is off. After so much manic movement and chaos, I relish the silence of my car's warm interior, the smell of the leather, the faint lavender scent of the dried bunch hanging from my rearview mirror.

Then I'm home, pulling up the long, steep drive-way. I stop at the top, waiting for the garage door to open. Home is a two-story red brick Colonial, white Ionic columns framing the wide white French-style front door, white shutters. Box shrubs trimmed in precise squared-off rectangles under the windows on each side, with a profusion of bright, colorful peren-nials in front of them and lining the ruler-straight, brick-paved walkway to the front porch. A pair of double-width garage doors, white wood with an X of black wrought-iron straps across each. Faux gaslight lampposts stand at the corners of the property, far cor-ner, on either side of the walkway, and on either side of the driveway, flickering their welcome.

McMansion it may be, and very much alike all the rest on our street, but it's home and I love it. It's the first and only house Adrian and I bought together and, as far as I'm concerned, the last. Every day, I pull up the driveway, stop here waiting for the garage door to trundle slowly upward, and I stare at my home, and I appreciate it.

I slide my car into its space, shut off the motor, and push open my door. Stand beside my little red convertible and stare at the empty space next to mine where Adrian's car belongs. Beyond it, occupying a storage bay, is a collection of mountain bikes, kayaks, stand-up paddleboards, bike pumps and spare tires and paddles and a shelf at the back littered with the detritus of life.

It has been a long time since Adrian and I used any of those things over there.

Years, in fact.

I close the door of my car, listen to the engine tick and pop as it cools. I finally summon the motivation to go inside; just as the garage door light flicks off automatically, bathing the garage in darkness. The house is silent, dark. I flick on the kitchen light, a small pool of incandescent yellow, limning the marble counters and stainless-steel appliances with sepia light.

Green numerals on the oven: 12:47.

I'm hungry. But food seems to require too much energy to prepare, even ripping open a protein bar or popping some popcorn in the microwave, or reheating leftovers. It's all too hard. I toss my purse on the island, fish my phone out of it, shuck my hoodie and leave it on the island with my purse—I'm going back to work in less than six hours anyway. No point in putting them away. I trudge upstairs. My footsteps scuff loudly on the carpet, and when I touch the doorknob to open my bedroom door, I'm shocked by a burst of static electricity, bright blue-white in the darkness of the hall. Sometimes, if I remember, I leave the TV on in our bedroom, just for the semblance of welcome.

I neglected to make the bed this morning. Only one side is mussed, slept in. Adrian has been on a research trip to the East Coast for the past week. Even though I'm dead on my feet, I force myself to bypass the bed. I have to shower, and scrub the day away. I strip out of my scrubs and drape them on the seaman's chest at the foot of our bed, for tomorrow. Toss my sports bra, underwear, and socks in the hamper. Turn the shower on and let it run to scalding and brush my teeth and scrape a brush through my hair.

I catch a glimpse of myself in the mirror. Black hair, so thick I've broken brushes trying to drag them through the waves. It hangs to my shoulder blades, dry and loose and brushed out. Shimmers, glistens. Adrian says he fell in love with my hair first, and then with the rest of me. I don't blame him—if I'm vain about anything it's my hair. It's never felt the touch of chemicals, and I religiously trim the split ends, condition, brush it out every night the way Mom used to. My olive skin is naturally tan and tans darker at even the least glimmer of sun. I'm slender, maybe a bit too slender, and my ribs show. But I've got abs, which is nice considering I never work out. I always drop weight when Adrian travels. I work twelve to eighteen hours a day as many days in a row as Dr. Wilson will let me, and I often either forget or don't have time to eat.

I've been spacing out in front of the mirror for…I don't know how long. Long enough that the bathroom is fogged with steam.

I linger in the shower long after I've shampooed and conditioned and scrubbed my skin. I soak up the warmth, let it loosen my tight muscles.

The water goes warm, then lukewarm, and I finally turn it off. Towel mostly dry, use my magic wand to brush and dry my hair at the same time: my Dyson hairdryer. God, that thing is amazing. My crazy thick hair would normally still be wet hours and hours after the shower, but that thing makes it so I can brush it and get it dry enough to go to bed without my hair being soaking wet.

I don't bother with clothes. Just fall naked into bed, climb under the covers. Bedside table alarm clock: 1:36 a.m. My shift starts at seven.

One more thing I have to do before I can sleep.

I call Adrian. It rings exactly twice, and then he answers. "Hi, baby." His voice is muzzy, thick and slow with sleep. "Doing okay?"

"Long. Hard. We lost someone."

"Shit." A sad sigh. "Work again in the morning, yeah?" He somehow convinced Lacey in scheduling to email him my schedule every week. He probably gave her a signed book or three.

"Yeah. Seven."

"You could've called me on the way in."

"I have to call you at night. I need to hear your voice so I can sleep."

"I know."

"What'd you do today?" I ask.

"Toured the site of the Battle of Yorktown." He's working on a Revolutionary War piece about a Redcoat who falls in love with the widow of a rebel…a man he killed. It's in the developmental stages, he says.

"Get some good material?"

"Eh. I think Yorktown is later than I'm planning on setting the bulk of the story. I might hit Lexington and Concord next."

"When will you be home?"

"Thursday, maybe Friday."

"I miss you."

He sighs, heavily. "I love you, Nadia. So much."

"I know," I say, smiling to myself.

"Don't you 'I know' me, woman." A snort. "I need some sugar."

I reach out, twist on the bedside lamp. Pull the phone away from my ear, switch to FaceTime. The screen resolves into a grainy image of Adrian, covered to his chest with a hotel comforter, lying down, smiling up the phone. I flick the blankets off, pan the camera down to show him my naked body. "How's that for some sugar?" I murmur.

He groans a laugh. "Aww hell, Nadia." A sigh. "So beautiful. Miss you so much."

"Get home and you won't have to miss me, because you'll have me." I turn the phone so it's on my face. "In fact, come home early, and I'll even take the day off work and keep you in bed with me."

"Make it two days, and I'll be home by noon Thursday."

I laugh. "Are you bartering with me, Adrian Bell?"

"Sure am."

I laugh. "Fine. I'll get all day Thursday *and* Friday off, if you're home Thursday by noon."

"You have a deal, my darling." He passes a hand through his hair, mussing the already messy blond locks. "But be warned, I won't let you leave the bed until at least midnight. I might even handcuff you to it."

I wriggle, smirking at him. "Oooh, threaten me with a good time, why don't you."

He scrubs his hair again, and I see a Band-Aid on his forearm, on the inside, near the crease of his elbow.

"What's that?" I ask.

"What's what?"

"The Band-Aid. Did you get hurt?"

"Oh, that. Uh, yeah, a branch caught me. No big deal."

"Hmmm. But it was bad enough you needed a Band-Aid?"

He typically refuses to use them. Usually he just rinses cuts out with soap and water and then super-glues over them. Which, as an ICU nurse, drives me a little nuts. So a Band-Aid is weird.

"Oh, well. My tour guide insisted. She was such an earnest, sweet little thing that I couldn't say no. She didn't know a thing about Revolutionary War history, bless her heart, but she was trying."

"Sweet little thing, huh?" I tease, my voice drily sarcastic.

"Oh stop. She was all of sixteen and it was her first job, and I guarantee you she got it because her mom worked in the gift shop or something." He yawns, and then I do.

"You gave me your yawn, asshole." I laugh.

"You work another double tomorrow?"

"Alan is insisting I take the afternoon off. So just the morning shift."

"Good man. I'll have to send him a bottle of whiskey or something."

"Alan doesn't drink. Send him some fancy tea instead."

"Oh, the irony," he laughs. "Buying tea as a gift while in Boston researching the Revolutionary War."

I want to laugh, but I'm having trouble keeping my eyes open. "I'll call you tomorrow."

"I love you." Pause. "Nadia?"

"Love you, Adrian."

"Nadia."

"Hmm."

"Diamond solitaire earrings, or a sapphire pendant necklace?"

"Neither. Just you. Snuggles and kisses and lots of sex and you making me that fancy pour-over coffee."

"Nadia."

"Sapphire. The only diamond I own is the one on my finger, the one you put there the day you proposed. It's the only diamond I want." I'm asleep, mostly. My brain and my mouth haven't quite gotten the memo, because I miss him so damn much.

"Talk to you tomorrow. Sleep good, my love."

"You too."

"Bye."

"Bye." It's whispered, barely audible.

I feel my phone slip out of my hand and thunk onto the floor, but I'm too far asleep to care.

Three

Magic; Lies

I WISH I COULD SAY I'M NOT A GOOD LIAR. BUT THAT WOULD be a lie.

I lie for a living—that's all fiction is, after all, when you drill down to the molten core of it: I, the writer, create in my mind a pair of characters, two people who did not heretofore exist, and I strive to make them seem real. I give them backstories. I give them foibles and flaws. Scars, peccadilloes, fetishes. Like you, like me. Then I come up with a way to force them into orbit around each other. This is the plot—the path of their orbits as they intersect, creating a necessary collision. The collision results in not destruction as in true astronomy, but creation. This collision is where the magic happens. It's the real lie. It's a lie that these people exist, that this story is real, or even possible. The happily ever after carries on after you've read those words: *The End*. You, the reader, come to me begging for that lie. You relish it. That lie provides you with comfort, with entertainment, with emotions your real life may lack. You know exactly what I'm doing, but like any accomplished magician, you don't know how I do it. Even the above explanation doesn't *show* you how I tell my lies, or how I perform the magic, the sleight of hand, the prestidigitation which turns ideas in my brain into real people on the page.

I am very, very good at this kind of lying.

My lies have won literary awards. They've been turned into movies, which themselves have won awards. Movies made from my books have launched careers.

I am also, perhaps unfortunately, good at lying in other ways. I just am. It comes naturally to me. I'm a storyteller. I could have been an actor, but I'm far too self-conscious for that. I comfort myself with the fact that, in general, I do not lie in everyday life. I'm not practiced at it. Lies do not come smoothly. I must work at them. Create them, smooth out the edges like a blacksmith with a hammer and anvil.

This is what I'm doing as I drive home from the airport: working on my lie. The best lies, as any accomplished liar knows, contain a counterintuitively disproportionate amount of truth. You can't tell a whole lie. As in, you can't create a whole fiction to cover your ass. For it to work your story has to be more truth than lie.

For example: I really did go to Lexington and Concord. I really did go to Yorktown, and there really was a blissfully, almost comically young and uninformed tour guide. I really did spend most of my time in the libraries in Boston and Philadelphia, researching. It really was a research trip. Ninety percent, at least, was research. This is the truth, and not a word of it is made up, embellished, or fabricated. The lie in this case, you see, is one of omission.

I'm leaving out the ten percent of the trip, the detour to Johns Hopkins Hospital in Baltimore, which happens to have one of the top oncology departments in the country. I'm leaving out the reason I was there in the first place, the reason for the entire research trip: an experimental variation of chemotherapy, designed to reduce certain side effects, such as hair loss and the violent liquid expulsion of poison from both ends of my gastric system.

It is successful for what it is: I still have my hair, most of it. It's more brittle, thinner, but it's there. And I only spend forty-eight hours or so being violently ill, rather than the days or weeks of the normal rounds of chemo.

How, you might ask, have I managed to keep all this from my wife?

And more to the point, why?

I've kept it from her via a very elaborately planned series of research trips, where I build my research schedule around the chemo and recovery days. If I'm still feeling under the weather when I get home, well, jetlag is a bitch, right?

I'm also traveling to receive the best possible treatments. Experimental stuff, cutting edge. I can afford it, and if it'll prolong the inevitable, I'll try it.

The inevitable being Nadia finding out I'm sick.

Sick.

Such a trite, flat, flimsy descriptor for this ninth circle of hell.

Sick is the flu. Sick is a cold, or you get pneumonia or something. Sick is...sucky but recoverable. It disrupts your day, your week, your month.

But this?

What I've fought hardest against is that when you get the C-word, you *become* it.

You're not just sick.

You don't *have* cancer—you *are* fucking cancer.

I hate that word.

I never utter it. Rarely even think it.

I'm sick.

That's it.

If I focus on that, on just being sick, it's manageable. It's a series of things, which need to be done, in order to not be sick.

Ready for the real leap of logic? Here goes.

If I'm just sick, it's no big deal. I can handle it. I can manage it. I don't usually tell Nadia when I've got a headache, or feeling feverish or coming down with the flu. See, she's a nurse. But with Nadia, it's not just a job. It's *who she is*.

When we first got serious, to the meet-the-family stage, I spent an afternoon with Nadia's mom. She told me a story about Nadia, when she was five, or maybe six. Very young. Precocious, serious even then. I could see it, little Nadia with her black hair in a thick braid, a pink ribbon tied at the end of it. She'd be wearing tiny shiny black Mary-Janes and white stockings, plaid skirt, white button-down—she went to a private Catholic school. Anyway. Nadia, young and serious, refused to go to school one particular day. Her daddy was sick. He claimed it was the flu, just under the weather, I'll be all right in a day or two, baby girl, just go to school. Nadia was no dummy. She knew. Daddy wasn't just sick, he was Sick. She saw it.

She categorically refused to go to school. No amount of threats of punishment or bribery could convince her. She had to take care of her daddy. And she did. A day, then a week. Then it was a month. She would give him his medicine, she would do her five-year-old dead level best to make him food, make him eat, spooning soup into his mouth and, being five, getting as much on them both as in his mouth.

"I let her," Nadia's mother had said, tearing up. "I shouldn't have, she was too young, I knew it then and I know it now, but...she just *had* to do it. I couldn't stop her. You know how she is, how once she's set on something, there's no stopping her. I knew then it was who she was—a nurturer, a caretaker. She takes care of people. If you'll let her, if you don't stop her, she'll take care of you, until there's nothing left of her. Nothing left of her *for* her."

She had stared me in the eyes. Taken my face in her hands. "You can't let her do that, Adrian. If you love her, you have to make sure she takes care of herself. If she gets a whiff of you being sick, she'll drop her entire life, her entire existence to take care of you. She won't sleep, won't eat, won't rest, won't do anything but care for you until you're better. It's…well, honestly, it's compulsive, with her. I hesitate to say obsessive, but that's pretty near the truth of it."

So, you see. I have to take care of her. If she knew I was sick, she would quit her job, she would baby me and sit at my side for every round of chemo and every experimental treatment, and she'd do her best to take the burden of my sickness on herself, and I just can't put that on her.

I hate lying to her.

Hate it.

I've never lied to her about a thing. Not a single other thing. Not even, when we were dating, and I got drunk at a party and made out with another girl. I told her, the very next day. She broke up with me, and I didn't see her for two and a half weeks, until she got sick of me sending her a dozen roses every day, box after box of chocolate, pages and pages of college-ruled notebook paper with "I'm sorry" written on it a hundred times. Mixtapes burned onto CDs of hand-picked songs. She finally realized, somehow, that it had been a stupid drunken accident. Honestly, I'd been so blitzed I'd thought it was Nadia. When I realized it was someone else, I stopped, threw up, and ran away. Stupid. But an accident. Not an intentional betrayal. I'd never do that.

I hadn't lied then.

I told her it was my fault the time I got into a car accident. I'd been messing with the radio and rear-ended someone.

I face the truth, no matter what.

But this is…

This is bigger than that.

I have to protect her. If she knew I had cancer, it would kill her right along with me. Her force of will is exactly that powerful. And I can't handle that. Can't have that on my conscience. I know she'll be angry. She won't understand. Hopefully, she'll never know. But if somehow the worst comes to pass, by the time she finds out, what's done will be done. She'll have anger to deal with as well as grief, but at least she'll be alive.

At a red light, two blocks from home, that's what I think: *at least she'll be alive.*

And it guts me.

She'll be alive.

After I'm gone—*if* I'm gone—she'll be alive.

The light turns green, but my foot is stuck on the brake. Horns blare, shouts are muffled and dim. I can't swallow, can't breathe. Force myself off the road, into the parking lot of a KFC.

She'll be alive.

I'll be gone.

I've never really allowed myself to even consider that truth.

Because this is Nadia. And my Nadia is loyal to the very bone, to the atoms. Down to her component electrons and neutrons, she's devoted to me. If I die, she will mourn me the rest of her life. And that life will be short, if she has anything to say about it. She won't just grieve, she'll wear black forever, like Queen Victoria is said to have done. She'll cut herself off from life. She will drive the empty shell of her body to work, and she'll put on a mask along with her scrubs and stethoscope and rubber gloves, and she'll care for the patients in the ICU, and she'll drive the empty husk of her body home again, and every thought will be about me. Grieving me. Mourning me.

She will be alive…

But not living.

I've been developing this story for her and, up to now, I think my subconscious has been telling me some truths. This could be my last story. I'll fight until there's nothing left, but I can't ignore the possibility. But this story, this love story I've been working on. It's about second chances. Moving on after loss. I think my forebrain was thinking of it as a poignant set of themes, disconnected from my life. But it's not.

It's more than that.

It's for her.

But…now that I begin to allow myself to really think about this, it's a big, complicated, thing.

Because she's complicated. Complex. Deep. For more than ten years I've loved her, and I'm still just beginning to plumb her depths, to understand her.

Then an idea forms.

Sitting in the parking lot of a KFC, two blocks from home, still a bit nauseous, whether from chemo or the cancer or this realization, I don't know—I understand what I have to do.

It's just going to require a lot of thought, a lot of care, a lot of planning.

Best-case scenario, it's all for nothing. I'll get the all clear, cancer free.

A niggling worm in my gut is worried, perhaps far more than worried, that it won't be for naught.

⁂

I wipe my face. I've been crying, apparently.

I collect myself.

It's eleven twenty-six, Thursday. I promised her I'd be home by noon.

I keep my promises.

I also promised I'd tie her to the bed and not let her leave for days, and that's a promise I intend to keep as well. That part is tricky, though. Chemo has a lot of awful side effects. It is poison, after all. One of those side effects is sexual. Not one of desire, oh no. That's as intact and fiery as ever. Energy, though, is an issue. As is physical ability to sustain the necessary hardness to act out that desire.

So this has to be carefully timed.

I just need a little help showing her how I feel. The emotions, the need, the drive, is all there. It's real, more powerful than ever. I just need a little help forcing my body to match my mind, my heart. My body is the weak thing, the failing thing. And I'll be damned and double damned if I'll let it slow me down, if I'll let it stop me from showing my beloved, beautiful wife how much I love her, how much I missed her, how much I need her and want her.

Nope, nope, nope.

So, I take a little blue pill, since I'm only a few minutes from home, and they take a few minutes to kick in.

I'm on our street when I call her. It rings exactly once.

"Hi," she breathes. "Where are you?"

"Passing the Johnstone's house."

She inhales sharply, and there's a smile in the sound. Not a grin, not a smirk, but that secret smile only I know. A half-curve of the right side of her mouth, eyes narrowing, jade-green eyes luminous and hot. It's a secret smile just for me that says *you have no idea what you're in for, buddy.*

"I just got home from work," she says.

"Have you showered yet?"

"Getting in right now."

"Don't."

"I smell like—"

"Nadia." I wait, and she's quiet; I'm pulling into our driveway. "Just stay where you are, like you are."

"I have to get work off of me."

"I'll do it for you."

"I don't want work on you."

The smell of sickness, she means. The indefinable scent of possible, potentially imminent death. The scent of sorrow, the tang of fear. It's palpable to her, and it's why she's such a fierce zealot about showering the moment she gets home. Protecting me, and our home, from all of it.

"Nadia."

A sigh. "Okay."

I feel a desperation right now. I haven't seen her, or touched her in over a week, and for us, it's an eternity.

But it's a desperation borne of...something more. Something else.

Something I dare not, cannot even give name to in the deepest, hidden sanctum of my own mind.

I leave my bags in the car. Bring only one thing: a small velvet box, in my hip pocket. I pinch my cheeks and slap them on the way up the stairs, to put color in them.

I feel the little blue pill working. It's me, too, though. It's not that I *can't* get hard, it's that it can be difficult to stay that way, to keep from blowing too soon. The pill just restores some of my former stamina.

Our bedroom door is closed. I smell her: she's put on perfume. Chanel. A gift for our fifth anniversary.

She's in the process of taking her hair out of the braid—that's part of her ritual, in the morning and when she gets home, like a warrior putting on his armor. She puts on her scrubs, bottoms first, then the top. Brushes her hair and puts it in a tight, severe braid, and then knots the braid into a bun at the top of her head. Some thick black eyeliner under her eyes. Moisturizing lip gloss—something I have bought for her in the past. Then she wraps her stethoscope around her neck, and she's armored against the day.

When she comes home, the stethoscope goes in her purse. She begins with the braid, unknots it. Slips the tie off the end, and slowly eases the locks out of the binding of the braid. She then shakes it out, the kinked tresses sticking to each other at first. Brushes it out. Then, and only then, does she begin removing her scrubs, top first, then bottoms. The shower is usually going, warming up. She'll brush her teeth.

When she gets out of the shower, she's a different woman. Softer, sweeter, warmer. Nurse Bell is harder, sharper, colder. Not unkind, not at all. Nurse Bell is the human definition of understanding and compassion and kindness. But it's a kindness that has seen pretty much the worst the medical field can offer.

Nadia feels me, hears me.

Pauses, hands up behind her head, about to free the last inch of braid. I slide up behind her. Capture her hands in mine. Bring her knuckles to my lips, kiss each one, pinky to thumb of her left hand, thumb to pinky of her right. Then I kiss each palm.

She holds her breath.

Her eyes are closed—I don't have to see her reflection in the mirror to know this. She always closes her eyes when I kiss her hands like this.

I love her hands. They are strong, efficient, capable, but they can also be soft and loving and clever.

Oh, the things she can do with these hands. I treasure the way these hands make me feel, and so I always begin our lovemaking by kissing them.

I finish unbraiding her hair; she's got her brush on the counter, waiting. I know how she brushes her hair. I slide the brush through her black locks, beginning on the left side and working my way around to the right. Then underneath, right back around to the left. And then in sections, until the kinks are gone and the wispy flyaways are smoothed down into place and her long, wickedly thick, raven-wing hair shimmers almost blue-purple and it's glossy again and perfect.

She just breathes, and lets me brush.

The shower is still running. I let it run.

She's antsy. Eager. Reaching behind herself, for me.

I let her.

Let her find my shirt hem, and let her help me shrug out of it. I match her, tugging the pale green scrub top off, tossing it into her hamper. Her turn. She fiddles blindly with my belt buckle, her body angled away from mine to make room for her hands, while her shoulders rest against my chest and her head leans on my shoulder, face turned to my neck, lips nipping and kissing at my throat.

While she fumbles with my belt buckle, freeing it and then working on the fly of my jeans, I caress her torso. Her taut flat belly, her sides, her ribcage and diaphragm. The elastic of her sports bra. I lift that up, off it goes I know not where. Cup her breasts, whisper murmurs of relief as I fill my hands with her flesh, then moan with need as she shoves at my jeans, my underwear. I help her, I kick out of them. I untie her scrub bottom, and she makes quick work of shucking out of them and her underwear.

We're naked together.

This is only part one. She wants everything. The shower, the bed, handcuffs, kisses, bitten shoulders, our walls echoing with screams.

But first.

Oh, first.

This.

I dip at the knees. She grasps me. Feeds me into her, and I stand up, fill her. She whimpers my name—*Adrian, oh god, Adrian*—and I cup her breasts in one hand, fondling each slight, small, round peak. With my other, I touch her, the way she loves and needs to be touched. She's tense. She needs this. She'll never take it for herself while I'm gone.

I move slowly, dipping at the knees and rising again, to fill her, to plunge. Her kisses rake along my jaw, her hand clutching at my cheek, her other hand awkwardly and clumsily scrabbling at my buttocks, helping and encouraging my movements.

We haven't said a word of greeting.

None is needed.

Just this. Hands reacquainting with beloved flesh, with the curves in which I delight, the hard angles of mine which she treasures.

I groan as I glory in the way she squeezes around me, in the way she gasps, in the way her knees forget to stay locked as I bring her to climax. Her eyes are open, as are mine. Watching us.

We can see where we're joined. She's leaning backward, into me, and I'm lifting. Circling her softness as she rises to the moment, moans becoming ragged, moans becoming my name chanted.

She comes.

I lift her in my arms—she's limp and boneless, for the moment.

"The water," she whispers.

"I've got it."

I settle her on the bed. Go back to the bathroom, shut off the shower; we won't be needing that for a while.

When I turn back to our bed, she's recovered. Posed. Sprawled out on the bed, spread-eagle. Touching herself. Massaging her breast, her sex. In one hand, she has two pairs of handcuffs, lined with some soft plush black material. She latches one set to her wrist and the bedpost. The key is in the hole, so I can twist it and release her, when she's ready.

She hands me the other.

I oblige. Cuff her other wrist to the bed, and now she's at my mercy. And I'm not going to be ready to be done for…oh, for hours.

We'll sleep, when we're finally done. Eat. I'll sneak another pill while she's not looking, and that's how we'll spend the next two days.

God, I'm such a lucky man.

She's a goddess, lying there, naked, flush with a fresh orgasm, writhing with need for me, begging me with her eyes to come closer. To take her. To use her. To show her how fully mine she is.

She doesn't need to say a word.

Doesn't need to hear anything from me.

This is our dance, and we've perfected the steps.

I take my time. Because thanks to the miracle of chemistry, I now have the time to lavish upon her. Used to be, I could do this with her naturally. Take hours to make her come a dozen times before I let her bring me to my own completion.

Maybe that's the storyteller in me; maybe it wasn't hours and hours. I'm no superhuman. But we would be in bed for hours. Again and again and again, and while we were waiting for my less-than-superhuman body to be ready again, we'd talk and confide and kiss, and when I felt myself stirring I'd crawl down her body and worship at the pink, lush altar of her womanhood until she begged me to stop, until she demanded I come up her and love her properly.

"Come fuck me, husband," is what she'd say.

I have her handcuffed and helpless, and it's her favorite thing, this. Helpless under my mouth. Because no matter how she begs, I won't stop. No matter how many times she topples into frantic delirium, I push her more, more.

Until she says those words.

It's a game.

How long can she go before she says it?

Now, with me gone for a week, it's either going to be mere seconds, or it could be hours. You never know with my Nadia.

I worship at her altar, and she screams and weeps and thrashes, locks her thighs around my neck and squeezes my face with those silky, powerful, pinioning limbs and takes all I can give her until she can take no more.

Momentarily limp, caught between orgasms, she shifts her thighs, hooks them around my waist. Her eyes meet mine.

Searches me.

I wonder if she can tell?

I worry that, sometimes. That she'll look into my eyes in a moment like this, and just *know*.

The moment passes, and her eyes see nothing but me, her husband, giving her all the pleasure and release and relief she can handle, and then some.

Her lips part.

Her tongue slides over her lips.

Drawing it out.

Four

Reunion; Observations

"COME FUCK ME, HUSBAND." I WHISPER THE WORDS, too shattered by his attention to speak any louder.

He prowls up my body. Kisses my belly. My diaphragm. Between my breasts.

I need to touch him. Hold him. It needs to be his turn.

But I'm still at his mercy.

He settles himself above me. Over me. Between my thighs. Buries himself in me. Face in my neck, then between my breasts as he moves.

"Let me loose, Adrian," I whisper, the words ragged and harsh.

He kisses my nipple and unlocks my left hand without looking. I lock my legs around his waist and free my other hand myself. Clutch him to me. I'm wrapped around him. Surging against him. Rolling with him.

How long was he between my thighs? I lost track

of time, but it was not a short while. He's sweaty. Something about the way his body feels under my hand, his muscles and flesh—something nudges at the back of my head. But I have no time for thoughts, no time for nonsense. I just need his pleasure.

I roll into him, and he lets me take him to his back. I manage it without losing him, without shedding our union. His hands cup at my backside, my shoulders, and I lean over him. Press my breasts to his face and clutch his head and despite my words a moment ago, *I* fuck *him*. Take no prisoners, unrelenting, all my pent-up need, all my stress and frustration of the week at work, the nights alone. I exorcise it all, on him. He knows my demons and he is the holy words and prayer which banishes them.

I feel him rising. It's unmistakable. His groans go softer, quieter. He's not a bellower, a roaring and shouting and punishing thrusts kind of man. He goes soft and sweet, quiet and intense. His fingers clutch hard into my curves and he hisses and whispers my name as I ride him, roll on him. Press my palms to his hips and sink down and push up and feel him throb and watch his face go through the beautiful, wild, fraught, shifting expressions of release, his eyes on mine, trying to keep his eyes open and failing, his teeth baring and clenching, brows drawn down, and then, god, oh god, oh god, and then I feel him give me his release.

"I love you, Nadia," he gasps, as he comes. "I love you—so—so fucking much."

"More," I demand. "More, Adrian."

He gives me more. Keeps going. Doesn't stop, and I take it all. Even when he's done, I don't stop. Not until he goes slack and falls out of me.

And then I collapse on his frame and his hands slide into my hair and his breath huffs on my temple and mine on his chest, and we're tangled in the blankets and sweaty and the handcuffs dangle from the bedposts.

And I know what's off, what's niggling in my side like a thorn.

He's thinner. Not significantly. But I know every centimeter of his body better than I know my own, and I know for a fact he's dropped weight.

But then, so have I, in his absence. Maybe, like me, he stays busy so he doesn't have to miss me. He'd forget to eat entirely when he's writing, if not for me.

The Band-Aid is gone, and there's no sign of a scratch. More of a poke. A small round hole, scabbed over. Days old.

It niggles at me. But he's my husband and he would never lie to me.

❧

Despite it being noon-ish on a Thursday, we sleep. I don't sleep well without him, nor he without me. So we make up for the week by crashing hard, after our vigorous reunion.

When I wake up, it's late afternoon. Sunshine is more orange-gold than yellow. His side of the bed is empty. He comes out of the bathroom, naked. Lean, hard, beautiful. Soft brown hair, usually neatly parted, now messy and scraped back. Stubble on his jaw. Patches of silver streak the stubble near his temple, over the back of his jaw, near his earlobe. He's only forty-one, but his father was almost totally silver by thirty-five so it's not unusual. I love it.

His abs stand out more starkly, even though he hates working out and rarely does more than an occasional jog—to fight the sedentary nature of the job of being a writer, he says.

Abs, ribs.

I notice for the first time that there's a tray on the foot of the bed. Two bowls of thick Greek yogurt sprinkled with granola, blueberries, cut strawberry quarters. A bagel each, liberally slathered with thick cream cheese. Two mugs, our special mugs, bought at a gift shop in Carmel-by-the-Sea, California, on our honeymoon. The mugs are hand thrown ceramic, each inscribed with "My beloved is mine" on one side, the inscribed words painted deep scarlet. On his, on the opposite side: "And I am hers." And on mine, "And I am his."

He's made us lattes. My mother gave us an

espresso machine for our last anniversary, and he has become very serious about his latte making. And I'm not going to argue—he makes a great latte, and god knows I love me a nice sugar-free hazelnut almond milk latte.

He knows exactly how I like it. Milk steamed extra hot. Just a dab of foam at the top. Very sweet.

The centerpiece of the tray arrangement is a small box, white velvet. He sits on the edge of the bed next to me. Grins at me. Juts his chin at the box. "Open it."

I hold the box in my palm, lift the lid. Within, a round bezel-cut sapphire pendant. Brilliant, stunning blue, almost the size of my two thumbnails together.

"Oh...my god, Adrian."

He's proud of it. "It's an heirloom Ceylon sapphire, almost two and a half carats." He lets me lift it out of the box, and the chain is delicate and filigreed, but substantial. Heavy. "The chain is platinum."

I unclasp the chain, hand it to him. He slides behind me, fixes it on me. The pendant rests about an inch and a half below the hollow of my throat, a little more than that above the cleft of my breasts.

"It's incredible, Adrian."

"I know I've been traveling a lot, lately," he says. His voice is heavy, serious. "I just...I want to thank you."

"Thank me?" I'm puzzled.

"For putting up with me leaving."

"Oh." I lift the pendant in my palm, gaze at it; it sparkles in the late afternoon sun, glitters luminous. "Whatever you need to do to write the best story possible, Adrian. You know I support you a thousand percent."

He cups my cheek. "I know." He seems deeply emotional, right now. I'll take it. "That's what I'm saying thank you for."

"Always, baby," I whisper. "No matter what."

"Promise. Promise me, no matter what."

"I already did promise you that, dork," I tease, reaching for him. "When I married you."

He responds readily, hardening in my hand. "Nadia."

I kiss him, leaning into him. Fondling him. "I promise, Adrian. Always, forever, no matter what. Anything, everything, always."

He huffs, growls. "Nadia…"

I smirk at the edge in his voice. "Yes, Adrian?"

"The way you touch me…"

I laugh. "I know."

"Stop," he whispers, "stop a minute. Let me—"

"Ah-ah," I whisper, push him to his back. "My turn."

"I'm not gonna last—" he starts.

I know what he's going to say before he does. "Good." I don't straddle him. I just sit beside him. Hold him, stroke him, touch him. "I don't want you to."

"I want to be inside you," he growls.

"I took all day tomorrow off, and I already had Saturday off," I said. "We have all the time in the world."

"But I need—"

I touch his lips with a finger. "What you need is to lay there and enjoy what I'm doing."

"Okay."

"Yeah?" I slow down, but add a twist. He loves the twist.

"God, yeah." A huff. "Do that again."

"What? This?" I do it again.

"Fuck, yeah. That."

"What if I do…" I lean over him. "This?" And taste him.

"Ohhhh shit, Nadia. You do that and it's over." He loses his voice, then. Because I'm not stopping.

He groans, and I'm loving him all over, with my hands, my mouth, my tongue.

We don't keep score. This isn't about what he did while I was cuffed to the bed. It's not even about the necklace currently draped on his upper thigh as I tongue him to ecstasy.

It's about how much I love his pleasure. How much I love the feel him abandoning control to me. Letting me show him my desire for his release. It's about…me.

I dreamed of this while trying to fall asleep, so many nights.

Now he's here and you bet your ass I'm gonna make my own dreams come true. After all, he's made the rest of my dreams come true.

Most of them, at least. Almost all of them.

I push that away, viciously. Later.

Now, it's him. This. Us.

It is over fast. I love it that way. I enjoy knowing I can make him lose it in two minutes flat, max. He's mine. I know him, I know what he likes. Inside and out, I know him.

When he's gone and done, I kiss his belly, his chest. His lips. He kisses me, unafraid to taste himself on my breath. He works into a sitting position, and we eat our yogurt and bagels, drink our lattes, and there's no need to talk. Our eyes say it all. The silence itself says everything.

And I'm fully aware that when we're done eating, he's going to keep eating…but me, instead of food. That might be part of it.

It's all a big complicated circle. And I feel no need to figure it out. It works, and that's what matters. I know him, he knows me, and we work together perfectly.

He finishes first. I'm much slower to finish, both my food and my climax.

He takes his time, this time. No hurry. Not a race to as many as possible. This is about making sure I feel every moment of it, fully.

And I do.

※

We watch a movie, and a second, until we're tired enough to sleep—well past three in the morning.

I wake to full daylight through the windows, and Adrian in bed with me, hard, grinning, waiting.

We take our time.

※

It's noon on Friday before I bother asking about his trip.

"It was a trip," he says, as if even talking about it is boring. "Libraries, historical battle sites, lots of driving around in rental cars. Nothing exciting."

"What's the story going to be?" I ask.

He's quiet. A long time, actually. Much longer than the question merits; he's always talked through his ideas with me, from inception to publication.

"I…" he sighs. "This one, I think…I think I need to sit on it a bit longer before I'm ready to talk about it."

I don't know what to make of that. "Um. Okay?"

I'm on my back, head resting on his bicep. Sheets around our hips. The afterglow is pungent. His finger idly, lazily traces figure eights around my breasts, circling one nipple then the other, back and forth, possessively, simply enjoying the privilege and right of touching my body.

He does not physically, audibly sigh again, but nonetheless, his pause before responses just…feels like a sigh. "I don't know how to explain it, Nadia. All my stories up till now have just sort of flowed out of me. Naturally, easy as breathing. Some have felt…bigger than others. You know what I mean? Like, not in terms of length, or even possible popularity, sales, like that. Just…the size of the story. The weight of it, inside me."

"Like when you wrote *Love, Me*?" I ask, referencing the book that put him on the literary map, and cementing his place in the public mind. "Because I remember when you first started talking about that idea, you said it felt big."

He nods. "Like that. But this one is…bigger. Just *more*."

"And you can't talk about it?"

He shakes his head. "Not yet. I need time to stew on it. I might need to get some of it down even before the research is done. I just feel it, Nadia. And it's not going to come out the way I usually work, so just…just be patient with me, okay? Just give me some space to do this one differently, is all I'm asking, I guess."

His words feel heavy. Like they are freighted with meaning I cannot quite fathom. As if the true depth of what he means is something he could not truly even put into language.

I lie in the silence. "Adrian…" But I don't even know what I'm trying to say, what I want to say.

There's something, but I don't have the shape of it yet. Like someone blindfolded me, brought me to a table, sat me down, took off the blindfold, and in front of me was a two-thousand piece jigsaw puzzle, but I didn't have the box for reference of what it was supposed to look like—I just had to try to fit the pieces together one at a time and get a feel for what it was supposed to be as I went.

He rolls over, curling his arm to pull me closer as he levers himself over me. Gazes down at me. His eyes are full of unconditional love, blazing hotter and clearer than the day we said "I do." Whatever the puzzle is, I do not have a single shred of doubt that this man loves me. I can rest on that. Whatever is going on with him, he loves me, and more now than ever.

I can taste the truth of that as he kisses me; it's written in the crush of his lips on mine. I can feel it as he touches his forehead to mine, breathing my breath. Times like this, we need no foreplay. No games. He kisses me, and I kiss him, and we wrap up together as if someone had filmed a braid coming loose and then reversed the flow, so you saw the braid twining itself together. Or, perhaps more apropos: a glass shattering on the floor, breaking into a million, million pieces, into glass dust and infinitesimal shards. Filmed, the flow reversed, so the dust assembles into shards, and the shards into jagged chunks, and the chunks puzzle fit themselves into sections and the sections fuse into the whole.

That's how we make love, in this moment. He kisses me, and I taste the absolute adoration on his tongue. I feel the fullness of his devotion as he fills me, bare within me, and then our love is joined, molded together in this sacred movement. We writhe together in an everlasting ouroboros, whispering love, worshipping each other by name, and the time it takes to reach our mutual completion is an instant, an hour, I neither know nor care, I only find awareness of him pulsing within me and my own shattering around him and our sweat commingling and lips touching and tongues tasting and gasps mashing into tangled groans.

⁂

Evening Saturday. Sunset a bloody orange fading to full scarlet.

I've lost count of the number of times we've made love since his return Thursday. We've screwed on the back porch with a bottle of wine as the summer fireflies flash orange in the dull heavy suburban Atlanta heat. We've fucked in the kitchen, me bent over the island, the marble cold against my bare breasts, his thrusts short and rough. We've languorously debauched in the tub, frothy mountains of bubbles revealing our union in brief glimpses of flesh as the water sloshes over the edge.

He's frantic for me.

Wild.

Rougher than he's been in a long, long time. Desperate, almost.

As if proving something to me, or to himself.

But after, as he holds me and nuzzles away our sweat and whispers *iloveyou* like a benediction in the slow silence, his gaze sometimes seems a million miles away, a thousand years away. Then I speak, and he's with me again, and whatever I saw in his eyes is gone and I doubt I ever saw it.

Saturday evening, and I'm making dinner. Spaghetti bolognese. Easy, quick. A bottle of red uncorked and breathing—Josh, my favorite brand. I've been battling my hair, brushing it out of my eyes with my wrist as I knead spices into the raw ground beef with my bare hands, blow it away with a huff, and finally I get sick of it. Wash my hands and head up to our bathroom in search of a hair tie.

I hear our toilet flush, a pause, and then flush again. When I go into the bathroom, there's a sour tang in the air. Adrian is wiping his mouth with a hand towel. Mouthwash bubbles as it swirls down the drain. I eye Adrian, waiting for some kind of explanation.

"I realized I haven't brushed my teeth since I've been back and they felt fuzzy." He brushes lips against my temple. "Dinner smells good—I can smell it from up here."

And then he's heading downstairs, leaving me in the bathroom wondering if I've missed something.

His toothbrush is dry. The bottle of mouthwash is still in the medicine cabinet—where I always put it. In the ten years we've been married, he has never one time put the mouthwash back in the cabinet when he's done with it, he just leaves it on the counter. It's one of those little things in a marriage that drive you bonkers, but aren't worth making a big deal out of. I just put it back, sigh and shake my head and sometimes mutter a few annoyed curses. I do things like that which prompt the same response from him, and it's just how it is.

But the mouthwash being put away…it sticks in my head as meaning something; I just can't put my finger on what.

He smelled like mouthwash when he kissed my temple. I scented it, briefly, faintly.

And something else.

Sharp, sour.

"Nadia?" I hear him shout. "Water's boiling. I'm gonna put the noodles in."

I set it aside. Later, I'll have time to puzzle over why he would lie about mouthwash.

But it sticks in my craw—whatever the hell that stupid phrase even means. What's a craw, anyway? I consider Googling the origin and meaning of the phrase, but it slips my mind and the rest of the evening passes in easy conversation and watching a sci-fi

thriller on Netflix and opening another bottle of wine
and then I'm tipsy and we sleep together, this time just
sleeping, and yet even as I drunkenly slumber, I dream
of Adrian standing in front of me, and he's just looking at me, and in the dream I NEED to ask him what
he's hiding, but my lips won't work, my mouth won't
open, and he turns away in the dream and the opportunity to ask him is gone. And when I wake up with the
sliver of silver moon hung in the window frame like a
stray fingernail clipping, I can't grasp the shape of the
dream, only the fleeting emotional substance of it.

Five

Whisky & Women

I'M HAVING TROUBLE WITH MY APPETITE. JUST…NOT hungry. Nauseated. I've been warned that with pancreatic cancer, having symptoms at all is not a good sign. The early symptoms tend to be vague, more generalized and not immediately tagged as symptomatic of cancer. Thus the fact that I didn't get mine diagnosed till it was already spreading, and fast.

It's already beyond my pancreas, so surgery wasn't an option even then, at the very beginning. Chemo isn't going to cure it. Just extend my life. Make it suck less.

People have lived for years with it, and others have died within months of first detection.

I'm maudlin, today. Nadia is at work, and I'm feeling like shit. Since she's gone, I let myself just wallow in the shittiness, a rarity for me. It sucks. It hurts. I don't want it. It's not fair. Wah-wah-wah. The river of bullshit from my weak mind and sensitive, *artiste* heart is sickening even to me. Fuck this.

I'm trying to force myself out of the funk when my phone rings. Oh, yay! A distraction.

"Hello?" I answer it on the third ring. Don't want to seem too eager.

"Adrian, hey. This is Nathan Fischer."

I blink. "Hey, bud. Long time no see, how are you?"

Nathan is a carpenter, real salt of the earth kinda guy. I met him on the set of *Love, Me*, for which I was a consultant and executive producer and he was a set construction foreman. We ended up spending a lot of time together during the filming, drinking whiskey in my trailer and talking about our mutual love of old Hollywood westerns. We still talk, every so often, still connect for drinks every few months. He sometimes gets contracted for jobs outside the Atlanta area—he's been in Glasgow for the past four months, working on a shoot for a miniseries, a WWI piece, I think he said. He must just be getting back into town.

"Doing good, man, glad to be home."

"You were in, what, Glasgow?"

"Mostly, yeah. It was a challenging set. Complicated and extensive. Looks good on the ol' resume, though. The director is getting a lot of attention, so having worked on his set will do good things for me."

"Good to hear it, happy for you."

"How's books?"

"How about we meet downtown for drinks and talk, huh? Usual spot?"

"Sounds good. See you in twenty?"

"For sure." I end the call; get my wallet and keys and head out. I still feel like shit, and drinking is probably not a great idea considering liver failure is what tends to be the real killer behind pancreatic cancer, but fuck it. I'm gonna live while I'm still alive.

Nathan is good people, and I always enjoy getting to talk to him.

We meet up at our favorite bar in downtown Atlanta. He's big, Nathan is. Six-four, and broad as a damn barn. Heavy shoulders, thick chest, thick arms. His hair is almost as dark as Nadia's, but he has tinges of gray at the temples. Short but thick beard, also streaked here and there with silver. He's the same age as me, forty-one. His hands always fascinate me—they're gargantuan, almost double the size of my hands; when we shake, his grip is loose and easy, but it's like shaking hands with a cinderblock.

He got here before me and ordered for us—we chose this bar as our haunt because they have a bewildering selection of whiskey and scotch and rye. He's ordered an obscure scotch, something he discovered in the UK, I figure.

It's just shooting the shit at first. He talks about the set in Glasgow, lots of building trenches and such, the challenge of making new wood look old and muddy and splintered and blasted, things like that.

Two doubles in, and I sense him going sour. He's

quiet, and I let it be. He does this when he's a few drinks in—goes from animated and easygoing to slow and dark.

"Thinking deep thoughts over there, Nate," I say.

He shrugs. "Nothing worth sharing."

"Try me." I don't usually push, when he goes dark like this.

He never wants to talk about it anyway, and seems to appreciate that I can just sit and sip and let him claw his way out of whatever pit the whiskey shoved him into. Today, though, I can't shake my own maudlin, my own depression. I've tried to fake it, hanging out with Nathan. A glance here and there from him, though, tells me he sees through it and is just being polite enough to ignore it.

"I will if you will," he says, his voice a low, bumpy grumble.

I sigh. Flick a finger at the bartender at the other end of the bar; she nods, brings over the bottle. "Breaking the mold here, my friend," I say. "But you've got a deal."

He waits until our tumblers are full again, two ice cubes each tinkling around the amber. "Truth is, I'm thinking about my wife."

This has me rocking back on my stool. "You're married?" I cough around a startled mis-swallow. "I've known you almost four years, and you've never told me you're married."

"Was."

"Past tense."

"Yup." A hefty slug from the tumbler. A hissed growl as it burns on the way down; this is thick, bold scotch, with a rough burn that only turns honey-smooth after you've swallowed it.

"Divorced?"

He shakes his head. "Nope."

"Shit." This hits close. "She, um…she passed?"

He harrumphs. "Hate that bullshit phrase. *She passed*, like she just sorta moved on, nice and easy. She died."

I take a more tentative sip. "You, uh. You want to talk about it?"

He's silent for a long time. "I've talked to a shrink. After she died. Every week for six months. Helped, I guess. Very least, I started to understand what I was feeling. Which is…it's a fucking lot."

My face burns. The whiskey is unsettled in my belly. I can't look at him—I'm scared he'll see the nature of my curiosity. "I imagine it is a lot."

"No. You don't imagine." His forefinger, the size of a frankfurter, if not thicker, taps rapidly on the bar top. "It's just so much, man. And it's all tangled together like one big rubber band ball of fuckedupness."

I go for a sideways bolt of honesty. "I don't know how to navigate this conversation, Nathan. I want to ask, but not if it's going to hurt you more. You want to talk, talk. I'll listen."

He humphs again, snorting into his whiskey, a narrowing echo of sound as he brings the tumbler to his lips through the snort. "You don't know what to ask?"

"What not to, more like."

He chews on the inside of his cheek. "Ask me about her."

"What was her name? What was she like?"

"Lisa. Lisa Leanne Fischer. Thompson, originally. She was tiny. Five three in socks, a buck ten soaking wet. Somehow made short and lean look curvy. Blond hair, blue eyes. Firecracker. Girl was hell on wheels, man. All attitude and sarcasm. Funny as hell." He sighs. "Most I've talked about her since she died. In therapy I tended to talk about how I was feeling, not her."

"Have you…" I hesitate. "I dunno how to put what I'm trying to ask."

"Just ask, Adrian. Won't offend me."

"How do you move on? *Have* you moved on?"

He shrugs. "I don't think I have. I don't know how. She was my first serious girlfriend. Dated for five years, junior year of high school to junior year of college for her, through my apprenticeship and journeyman carpentry programs for me. We eloped." He laughs. "Her parents hated me. She was from money, like old South money. She didn't want anything to do with it, so when they refused to bless the marriage, she said fuck 'em and we eloped. Drove to Vegas, got married by Elvis."

"Legit?"

He snorts, laughs louder. "Yeah. Sober as a post, both of us. *Then* we got drunk and blew a couple grand at the blackjack tables and slot machines. Came home, got an apartment together, and that was life." A long silence. "Then a semi driver fell asleep at the wheel, crossed the center line, crushed her little Camry like a can of Coke. Killed her instantly. She was on the way to meet me for dinner after work. Phone rang while I was sitting at our table, waiting."

"Jeez, dude. I'm so sorry."

He nods. "Thanks." He shakes his head, then. "How do you move on, man? I went on a date, a few weeks ago. Girl I met at a coffee shop. I couldn't handle it. How do you tell a girl you just met that you've got dead wife? When do you mention it? Second date? Third? You gotta explain why you're so grumpy, closed off. But you tell her too soon, it freaks her out. Makes her think you're trying to...replace her? I dunno. I think that, myself. How do I replace Lisa? I know in my head that I can't, that I'm not going to do that. But tell that to my heart." He throws back the rest of his whiskey. "It's a tough row to hoe."

"I..." I want to say this is valuable insight, but that would be crass and would open up a conversation I'm not ready to have with anyone. "I guess you're right when you said I can't imagine."

"God damn but I hope you never have to, my friend."

"Me too," I whisper, but it's lost in my tumbler.

I won't have to. That's the problem. I know, I know, there's still a chance I'll make it through this. The experimental chemo might work. I've been loathe to try radiation. Surgery's out. But in my heart of hearts, deep down, I'm absolutely terrified because I don't think I am going to make it through this.

And it'll be Nadia sitting here, having this conversation with someone.

That's when it hits me.

An idea, or rather the completion of the idea I had earlier.

I can help her.

No one knows Nadia better than me, not even her. I know how she'll react—and predicting human behavior is what I do. It's part of the magic trick of inventing people. I can help her, when I'm gone. But in order to do that, I have to start now.

"Tell me about your wife," he says, apropos of nothing. "Nadine?"

"Nadia."

We tended to stick to whiskey and westerns, old girlfriends, epic party stories. Macho bro-y stuff.

"Sorry, I knew that. I'm a little drunk."

"It's cool." I sigh. Here's a topic I can wax poetic about endlessly. "What do you want to know?"

"Whatever." A pause, ice tinkling as he swirls it in the dregs. "What made you fall in love with her?"

"Oh, man." I laugh, scrape a hand through my hair—wince when my hand comes away with loose hair stuck to it. Fucking chemo. "Honest answer? Her ass."

He chortles. "You fell in love with her ass."

"Yup." I'm tipsy enough that truth is easy, too easy. "She's tall, man. Five-nine, almost five-ten. Slender. Not skinny, just slender. Tits are a handful, just barely. I like it that way. But her ass, man."

He shakes his head. "Lisa was like that. Similar build. Got me every time she turned around. Like *damn*, would you look at that ass?"

I laugh, nod. "Exactly. Serious, though, that's what I first noticed about her. I was in the English program, she was in nursing school, taking a creative writing course I was the TA for. Taking it just for kicks, 'cause she likes a challenge." I let my mind float backward in time. "She wasn't a great writer. Shit at spelling, like to the point where it was comical. But what caught my attention was her focus. She would be at her desk writing, and her concentration was just total. But…god, how do I put it? It's different than when you love something and get lost in it. That's easy, right? For you, when you're in the workshop building something, you get in the zone, right?"

He nods. "Oh yeah. More so when I'm doing something for fun. Whittling gets me like that, as opposed to, like, building a chair or a bookshelf or a set. That's work. Whittling an owl or something, that's when I get what you're talking about."

"For her, writing was the other kind of concentration. A skill, you know?"

He nods. "Yep."

"That's what got me. Her ability to truly focus. It's sexy."

He rubs the back of his head. "Never heard anyone say concentration is sexy, but I get what you mean."

"Last day of class, last assignment I handed back to her, I put my number on it. Two days later, she called, and we went out. And I discovered that she's quick-witted, that she was demanding, but always more demanding of herself than anyone else. I discovered that she hates downtime, hates being idle. Hates being bored. Hates waiting. Which is why her ability to focus so totally is sexy, because her nature is the opposite. It's a sign of a strong mind."

"Lisa was crazy smart," Nathan says. "She went to MIT, but she was so ahead, so smart that a tech company here in Atlanta hired her before she even graduated. She could do shit with computers that's just magical. Like that cello guy, Yo-Yo Ma. She was like that, but with computers."

"Smart is sexy."

He nods. "Sure is."

I eye him. "Nathan, do you think maybe you can't move on because you don't really want to, deep down?"

He doesn't answer for a long, long time. "Fuck." His glass is long empty, and he's just twirling it on a bottom edge. "Yeah, you may be right."

"I just—"

"I'm lonely, dude. Go home alone every night, sleep alone, wake up alone…it sucks. After nine years of going to sleep next to her and waking up next to her, being lonely just fuckin'…sucks. So part of me really does want to move on. Find someone. But…I don't know how. How do you explain yourself to someone new? There's so much in here," he taps his forehead, "and here," his chest, "and I just…I don't know how to go about showing it to anyone. She just *got* me. Lisa, I mean. We had years together to figure it out. We were young. It was easy. Feels different now. I feel…heavy, inside."

"Would you? If the right person came along… would you?"

"Try?"

"Yeah."

"Yeah, I would. I really would. I'd fuck it up, probably, but I'd go for it. I guess deep down, I know Lisa would want me to. I guess part of me wants her permission, and I don't know how to reconcile that."

I nod. "What would you do differently?" I'm

pushing it. I know I am, but I'm in the grip of an idea, and it's making sense of my desperation, that fierce furious desperation I feel all the time now.

"Be home more. Talk more. Tell her how I feel more openly. She was always after me to open up, but I couldn't figure out what the fuck she meant. And I think I get it now. I think I could do that better, now. I'd do things for her. So she'd know." A gruff clearing of his throat. "I'd treasure each moment, because we ain't guaranteed a single goddamn one of them."

Fuck, that hits me like a javelin. It punches into my chest so hard my breath whooshes out like he physically punched me with his giant cinderblock fist. Might as well have. Hits me so hard I get nauseous.

He notices. "Dude, Adrian, you okay?"

I nod. "Yeah," I rasp, hoarse. "Swallowed wrong."

"Bullshit."

I glance at him. "I'm sorry?"

He eyes me. Eyes somewhere between brown and gray, deep, serious. "That was rank bullshit. You didn't swallow wrong." He clenches his fist, taps a knuckle on the bar. "Adrian, why're you asking me this shit?"

"Curious."

He nods. "You're lying."

I laugh, but it's bitter, morbid. "Yeah."

He lets out a long breath. "All right. Keep your lie. You got your reasons, I guess." He tugs a card out of his hip pocket, hands it to the bartender. "On me."

"Nathan, let me—"

"On me."

"Okay," I say. "Thank you."

He shakes his head. "No, thank you. I needed this, man. More than you know. Getting home today, to *that* home, alone, it just…it hit me and I couldn't be alone. And you were the first person I thought of."

"Honored to be, buddy. Honored."

The bartender hands him the black plastic tray with the receipt; he tips generously, totals, scrawls a sloppy signature. He stands. Claps me on the shoulder, gently, but it rocks me forward with a jolt. "You want to unburden yourself of whatever it is you're carrying, Adrian? You let me know."

I want to, in that moment. So damn bad. "Some burdens can't be put down, my friend. But thank you. I know you mean it."

"Yeah, I guess I get that." He stumbles a bit.

"You're not driving are you?"

He shakes his head. "Nah. I knew I couldn't go home tonight. So I got a hotel a couple blocks away. Bottle of Blanton's waiting for me. I'll deal with going home tomorrow." He juts his chin at me. "You're not driving either, I take it. You had as much as me, and you weigh probably a good buck less."

"I got an Uber here. When we sit down to drink, we don't mess around."

I stand up, and we man-hug, and then he ambles

away—his tread is heavy, as if that weight he talked about, feeling heavy, inside, was nearly too much to stand up under.

I watch him go, and I knew then, down to my bones and in my balls and in my blood, what I had to do. It hurt. I wanted to deny it. To put it off. To fight, to hope; I would fight, I would hope, until the bitter end, I would. I'd hope this would all be for nothing. Wasted effort, wasted time. Wasted pain. Wasted sacrifice. But I knew I had to.

For my conscience.

For Nadia.

Six

Whispers & Wine

Being married to a writer is hard. Don't let anyone ever say different. They're aloof, when they're writing. It's not you, it's them. They don't mean to be, it's just the job. That notebook opens, that computer turns on, keys start clacking, pen starts scribbling—that person is gone. It's the story, then, and it takes them.

He usually writes with his office door open, some classical music on in the background, cello or guitar or piano.

A month after his trip up to the East Coast, and he's got his office door closed, locked. Silence, but for the *tick-tick-tock-tick-tickety-tickety-tock-tock-tock* of the keyboard. Fast and loud, meaning he's really moving. Adrian is gone and all that exists in that room is a conduit, fingers and a story.

I'm worried.

He comes out after eight hours in there, looking wan. Shaky. Thin. In the words of Bilbo Baggins, he looks like butter scraped over too much bread.

I've made a pot of stew, left it to simmer for him. I'm reading, my day off. He comes out, props himself against the range with one hand, lifts the lid of the pot. Sniffs.

"It's been ready to eat for hours, babe," I say, rising. "Let me get you some."

He waves me off. "Nah, nah. I'll do it."

I sit back down, and he ladles himself a bowl. Brings it to the couch where I am. Eats in silence.

"Adrian, are you okay? I'm worried about you."

He eats steadily, mechanically. "I'm okay."

I frown. "I'm not just your wife, you know. I'm a trained medical professional. And I don't think you are…okay, that is."

He stops eating, abruptly. Sets the bowl on his thigh. Sighs. "I know. I just…I have to write this."

"That's not an answer to my question, Adrian."

"I know, I know." He finishes the last few bites. "That was great, Nadia. Thank you."

"You're welcome. Now talk to me, honey."

He blinks. His jaw works. His eyes drop; embarrassed, angry, bitter, sad—I can't tell. "I can't."

"You're hiding something." I blurt it out—I feel the words topple out of my mouth like stones tumbling down a hillside.

"Yes."

My heart sinks. Pangs. "If you try to tell me you're having an affair, I'll just laugh. And then murder you in your sleep."

He snorts. "Not in a million years, my love." He gives me his eyes, open and frank, at least in this. "Never."

I know it's true. My heart knows it. "Then what?"

He shakes his head. "Not yet."

"Adrian, please."

He sets the bowl on the coffee table—the spoon clatters noisily. His eyes are gray, almost silver. Turns to face me, those eyes heavy, hiding something. Sadness, I can see it. Panic. Desperation.

For the first time since I met him, I don't get what I ask for.

"Nadia…" He ducks his head. Seems to have trouble breathing. "Not yet. Please. I love you. More than I can ever—more than I can ever fucking express. I just…"

I palm his cheeks. "Make me a promise and I'll let it go."

"Okay?"

"You ask me for help, if it's something I can give. Anything. My last breath, you ask for it—I'll give it. You love me; you're mine and no one else's. You don't leave me. Promise."

This is, suddenly, everything.

One of those moments that are etched into your soul, a mile deep.

He blinks. Tugs away, ducks his head. "Everything I do, Nadia, I do for you. Never doubt that."

"Adrian, you didn't—"

A harsh sigh. He visibly rallies, gathers himself. Looks me in the eye, clear and strong. "I promise. Whatever you can do, I will let you do. I'll ask. I'm yours. Totally. More now than when we exchanged rings. Forever, I'm yours. I will never…" he falters here. "I won't leave you. I swear on my soul."

"Okay." I clutch him to me, and I feel him breathing hard. "Okay, Adrian."

"Okay?"

I nod against his shoulder. "Okay."

I want to hold him forever. As if to let go, now, is to somehow let go in some deeper metaphysical way I cannot truly grasp. But I do. I let him go. "Go back to work, babe. I can feel you needing it."

"Just a little more. Then I'll come to bed."

"I work—"

"Seven to three tomorrow, noon to midnight Wednesday, seven to three Thursday and Friday, off the weekend." He smirks. "I know your schedule before you do."

I laugh. "Yeah, yeah. Creeper."

He pauses at the door to his office, which I can see from my place on the couch. "Nadia."

I pick up my book. Smile at him. "Yeah?"

"You're cute. I like you."

"You gonna keep me, then?"

He laughs out loud. "Yeah, babe. I know a good thing when I snag it, and I ain't letting go of you." His words are light, but I feel like if I were closer, I'd see a heaviness behind them.

I feel the pilot light of my panic furnace kick on. *Whoomp.* Just a simmer, at first. But it's growing. And the more he dissembles, the higher the dial will go. He knows he can't fool me, not for long. So now he's not even trying. He's still not talking, not sharing: I still can't get through.

I know him, though.

He can't hide anything from me for long.

But for the first time, I wonder if I want to know.

If maybe this is something I'm better off not knowing.

"Beaches!" Tess garbles, around a mouthful of mint chocolate chip ice cream.

"Hell no!" I shout from the couch, flipping through Netflix. "I need the opposite of sobbing my eyeballs out. *Dumb and Dumber*?"

"'Hey, you wanna hear the most annoying sound in the world? AAAAAHHHHHH!'" She does a gratingly accurate impression of Jim Carrey in that scene, to the point that I throw a throw pillow at her face from across her living room.

"Is that a yes or a no?" I ask.

"Nah," she says, batting it aside. "Seen it a bazillion times. *Far and Away*?"

"'Tell me you like my hat, Shannon,'" I quote, in a terrible Irish accent. "Nuh-uh. *Eat, Pray, Love?*"

She brings over the gallon of ice cream, hands it to me, and returns to her kitchen, where she peruses the wine rack in her pantry. "Josh, Joel Gott, Jordan… Decoy, Duckhorn…"

I twist on the couch, to stare at her. "Tess McAlister. Do you have your wines alphabetized?"

"No," she says, her voice defensive and sullen. "Maybe. Yes. Shut up. I was bored, okay? Clint was in Milwaukee for two damn weeks, and I was bored out of my fucking mind. So I alphabetized the wine. And the DVDs we haven't watched in like, five years. And the, um, soup."

"Soup?" I take a bite of mint chocolate chip. "You alphabetized your damn soup? If you're that bored, you need a hobby. Needlepoint or some shit."

"By that point, I'd crocheted an entire scarf, done about fifty word searches and three crossword puzzles, and only cheated twice on the crosswords, by the way and thank you very much. I even did fucking Sudoku, and you know numbers make my nose bleed. I watched an entire season of Grey's Anatomy, and all three *Lord of the Rings* movies, *with* commentary and bonus features."

I laugh. "At that point call me. You can organize my pantry for me."

She fakes a violent shudder. "No thanks, bitch, I've seen *that* abomination."

"Shut up, it's not that bad."

"You have chicken stock next to coffee beans and ketchup with soup. It is exactly that bad."

"Which is why I need your organizational magic."

"You couldn't pay me enough."

"*Anyway. Eat, Pray, Love*, and…Joel Gott. Yes?"

"Agreed." She withdraws the bottle, uncorks it, brings it and two stemless wineglasses over, sits on the couch beside me, and pours us each a generous glass, and by generous I mean nearly to the brim. Then, she grabs her gavel—an actual antique gavel, once used in an actual courthouse—and slams it down three times. "I hereby declare this Period Party in session. May our cramps be gentle and our bleeding light."

"Amen, and so shall it be," I intone, getting into the spirit of things.

We find the movie we'd agreed on, get it going, and share the gallon of ice cream while slurping wine; we have an ongoing contest to see who could slurp the loudest before the other one gets pissed off. So far she always wins, thanks to misophonia.

Tess is my best friend, and really, my only friend. Adrian and I have lived in Atlanta for six years, but my work schedule sort of precludes a social life. Tess and I went to college together, and she and her husband Clint moved down here from Pennsylvania shortly after Adrian and I moved here from North Carolina. The moment her moving truck arrived, we picked up our friendship where it had left off. During college, she and I and the girls in the rooms around ours instituted what we called the Period Party, where we'd get together once a month, usually around the same time because these things tend to synch, and eat garbage and get drunk and watch movies and commiserate about nature and men and life. When Tess moved near me, we started it up again, just the two of us.

We finish the ice cream and the wine—well, the first bottle—and have to take a pause break to take care of bathroom issues related to the reason for getting together. Tess brings another bottle, but this time it's not wine, it's tequila.

I frown at the bottle of Patrón. "Um. Are we escalating this party to upper management?"

She nods. "I got an email while I was in the bathroom."

"At ten fifty-five at night?"

"From Clint."

"He's in Chicago, right?"

"Supposedly." Her eyes are red-rimmed.

"Oh. Oh no."

"He's filing."

"What? For divorce? *Why?*"

She sits down, pours tequila into her wineglass, shoots it, hissing. "I guess these business trips he's been going on for the last few years haven't been all entirely business. He's been seeing someone, and by seeing I mean fucking. From his department, I guess."

"Tess. God, no." I wipe my face, as if to wipe away disbelief. "And *he's* filing?"

She nods, shoots another. "Yup. He's giving me the house, my car, and fifty percent of our financial assets, either cashed out or transferred to me through some banker mumbo jumbo I don't give a shit about. All he's asking is avoiding court, squabbling over bullshit. And I'm fine with that."

"No, you're not."

She laughs bitterly. "No, I'm not. But I don't have the heart to fight. He's been miserable for years. I thought it was me. I've tried everything, Nads. I pulled back my hours so I could be home more, but he increased his, started these trips. I moved my yoga area in the basement up here so he could have a man-cave... he never uses it and isn't home to use it anyway. I...I spent a thousand dollars on lingerie, went on this whole spice-up-the-bedroom campaign. Started blowing him the moment he walked in the door, cooking in lingerie. Surprising him in the shower, everything I could think of. He'd let me do shit for him, but then blew me off as soon he got off. Nothing was enough."

"Tess, come on. You know this is on him."

"Damn right it's on him. But it makes you wonder—what's wrong with me, you know?"

"Can I just say *fuck him* for telling you via email?" My voice goes shrill with rage. "Fucking *email*? What a pussy."

She glares at me. "No, don't you dare denigrate the sacred pussy that way. Pussies are strong. Powerful. Mysterious, sexy. We have babies with our pussies. He's a limp cock—funny-looking and dangly and useless."

I nod. "Truth, babe, truth."

"He's a limp dick," she repeats. "Good riddance." Another shot. "I'm not sad. I'm angry. But I also think I knew. His business trips suddenly went from a couple days to a week max to a week, two weeks, and from one every couple months to at least one a month. I think half that time has been actual business, and the rest is vacation and dicking his assistant or whoever this bitch is."

"I'm sorry, Tess. You deserve better."

She huffs, squaring her shoulders. "I'm not going to wallow. I'm signing his stupid papers, taking my maiden name back, and going on the warpath."

"Warpath?"

"Against men."

"Meaning?"

"Meaning I started dating Clint in high school. I went to college to be near him. Chose a job that would enable his career. Worked from home to take care of Yvette." Their daughter, now eighteen and going to college—Tess is a few years older than me, and they had Yvette young. She pours a shot but this one she hands to me. "I know, I know, you have to work tomorrow. Just do a couple shots with me, Nads. Please."

"Fine." I take the shot, coughing and hissing. "But only for you, because I love you and this sucks. God I hate tequila."

"It's the glorious juice of forgetting."

"It's the glorious juice of getting arrested for reckless behavior, public intoxication, and public urination."

She flips me off. "That was one time, bitch, *one* time."

"What's the warpath, though? Because I'm not following."

"I'm gonna sow my wild oats, Nads. Yvette comes home for major holidays at most, and now I'm single again, so I'm gonna go out and get all cougar on Hotlanta."

"No one here calls it that."

"I know. I was being funny."

"Well. Use a condom and take Ubers. Last thing you need is a DUI and an unexpected pregnancy."

She waves a hand. "Psshh. I'm perimenopausal already, so that's not an issue. Uber is magical, though."

"You're only just barely over forty." I frown. "And I don't think being perimenopausal means you're no longer fertile. You have to be through it all the way."

"I'm forty-two, and my mom was menopausal by forty-five. And I'll be careful." She points at me with her spoon. "You're next, so pay attention."

"Am not. I'm thirty-nine, so I'm a baby compared

to you. I've got years to go, still." I hate my next words even as they emerge. "Fat lot of good they'll do me."

She pours me another shot—it tastes funny, with the residue of the wine mixed in. "Nothing, still?"

I shake my head. "Nope. I'm fertile Myrtle, according to tests, but he's not."

"Shooting blanks?"

I nod. "Seems that way."

"What about—"

"Tried it, twice. Didn't take. Haven't had the courage to try again." I twist my wedding band. "Plus, he's...I don't know."

She slowly sets the bottle down. "He's what?"

"Lying about something. Or, hiding something, rather."

"How do you know?"

"He told me."

She laughs in disbelief. "He *told* you he's hiding something?"

"Yeah."

"But not what?"

I shake my head, tears stinging my eyes, words now clogged in my throat.

"He's not cheating is he?" She sounds like she finds that as hard to believe as I do.

"No." It's barely a word, more of a hissed sound.

She huffs. "Yeah, I can't believe that of Adrian. No man has ever loved a woman the way Adrian loves you." A shake of her head. "So that being true, what could he be hiding?"

I shake my head and shrug, fighting sobs. "I..." One escapes, a low ragged one. "I'm scared, Tess. Really, really scared."

"Like, you think he's sick or something? And trying to hide it to protect you or some macho bullshit like that?"

I nod. "He's losing weight. I think he's secretly throwing up. I think his research trips aren't all...just research."

"Why hide it? I don't understand."

I wipe my face with both hands, rub vigorously. "Because he knows me. He knows I would full Amazon on his ass. Take care of him, baby him. I'd quit my job to nurse him. I'd sell my fucking soul for him, and he knows it." I now take a shot for me. "My dad died young, you know that. When I was six. He died slow, and I...it's why I went into nursing. To take care of people, the way I did Dad."

"Nadia, Jesus. You were *six*."

"Some things you don't forget," I say. "So Adrian... he thinks he's protecting me from him, from myself."

"It's bullshit. You deserve to know."

"One time, when we were first married, he lied about being sick. Toughed it out, pretended he was fine. And then his appendix burst and he almost died. I was so mad at him, Tess, you don't even know. He wasn't sorry at all. Not a word of apology. Told me he did it for me and he'd do it again. And he has, our whole marriage. He refuses to let me nurse him. Says I do it enough for work, so he's going to be my husband, not my patient."

"Wow."

"Won't even cop to having a damn cold." I speak like I have a stuffed-up nose: *"He'd dalk lide dis,* and have the balls to be like, naw, I'm fine. Just a stuffy nose. Flu? Waits till he can't stand up before admitting he's sick, and then he locks himself in his office with a water bottle and an iPad and doesn't come out till he's on his feet again."

"I knew he was stubborn, but damn."

"So I guess I should expect this from him, but…" I shake my head again. "I have no proof that's what it is. I just know he's not okay."

"What are you going to do?"

"I don't know. I can't make him tell me. I mean, I can put down an ultimatum or something but…I don't want to do that."

"So you're just gonna wait him out?"

"He's not lying out of malice, or…or to like, hide something he shouldn't be doing. It's not a white lie, because that's bullshit anyway, but it's…I don't know. He has good reasons, in his mind. I don't know, Tess. I just don't."

We both cry, then.

"What a pair we are today, huh?" Tess says.

"Yeah," I whisper. "No kidding."

"Call in tomorrow," she suggests. "Get hammered with me."

I shake my head. "I think I have to start saving up my liver function. Just a hunch. Plus, we're already short-staffed tomorrow, that's why I'm working a double—I'm covering for Rachel."

"Fine. Lame-ass."

"Not lame—responsible."

"Lame."

"Shut up."

A companionable, sorrowful, angry silence.

"I'm gonna sell the house. Get a condo downtown." She flaps a hand. "It's too much house for one little old lady."

"Little old lady my ass."

"It's too much house."

"I know."

"Nads?"

"Tess-icles?"

"You know I'll be here for you. No matter what."

"I know. Same."

"Am I allowed to be angry at him for you?"

"No."

"You're too nice."

"He's my husband."

A sigh. "Yes, he is."

"Condoms, Tess. They're not just for pregnancy. You also don't want syphilis."

"Shush. I know. I'm forty-two, hon, I know how safe sex works."

"You do not. You've never slept with anyone but Clint."

"Have too."

I sit up and look at her. "You have? Who?"

"We were on a break." She snickers at the *Friends* reference. "It was freshman year of college. I fucked a guy on my debate team."

"Oh. Oh god. And how was that?"

She snorts. "There's a reason I went back to Clint. He's a douchebag, and I'm realizing he always has been. But god, the man can screw like nobody's business."

"Well, like more than just your business, it seems."

"Too soon, Nads. Too soon."

"No it isn't."

She snickers. "No, it's not."

I sigh. "I'm gonna go."

"You should wait a bit longer. It's only a few blocks, but still."

"I'll walk."

"It's nearly midnight."

"We could borrow Rufus. Toby is always awake till at least two."

Toby: Her gay next-door neighbor owns Rufus, a Rottweiler the size of a 747. The dog is sweet as sugar to Tess and me, but to anyone else? Don't get too close, is all I'm saying.

"Good plan."

Toby answers the door wearing a pink kimono, sipping something vividly orange from a martini glass. "Ladies? Here to party, are we?" His voice is deep, smooth, and masculine—not a hint of a lisp or affectation. You wouldn't know his orientation from talking to him, or seeing him in his business suit at nine in the morning.

"We already did our partying," Tess says.

He glances up and to the side, thinking. "Oh. *That* party."

"Right."

"And you're out of booze? I'm making these martinis. I could whip up another batch."

"Actually, we just need to borrow Rufus so we can walk Nadia home."

"Ah. By all means. Rufus!" He calls the dog like you'd call for a person in another room. There's a scrabbling of paws on hardwood, and a short-furred brown bear appears next to Toby. "You want to go for a walk?"

Rufus barks, and I feel the bass of it in my gut.

"Say his name, pat your thigh, and tell him to heel," Toby tells Tess. "He'll stick right by you."

I eye the dog nervously. I've only been with him around Toby. "Um. Do we need a leash?"

"Nah. A cat could run in front of you—unless you tell him to go, he'll stay on your heel. I paid a shitload of money in dog training, but it's worth it."

"And if someone makes trouble?" I ask.

He laughs, a morbid chuckle. "You call me, and we get rid of the body."

"Oh." I giggle, inappropriately. "Wait. Can you really do that?"

"I'm a deputy DA, sweetheart. Yeah, I can do that."

I pat Rufus on the head. "Good boy, Rufus. Nice pup."

Rufus barks again, and it startles me even though I'm expecting it. He's got a big doggy grin, happily waiting for the walk.

We go slow, talking about less heavy things; as promised, Rufus walks next to Tess's heel as if tethered there by an invisible leash, exactly one step behind and to the right of her—he's tall enough she can rest her hand on his shoulder as they walk, and I notice his eyes are constantly roving, his nose sniffing, alert, watchful.

Tess walks me home, takes me to my door. She hugs me. "When it's time to go to court to end this whole shitshow, you're gonna go with me, right?"

"Wouldn't miss it for all the Josh in California."

She holds my arms. "Nads…"

"I'll let you know when I know anything. But for

now, if you were to suddenly develop an urge to pray, I wouldn't mind a few prayers."

She snorts. "Maybe we should go to church together this Sunday."

"'Dear God, I'll go to church at least once if you promise to perform a miracle for me.'" I roll my eyes at her. "Not sure that's how it works."

"Worth a shot?"

I nod, suddenly exhausted. "Yeah, maybe it is."

Another hug. "I love you, Nads."

"Love you too, Tess-icles."

When I go inside, Adrian is still in his office. Click-click-click, goes the keyboard. There's a cough, a wet one, and I'm not sure if it's him throwing up or coughing up blood, but it sounds *awful*. A groan.

"Adrian?" I call, through the door. "I'm home."

"Hiya, babe." He cracks open the door, leans in to kiss me. "Have a good time?"

I shrug. "Not really that kind of a party, but it was good to see Tess."

He's so pale, so thin. His cheekbones stand out more now. Our conversation over that bowl of stew was a month ago, and there's no denying something is physically wrong.

His eyes are haunted. He's working all the time. Sometimes I come home from work and he's gone. Or I wake up and he's left before me. I don't ask where he's going, but I know I'm going to find out soon.

I can feel it.

And I don't want to know.

I have to know, but I don't want to.

Panic burns hot, deep down.

He pulls me inside his office, wraps me up in an embrace. He's as strong as ever, it seems. He grips me fiercely. "I love you," he whispers.

"Tell me."

"Soon." A sigh. "Soon."

"When?"

He touches his forehead to mine. Kisses my hair, my temple. Then reaches back and picks up something off his desk. "We're going on vacation." A seeming non sequitur.

He hands me two first-class tickets to Paris.

"Paris?" I want to be excited, but fear is what I feel.

He nods. "Paris, for a month."

"A *month*?"

He winks at me. "Pack light. You won't need much clothing."

I roll my eyes. "We're not going to fly all the way to France to spend the entire time fucking in the hotel room."

He kisses my temple. "No, we're not. Not the *entire* time, at least."

"A month. I've saved up a bunch of sick days, but..."

"I've already worked it out with your boss. It's

covered. You have three weeks off, paid, the fourth used as sick days."

"Sneaky, sneaky," I laugh, and lean against him. "Just come to bed, Adrian. Please?"

He glances over his shoulder at his laptop, open, the blue-white light illuminating the otherwise dark room. "Okay. Bed, then."

I smirk up at him. "I'll make it worth your while."

He palms my butt. "You always do, my love."

"Ah, the old ass grab. The most romantic move in any man's repertoire."

We tease each other all the way upstairs, and my heart is in it, my body is in it, and even most of my mind. But there's a part of me that notices how he always manages to pull my attention away from the issue without answering any questions, manages to deflect away from his refusal to talk to me about what's going on with him.

A month in Paris, I reflect, as I lie awake, afterward. He's snoring beside me, turned to face me, one leg thrown over mine, his manhood slack and wet against my hip, hand flung over my breast.

A month in Paris is way more than a vacation.

Fear is building. Panic. Desperation.

"Don't leave me," I whisper to my sleeping husband. "Please, don't leave me."

Never. I won't leave you. I swear on my soul.

Keep that promise, my love. Please.

Seven

The Truth Will Out

"WELCOME TO CHARLES DE GAULLE INTERNATIONAL Airport. The local time is 1:43a.m...." the message continues with announcements and information, and then everything is repeated in French.

We packed light. One suitcase each, one carry-on each, plus one extra empty suitcase each. I've rented a flat in the 4th Arrondissement, Le Marais: trendy, hip, close to all the best of everything Paris has to offer... or so said the travel agent I hired to set this all up. Not knowing any better, I went with her expertise. I mean, she *did* have a French accent, and her name *was* Eloise Gautier, and her office *is* in Paris, so it stands to reason she'd know.

She told me our flat is a top-floor corner spot, with the most romantic view of the Eiffel Tower you can ask for. I paid extra to have it stocked with hand-picked red wine and champagne, stuffed to embarrassment with profusions of roses and bouquets of wildflowers, to have the fridge filled with cheese and strawberries and blueberries and yogurt and charcuterie meat and baguettes in the breadbox. Candles everywhere—I send a text when we're leaving the airport, and the agent will send someone to light the candles. We have a car service, available to us twenty-four seven for the duration of our stay. I've scheduled a personal shopper for Nadia, and took out a credit card with an eye-watering credit limit.

I've also got essentially a bucket of high-dose painkiller narcotics, not just the good stuff but the best stuff. I sampled them a few days ago, when I first got them, and whoa. Seriously whoa. I have to be careful, judicious. Mainly at night, so I can sleep, or only during the day if it's too much to bear.

I've gone all out for this trip. I cashed out a bunch of investments to pay for it, and did some financial jujitsu with the rest, moving them to less risky, more stable portfolios, and all solely in Nadia's name. I've done a lot, the past couple months. My final book is done. The arrangements have all been made.

The entire reason I booked this trip in the first place is because I met with my oncologist, Dr. Jerry Lowell, not that long ago.

"All we can really do at this point, Adrian," he'd told me, "is try to make you as comfortable as we can. We can keep doing chemo if you want, it'll push things out a few more weeks, maybe a few more months at most. But…in the end, there's really nothing else we can do."

"Say I stop all chemo, all treatments," I'd said. "How long?"

"Two, maybe three months. Three and a half on the outside."

I'd nodded. "I had a feeling." My eyes had burned, and Dr. Jerry had the decency to find something on his computer to do while I fought for composure. "So, how do we make me comfortable? Meaning, I want to be able to enjoy the time I have left with my wife as much as possible."

He'd nodded, and explained my options to me.

So now, here we are. Paris. The trip of a lifetime. Of course, we've been here before. London, Hong Kong, Tokyo, Berlin, Perth, Dublin, Reykjavik, lots of places. Signing tours, film publicity tours, that kind of thing. But they had always been for work. We always took a few extra days around the event to see the sights and play tourist, but we've never taken a major vacation like this without there being some kind of work event connected to it.

This is…not goodbye. Not yet. This is…I don't know what the hell it is. Time with my wife, my best friend. An epic send-off. Memories to hold on to as I near the end.

I push my morbid thoughts aside as we slide through Paris traffic. I'm holding her hand, watching her more than the sights. She's radiant, lovelier than ever. She had her hair trimmed, three inches off the bottom. Got a manicure, a pedicure, the works. Her eyes soak up the sights.

I'm going to make this the best month of her life. Take all the drugs to kill the pain and fight the nausea. Pretend it's a stomach bug that won't quite go away. There'll be time, later.

I know she should have more time to adjust, but… selfishly, I can't give her that. I want this time for us.

Us without

The Big C

between us, hanging like a bloody carcass, dripping effluvia all over our joy.

No. This trip is about us.

The first two weeks have been magical. We spent it walking, shopping, sitting in cafes sipping espresso and eating flaky, delicate pastries.

We attended Mass in Notre Dame at midnight. The nave was bigger than belief, the vaulted ceiling dark with age. A beautiful young woman in a blue gown sang an aria in Latin, sang it with such holy, reverent beauty that we both wept.

One day we strolled across the Pont des Arts bridge with hundreds of padlocks on it—there was signage posted in English and French prohibiting further locks, because the weight of them was beginning to compromise the integrity of the bridge, but we stood there at the apex of that romantic bridge at sunset, watching the water flow underneath like a ribbon of silk blowing in a silent wind. The locks caught the light, reflected and refracted, and each one represented a love story. We examined some of the locks and pretended we could determine the details of the lives of the people who'd put them there.

We lay in the long green lawn under the dizzying height of the Eiffel Tower, listening to the chatter of a dozen languages, watching lovers take selfies.

We made love, endlessly. I required a lot of chemical help, now, but she didn't need to know that. All she needed to know was that I loved her, that I worshiped her body, that I treasured her.

I barely sleep anymore. It's like my mind, now that the end grows near, refuses to let miss even a few hours of life.

I watch her sleep.

I write poems to her, about her, for her.

I write vignettes, remembering our life together. That time we tried to adopt a dog from a shelter, and it turned out to be a wild monster of destruction, sweet and hysterical but obsessed with eating couches and shoes and counters and cabinets and even, when locked in the garage, my lawnmower. It ate my fucking lawnmower. The final straw for it was when it ate Nadia's Michael Kors purse—literally ate it, devoured every last scrap of expensive leather.

There are a thousand stories, and I lie awake and try to remember them all, write them all. What I'll do with the collection, I don't know. Maybe nothing. Maybe it's just for me.

She wakes up, sees me in the bed next to her, my laptop on my thighs, the screen glow lighting my face. Snuggles closer. Kisses my shoulder.

⸎

It's taking more and more drugs to act normal.

We have a week left. I feel my body shutting down. I feel things beginning to fail.

I'm not ready, goddammit.

I mean, in terms of "wrapping up my affairs" I'm as ready as I can be. It's all arranged, everything is taken care of. She won't have to do a thing, after I'm gone.

Sometimes, when I do manage to catch a little sleep, I wake up and see that she's watching me.

Once, after a long night of sex and wine and French TV, I fell asleep on the couch and I woke up curled on her lap like a cat, and she was stroking my hair, what's left of it, and she was crying.

She knows.

But when we're awake, we pretend this is just a vacation.

It's what I need, and she knows it. She needs it too, but I'm not sure she realizes the depth of that, just yet.

I had to convince her to splurge on the shopping trips. She's a naturally thrifty person, doesn't let herself spend a lot very often. One time I wanted her to buy a Porsche, but she settled for an A5. I wanted her to get a Chanel bag, and she bought a Louis Vuitton.

This time, I insisted. It's taken care of, I told her. So she did. Reluctantly at first, but when she saw the way it made me smile, she let herself get into it and enjoy the splurge.

We wake up to our last morning in our Parisian flat.

We pack up, and I tell her to leave everything but her carry-on and purse, it'll all be taken care of.

We haul our carry-ons down to the cafe a half block from our flat, where we've become regulars this past month. We get espresso and *pain au chocolat*, sit one last time watching the passersby, gazing lovingly at each other.

"Thank you for this," she says, finally, after a long thoughtful silence between us.

I've been getting emotional, lately. I have to fight it so she doesn't misinterpret it. "No, Nadia. Thank you. You've made this best month of my life." I have to clear my throat, look away.

She reaches across the small round table, through the wreckage of espresso cups and pastry platters and crumbs. Takes my hand. I have to look back, at her, meet her eyes.

"Best month ever," she agrees.

It's there, unspoken.

Not yet. I silently plead with her to not ask, not yet.

She doesn't.

⟋⟋⟋

Touch down, Atlanta.

Home.

Unpacking.

I'd arranged for the house to be cleaned in our absence, the fridge emptied and restocked, bed linens refreshed, fresh flowers everywhere. So it'd be a welcoming homecoming.

⟋⟋⟋

It's impossible to ignore reality, now.

Finally, I know it's time to tell her. I loathe this. She'll be angry I've waited so long. There's so little time left.

It's hard to get out of bed the next morning. So, for once, I don't.

Nadia comes in with coffee, a mug for each of us. I take mine, sip at it.

"We need to talk," I whisper.

She nods, but is already blinking hard.

A brief, hard pause.

"What is it, and how long?" she asks.

"Pancreatic. End-stage…" I have to pause for courage. "Probably another month or two." Getting those words out is the hardest thing I've ever done in my entire life.

"*Adrian.*" Her hand trembles. She comes perilously close to spilling scalding coffee on her hands, so I take the mug from her and set it on the bedside table.

She stands up. Paces away.

I give her space.

She turns around, and I see that anger I know I deserve in her eyes. "A *month* or two?"

I nod, shrug. "There's no way to know for sure." I try to swallow, but can't. "This isn't exactly scientific here, but…I can feel…it. The end. It's not far off."

"No…" she hisses. "No, Adrian, no."

I don't know what to say, now that this moment is here. "I'm sorry I kept it from you."

She laughs bitterly. "You thought you were. But I've known all along."

"Then you know why."

"Yes." She sits, takes her mug back, and curls both hands around it.

Her thick black hair is loose, wild as thunderclouds. She's wearing my UNC T-shirt, and little boy-style briefs with flowers and hearts on them. They're so fucking adorable on her it makes my chest hurt. Sunlight shines early morning yellow-gold through our bedroom window; it's open, that window, letting in a breeze that wafts her hair playfully. A robin sings on a branch just outside. I can see it, the robin, redbreast puffing and fluffing, fluttering its wings, lifting its head and calling to the sky.

She tucks her bare thigh under the other, all but sits on me. She's battling more emotions than any human should experience all at once.

"Yes," she finally repeats. "I understand why. Doesn't mean I'm not mad at you for it, though."

"I'm sorry, Nadia. I just...I couldn't let it be your burden."

"You fought it?"

"For a year and a half. Mostly chemo. Surgery was never an option—didn't find it till it was too late for that."

"A year—" Her voice breaks. "A year and a half? Fuck you, Adrian. A *year and a half?*" She ducks her head, and a tear slips down her nose. "I'm your *wife*. It was my duty and burden to help you bear this."

I touch her chin, but she pulls away. "No, Nadia, it wasn't. You couldn't have healed me, not even with your force of will."

"I'm so angry with you for this, Adrian. So angry."

"I know."

"But you did it anyway. You knew I'd feel this way."

"I couldn't tell you. I tried. Right at the beginning. I almost told you. But then I...I thought about you wanting to push my wheelchair to and from chemo, and holding trash cans for me to puke into, and...I just couldn't. You couldn't have changed anything, Nadia. Chemo is boring. It gave me a little extra time, but that's it."

"I should have been there with you."

"I don't know how to say this without it sounding harsh or mean, but...I didn't want you there. It's dark and brutal and cruel and evil, Nadia. I needed you to be *you*—to be innocent and beautiful and *good*. I needed you to come home to, to be my brightness when I felt dark. I'd feel sorry for myself and then I'd come home and you'd kiss me and you'd look at me like I'm the best thing since red wine."

She sniffles a laugh, wet around tears. "You're not *that* great," she teases.

Silence.

"So, how does this work?" she asks, finally.

I shrug. "Hell if I know. My first time dying of cancer," I quip, but it's bitter and falls flat, and she flinches. "Sorry. I'm not flippant about this, I swear. But sometimes humor is the only way I can face it."

She takes my hand. "Since you kept it from me for so long, I think it's only fair we do this my way."

"'Oh good, my way... What's my way?'" I quote.

"'The moment his head is in view, *smash it with the rock!*'" She continues the *Princess Bride* quote, mostly correctly.

"'My way's not very sportsmanlike,'" I finish.

She laughs, but again it's more of a wet sniffle than a laugh. "We should watch that."

"Nadia."

She shakes her head. "My way is I quit my job, or take an indefinite leave. You let me take care of you. We spend this time together. Like in Paris, but at home, and—and all the way to...to the—the end."

"All right." What else is there to say?

She's blinking hard, head tipped back. "You're sure there's nothing...they can—they can do?"

"I'm sure." I wave a hand. "I could do more chemo, but at this point even the most aggressive chemo is just going to make my last few weeks or months a misery. Chemo fucking sucks...it sucks, it really, really, really sucks."

She nods. "I've done shifts in the oncology ward."

"I guess, if it can't be cured, and there's nothing else that can really extend my life in any meaningful way, then...I'd just rather go as peacefully as I can."

She's chewing on something. "What...god, I don't even know how to ask it. What will it be like? Do you know?"

I shake my head. "No, not really. I've wondered more than a few times myself, especially recently, but it feels sort of—I don't know, defeatist? Morbid?—to Google or ask the doctor what dying of pancreatic cancer will be like. Not fun, I can tell you that. But I've got…" I tug open my bedside drawer and pull out my little leather satchel of pills. "This. A veritable pharmacy of shit that's supposed to take the edge off. So I guess I'll just get all strung out and…we'll be together through it."

She's sorting through the bottles, reading the labels with a certain professional curiosity. She lifts one. "Adrian. Really?"

I know what's she's got: the little blue pills. "I get by with a little help from my friends," I say, trying to smile. "I just needed…I needed you to—to know that I still…that I'm not—"

"Oh, Adrian…" she chokes out.

"It's taking so much from me," I say, swallowing hard, my words feeling thick and slow. "I wasn't going to let it take that. I don't need them, especially when I'm not doing chemo, which I haven't since I was in Boston. It just helps things…last longer. Helps me out, when my body is using all its resources elsewhere. Doesn't leave a lot left over for sustaining erections, or sexual stamina."

"Coulda fooled me," she whispers. "*Did* fool me."

A long pause.

"I have another question," she whispers.

"'Kay."

"Is this why we haven't been able to conceive?"

"Didn't help," I admit. "Chemo kills everything—it doesn't discriminate. So yeah, it killed all my swimmers. But I also think there was an issue there before, honestly. I remember when Mom was in the hospital she was kinda delirious for a while and was just rambling, and she said she and Dad tried for years before they had me, and were never able to conceive again, which makes me think I'm either sterile or I just have shitty sperm." I take her hand again. "So, I'm sorry for that. I'm sorry I couldn't…" My voice breaks. Fuck, this is hard. "I'm sorry I couldn't give you that."

She shakes her head. "Don't apologize."

"I know you want a baby, more than just about anything."

"Well, I did. Now I just want you to…to not fucking *die*."

"Yeah, I wouldn't mind that myself." I cup her cheek. "Still. I'm sorry, Nadia."

She sets her mug on the side table, roughly, the coffee sloshing over the rim and dribbling down the side, smearing in a ring around the base. Climbs onto me, stretching onto my body, curling her hands behind my head, breathing in my scent and clinging to me.

"Hold me," she whispers.

I hold her.

Eight

i love you, for the millionth time

IF I CLOSE MY EYES AND FOCUS, SOME DAYS I CAN *ALMOST* pretend we're just on an extension of our Paris vacation.

We sleep in late, stay up late watching movies and bingeing all the shows we used to talk about watching but never got around to. We just sit together in the living room and listen to entire movements of classical music. Sometimes just sit and breathe together. He cooks, when he can. Or we cook together. Or I cook. Some days, neither of us has the energy, so we just order a pizza.

My favorite, though, is reading together. It's approaching winter in Atlanta, now, so the days are cooler. We turn on our gas fireplace and sit on the couch and Adrian reads to me. At first, it was just once in a while. But gradually, it becomes our Thing. We stopped watching TV. I'd buy books on Amazon, print or e-book, depending on the price, and he'd read to me. Sometimes when his voice got tired, I'd take over, but I'm not as good at it as he is.

He reads to me for hours. We read everything together. We go through the entire Little House on the Prairie series in a week. We read Nora Roberts, Stephanie Meyer, Harry Potter, we even start on the Game of Thrones series. Sometimes he reads from one book in the morning and a different one in the afternoons, after lunch.

But as the days crowd together, one after another, never leaving our house for much of anything, it becomes harder and harder to pretend that what's happening isn't real.

I want to keep pretending.

Pretend the days reading on the couch are just a magical interlude before our regular lives resume, me working in the ICU, him writing and researching.

But I can't.

He needs more and more pills to keep the pain and nausea and everything else at bay, and then it gets to the point of diminishing returns, where the drugs take away his lucidity along with the pain. And he hates that, more than anything. Says he'd rather be present with me and in pain than lost in narcotic la-la-land.

I try to make him promise that when it's bad enough, he'll take what he needs to be comfortable, but he refuses.

"We're doing this your way," he says. "And I wouldn't have it any other way. But I'm going to live out my remaining days on *my* terms. And I'm going to be *here*, with you."

A month after his reveal, his doctor makes a house call. Wonder of wonders—but then, Adrian has always had a way with people. After a checkup, some poking and prodding and questioning, the doctor says there's no point going in for MRIs and all that. Meaning, don't waste your time learning what you already know. He prescribes what he calls the nuclear option, some kind of strongest-possible opiate.

If you just want to float away, he says. I'm sure I'd know what it is, but my eyes are too blurry with tears to read, and it doesn't matter. He won't take it.

Not yet, anyway.

༺❦༻

I read to him, now.

༺❦༻

Tess shows up. Adrian does his dead-level best to get me to go out with her, just for an hour, just to breathe. Begs me, pleads, tries ordering, demanding.

I won't.

I can't.

I fucking *can't*.

So Tess brings a spread of food from our favorite restaurants in town. And every day after that, every single day, Tess brings us food. Carryout Chinese, Thai, Indian, Mexican, homemade casseroles and pots of Spaghetti bolognese and lasagna and platters of hot grilled PB&J and boats of tomato soup with triangles of grilled cheese.

One day, she brings over a bag of marijuana and a pipe, and we get Adrian stoned out of his head. Where she got it, hell if I know, but it helps him in some ways more than even the narcotics. So she keeps bringing it.

I've stopped drinking almost entirely. I want to be lucid, to remember.

The pain is too much to bear, and I know no amount of alcohol will help.

I smoke with him sometimes, but mostly just so he doesn't feel alone in it. "I hate partying alone," he says, with a tired smile.

Tess, god, what would I do without her? Adrian falls asleep around three in the morning most days, and when I let it slip to her, she starts sneaking in at 3 a.m. every fucking day with a bottle of Josh and her iPad Pro and a big bag of Skinny Pop, and she makes me sit outside with her on our back deck covered in a huge, thick blanket she got on Etsy, and we drink wine from the bottle and watch mindless comedy and action flicks and cheesy romances. So much for not drinking, right? But it's the only way I manage to find space to breathe.

Every other moment of my day is consumed with…It.

We don't use the word. We don't talk about death.

Tess never asks how I am. She's just there.

꧁꧂

We're a few days shy of three months from when he told me.

He's been in bed more often than not, and I just sit with him and we keep the TV on, or I read to him until I start to lose my voice.

We're halfway through *Casablanca*.

Play it, Sam. Play it like you did for her.

Adrian turns it off, and his head swivels slowly, heavily over to me. "Nadia."

I swallow hard. "Yeah, baby?"

"I need you to help me move to the guest room."

"What? Why?" I sit up. "This is our bed."

He closes his eyes. Even that seems hard for him. "I'm not going to die in our bed. I won't do that to you."

"Adrian, goddammit. No. I'm not, I won't. This is our bed."

"Nadia—"

"No. Not a fucking chance."

"I will not haunt this room for you. This bed. I won't do that."

I blink, but the tears win. "Adrian, you big dork. You're going to anyway. You think you're just…written into my life on this bed? You're in everything. Every room in this house, Adrian."

"We *have* christened just about every horizontal

surface there is, and quite a few of the vertical ones, too." He smirks, and for a second he's the old Adrian, wry and provocative, and horny *all—the—damn—time*.

I laugh through the tears. "Exactly. You being in the guest bed isn't going to make a difference."

"Yes, it will."

"You promised me we'd do this my way. This is my way. Here. Together. Our room, our bed."

He grimaces, and after a few minutes, whatever it is, it passes.

He squeezes my hand, and that's all there is to say.

I'm glossing over the details of taking care of him, especially as he gets too sick to do certain things for himself. Or loses control over things. He wants to hire a hospice nurse, but I tell him I'm professionally insulted by the suggestion. I'm a nurse, dammit. It's what I do.

No, he's not my patient, he's my husband.

I'm going to take care of him my damn self. No matter what it requires.

The last days are slow.

An hour passes like taffy being stretched out.

Sometimes it begins to feel like I've always been here, like this, with him. Sitting in our room, on the bed next to him, holding his slack, cool, dry hand.

Pretending to read a book and really just listening to him breathe.

It's slow, his breathing. Rattling.

I call the doctor, and he comes, and his face confirms it.

There's no one to call, no one to tell.

When we first met, in college, we bonded over the fact that both of our parents died young, and we were only children. The Lonely Club, we jokingly called it. Orphan humor—you wouldn't get it, unless you get it.

So tThere's no one to notify that the end is nigh. He tells me he's made arrangements through his attorney to inform his publisher and agent and all those people, after he's gone. He doesn't want anyone to know till after.

So…there's no one to tell. Not now.

Except Tess. She comes—she packs a bag and moves into our guest room.

She cleans for me, reminds me to shower once in a while.

Tries to get me to eat, but it seems pointless.

Even going to the bathroom is too much time away from his side.

He wakes up. Takes my hand. "I love you, Nadia."

I can barely get the words out. "I love you more, dork."

He tries to laugh. "I'm not a dork, I'm a nerd."

"Oh, right."

"I think it's time for me to…to float away, Nadia."

I try to say okay—my mouth forms the word-shape but no sound comes out. I nod, blink the tears away. "I love you," I whisper. "I love you."

"'Don't cry for me, Argentina,'" he murmurs, referencing one of my favorite musicals. "'The truth is, I never left you.'"

Even now, he's trying to make me laugh. He gets me. He's always just *gotten* me. Who else ever could, the way he does?

I want to be grateful about this. But it hurts to goddamn bad.

I squeeze his hand so hard it must hurt. "Don't leave me, Adrian. Please. You promised you'd never leave me."

"I'm not leaving," he says. "If I could stay, I would. I'm trying. I've been trying. I'm not leaving you, Nadia."

"But you are." These are not words; they are sobs that sound like words. "And I don't know how to live without you."

He's suddenly fierce. "You make me a promise, Nadia Bell. And this promise, you keep. After I'm gone, you remember this promise, and you fucking keep it. Swear." His eyes blaze.

I'm startled by the ferocity. "Okay, I—I swear."

"*Live*," he snarls. "You don't stop living. You don't fucking give up. Mourn me, as long as it takes. Remember me." He clutches my hands in his, so hard my joints and bones throb. "Love again. Don't spend the rest of your life alone."

I shake my head. "I can't—you're my husband, Adrian. How can I...?" My voice cracks, breaks, and words fail me.

"Promise. You have to promise, and not just to get me to shut up. Promise and mean it."

I can barely see through the tears. My head drops, touches his chest. I'm wracked, shaking. "I can't, Adrian. You're it."

"No. I'm telling you. Promise me. Please, Nadia. It's what I want for you. As your husband, as your best friend. I don't want you to be alone. Promise me." His voice crumbles. "Please."

I can't look at him. "Okay. Okay, Adrian. I promise."

"Look at me." He touches my chin. "I know when you're lying."

I look at him—it takes everything, but I do. "I promise."

He nods. His head goes slack against the pillow. "Thank you."

"I love you."

"I know."

"Don't you quote *Star Wars* at me, mister."

A soft huff. "Fine. I love you too." A long, long, long silence. "I'm ready, now."

"Don't you lie to me."

"You...you know me too well, don't you?" Another silence. "Fine. I'm not. I never was and I never will be. But...I think I'm as ready as you can get."

It takes me several minutes to compose myself enough that I can see what I'm doing. I find the pills, the Nuclear Option. Whatever the fuck it is. I still don't look.

He takes it.

Clutches my hand. "I love you more than fucking life itself, Nadia. Never forget that. Wherever...wherever I'm going, I'll love you there too."

I hold him.

Cling to him.

His arms are around me, clutching.

"I love you," I whisper, for the millionth time.

For the last time.

How long, then?

An hour? Five minutes?

His arms go weak. Slack.

His breathing slows.

I start to shake, trembling like a leaf, like I've been outside in -20 degree weather for an hour.

No, no, no, no, no.

It's so subtle I barely notice it, for a moment.

I look at the clock: 3:33a.m. He always called three in the morning "zero hour."

Figures he'd choose that time.

⸙

I cry, and I cry and I cry and I cry.

Until I'm dry, and hoarse.

Tess comes. Tries to pull me away, but I refuse. Fight her off, even though I know it's her.

⸙

Stronger hands, stronger arms.

A pinch to my arm, because I won't leave him.

Darkness, blessed darkness.

⸙

Can I just stay in this place? This quiet? This solitude, where there is nothing, and so much of it?

The world is cruel, and I don't want to go back.

❧

Take me with you, Adrian.

❧

You promised. I almost hear him.

❧

I promised.

Part Two

Drowning

Nine

72 hours

"*THE LORD IS MY SHEPHERD, I SHALL NOT WANT. HE MAKES me lie down in green pastures; He leads me beside quiet waters. He restores my soul; He guides me in the paths of righteousness for His name's sake. Even though I walk through the valley of the shadow of death, I fear no evil, for You are with me; Your rod and Your staff, they comfort me. You prepare a table before me in the presence of my enemies; You have anointed my head with oil; my cup overflows. Surely goodness and loving kindness will follow me all the days of my life, and I will dwell in the house of the Lord forever.*"

The minister's voice is what Adrian would have called mellifluous.

Why is it always that Psalm? What does it have to do with death, and mourning, and funerals? I admit I've not really read much of the Bible, but I feel there has to be a more appropriate passage to read at funerals, but it's always that one.

I'm numb, at the moment. I'm like a gourd that

has been scooped out until it's hollow. That's me, the hollow pumpkin lady.

A murder of crows perches in a giant spreading oak tree behind the minister, seven or eight of them all in a cluster on three branches. They're silent. Watching us. As if paying their respects.

Then one of them leans forward, caws raucously, once, and takes wing. It shits on the minister's shoulder, and for some reason this just strikes me as almost unbearable funny. I have to bite my tongue until I taste blood to keep from snickering at my own husband's funeral.

This isn't grief, or sadness, or mourning. This is a void. Emotional emptiness. All of my sadness has been burned through, all my grief used up. There is no more panic. No more desperation. I feel nothing, and I wallow in it like a sow in muck.

It will break, and soon. I know this. I can feel it coming, the tide of sorrow. I feel like someone standing on a beach, watching the water recede, leaving fish flapping and crabs snapping and fronds of seaweed laying limp…watching this means a tsunami is coming.

If you see the waters recede, then it's usually already too late to run.

So it is with me. There is no stopping what's coming.

But it's not here yet.

He's been dead three days. I have no clue what happened after he breathed his last breath. It's not even a blur. It's nothing. Vacant. A bare dirt patch in the landscape of memory.

I remember lying in our bed, feeling his warmth recede from the sheets.

I think Tess was there, maybe she spoke to me, maybe she simply sat next to me. I don't know.

I haven't wept. I wonder if I will.

Ten

7 days

A WEEK.

I'm still numb.

But now the numbness is not a comfort, not a balm of nothingness, not a balloon of calm in a world of pain and chaos and grief.

Now, numbness is...a sickness. An inability to cope. To accept.

I recognize the stages of grief within me, I know where I am in the process. I'm stuck.

Grief is building inside me. To continue the tsunami metaphor, Adrian's death is the earthquake far out at sea, a mile under the surface. Right now, the tsunami is racing toward the shore, maybe only a foot high, but moving with jet-plane speed, with monstrous energy.

At the funeral, my mind saw the waters pull back.

Now is the seconds or minutes before the freight train smashes into shore. I'm waiting for it.

I'm pregnant with a demon of grief and sorrow.

Grief, and Sorrow. In this, they deserve the title, the capital letters.

I cannot do anything.

I've barely slept since he died. I cannot eat. Tess has to force me to sip water.

What do I do with the hours? I don't know. Sit, or lie facing the window in our bedroom, watching the sunlight travel in an arc across my bedroom floor. It's abstract, the passage of time. Not a real thing. It feels like a movie montage, where the widow lies in bed and the camera remains still, a time-lapse of sunlight moving across the floor—it's real. It's me. I'm that widow.

A widow. I'm a widow.

Then it begins—I feel something, at that realization.

In my rotation in the ER, a gunshot victim said he didn't feel pain at first, more of an impact, a physical blow but not pain.

This feels like that. The first blow, the impact before nerve endings have a chance to kick in and relay the existence of agony.

Eleven

14 days

"…Closing on it tomorrow," Tess is saying. "I was thinking I'd move in with you."

I blink. "Oh." I'm physically present, but mentally absent. "Wait, what?"

She touches my cheek. "I'm closing on the house tomorrow. I've sold it fully furnished. I've packed up my clothes and the shit I care about, hired a company to clean it out to create a blank slate for the new owners."

I have a real, original thought for the first time in two weeks. "You sold your house?"

"Yeah." She's very patient with me.

Another thought occurs. "Wait. Your divorce. I promised I'd be there."

She gives me a small, sad smile. "It was the day before…um…"

"Say it."

"The hearing was the day before Adrian…ahhh… passed away." Her voice breaks on that phrase. "I went in three-day-old yoga pants, no underwear, no bra, a stained T-shirt, and my fuzzy pink slippers. I told the judge I didn't give a single shit about anything at all, I just wanted to be done, divorced."

"Was he there?" It's like my brain is being operated by something other than me, functioning for me.

Tess has been there for me through this, and I have to give back to her. I have to be her friend too. But where this thoughtfulness is coming from, I don't know. I'm still numb.

She nods. "Yeah, he was. He looked like he was trying to look guilty, or chagrined, or something, but couldn't quite manage it." She shrugs. "It's weird how little of a fuck I give about him. Like, I'm not even sad. I'm barely even angry anymore. I'm not, like, happy, or relieved. I didn't want to be a divorcee. But now it's over and I'm just...ready to move on. I just simply do not have a single feeling to spare for Clint McAlister."

"How is Yvette?"

She sighs. "Not exactly sure, quite honestly. She asked why we were getting divorced, so I told her the whole actual truth. She's eighteen, so I guess I didn't see the point in dissembling, you know? I think she's hurt that it's happening, but when I sat down with her via Zoom the other day and told her I was taking my maiden name back she was, like, fiercely in favor. She asked if she could hyphenate her name, so she'd be Yvette McAlister-Tailor. I told her to wait and think on it awhile. I just wanted to be assured that she didn't mind me doing it. She said she understood, and she's in support of me going back to being Tess Tailor."

"I'm sorry I missed it, Tess."

She shakes her head. "Don't be. It was supremely lame and anticlimactic. The judge started in on this whole spiel, and I politely interrupted and said could we dispense with the bullshit and just get to the part where we sign the papers? And she asked Clint if he felt the same way, which he did, and then we both signed and that was that. She pronounced our union divorced. Boom. I got the house, my car, and I chose to take the cash-out option he offered which is actually pretty sizeable. Maybe he was hiding things so I got a shit deal, I don't know and I don't care. I'm selling the house for nearly a million and netting over half a million, plus another hundred grand in investment cash-out, so I'm fine. I'll have enough to find a killer place downtown and that's all I really care about."

"Tess, I'm sorry I've been a shitty friend to you lately," I say.

"Oh, what a pile of moose poop," she says. "This is what we do, boo." She hugs me. "I'm here for you, which brings me back to my original question. Can I move in with you for a while? I'm not quite ready to start looking for a new place yet."

I sigh. "Is that the real reason, Tess?"

"Fine. I'm worried about you. You need me. I need to be here with you until I'm sure you're okay."

"I'll never be okay again, Tess."

"Yes, you will. It'll take time, but you will."

I shake my head. "I don't see how." I look down and find her hand. Hold it. "You come live with me as long as you want, and when you're ready to move out, do it. I don't want you to worry about me. You need to live your life too, Tess. I don't want you babysitting me indefinitely."

"It's not babysitting. It's being there for my best friend when she needs me, just the same way you'd do the same for me." She smiles brightly. "And now we're roommates again."

"Thank you, Tess." My throat feels tight. "You've done so much for me, I'll never be able to thank you enough."

She hisses, hands raised palms out. "Stop, stop. Don't make me cry. Right now, let's get practical. We're going to need supplies: several boxes of tissues, lots of ice cream, and lots of wine."

"Not wine," I say. "Anything but wine, and especially not *red* wine."

I don't have to explain to Tess, of all people, that red wine was Adrian's and my thing.

"Know what you *do* want to drink, then?"

What was it we used to drink in college?

"Remember the parties we used to throw back in college?" I ask. "We'd buy six bottles of the cheapest vodka we could find, a bunch of two-liter bottles of soda water, and a bag of limes. And we'd mix it all together in a punch bowl."

She snickers. "Hell yeah, I remember. Un-punch, everyone called it."

"I'm going to need that, I think."

She frowns at me. "Nadia, love. I'll enable you only up to a certain point. But eventually, you have to grieve. I know maybe you're not there yet. And I grant that you have the right to deal with this however you need. And if that means going on a bender, I'll be there with you every step of the way. But you have to deal with it, at some point."

"I don't know how. It's like the ability to feel it, to let grieving take over is…stuck. I can't. I just can't. Like when you're hammered and need to throw up but can't."

"Okay, let's get wasted then, huh?"

I manage to give Tess a small smile. I need to feel something besides this emptiness, this drowning nothingness.

Something. Anything.

Twelve

18 days

I'VE SPENT THE PAST THREE AND A HALF DAYS DRUNK. IT WAS glorious at first. We'd watch stupid movies and stand-up specials and laugh our asses off, and I know I was faking laughing harder than was necessary.

I'm drunk right now.

But it's not so glorious.

I'm splayed sideways across my bed, and I can't get up. The room is spinning. I'm delirious. I wonder if I've slept more than two or three hours at a time since…That Day.

I've eaten little besides Skinny Pop and cheese sticks and Costco peanuts. Tess tried making Mac 'n Cheese at some point, but we were both so wasted we let the pot of water burn dry, spilled noodles everywhere, and decided it was best to stick to easy stuff so we didn't set the house on fire. We only had the one between us, after all.

She'd gone out, the day we agreed to go on a bender, and came back with a whole case of Grey

Goose, several 24-packs of various flavored sparkling water, and several bags of limes. And one large punch bowl. We mixed enough for roughly sixty people, and we've been working our way through it.

All day.

Well into the night.

Tess passes out first, because she's just going along with me, and because I think she's actually feeling more emotions regarding her divorce than she's willing to admit.

But me?

Oh, me. I'm a colossal fucking disaster.

I still can't cry.

I can't even think his name, never mind say it.

I'm a sieve for vodka soda. I pour it into me, and it burns through me, and nothing is left but ice-cold misery.

When will I break?

When will the waves come?

I'm afraid of it, at this point. Terrified.

It's going to hurt so fucking bad, when it hits.

Thirteen

21 days

"Tess, I need you to do something for me."

"Anything."

"Sober up, and then go find some Ativan."

"Why?"

"Because I'm going to freak out. It's coming. I can feel it. And when it does, I'm scared it's going to be really, really bad."

"What does Ativan do?"

"It'll knock me out. You just stab it into my arm or shoulder. It's for seizure patients, to stop seizures. It's also used when someone has an hysterical episode and is at risk of self-harm."

"Nadia…"

My eyes blur and sting. I blink them away. Not yet, dammit.

"Tess, please. You have to."

"You're scaring me, Nads."

"That's because I'm scared."

"That bad?"

"It's going to be bad. Really, really bad. It's coming and it's going to be the worst thing you've ever seen."

"Okay. I have a friend, or more of an acquaintance really. He can get me some, I think."

"Do what you need to do. Just get some."

"All right. I will."

"But first, I need more vodka."

"How many fingers am I holding up?"

"What fingers?"

"Very funny. How many?"

"Tess, listen to me. Listen."

"No, stop, just stop. Here, take mine. There you go."

I take a sip. "This is water, goddammit."

"I stopped drinking two days ago."

"This isn't going to be a wine-and-ice-cream kind of crying, Tess. It's going to be me in the tub screaming at the top of my lungs. Or something. I don't know."

"You're being very analytical about this."

"I think I'm having an out-of-body experience. I'm not me right now. Nadia Bell is out to lunch. Somewhere out in space. I don't know who I am anymore. I don't know what life is anymore."

"You know a lawyer came by yesterday morning?"

"A lawyer? What? When?"

"There was a scheduled reading of the will, and I guess you missed it."

"The will?"

"Adr—"

"Don't say his fucking name!" It was an explosion, like she'd stepped on a landmine. "Do fucking not say his name."

She pales. "I'm sorry. I'm sorry. Jesus."

I swallow hard. "No, I—I'm sorry. See? That's what I'm talking about."

"Here. Drink this."

"Vodka. Thank fuck."

"I told him you'd call him, or I would, when you were ready."

"Okay." Burning, burning, burning behind my eyes, in my brain, in my chest, where my heart used to be. "I'm sorry, Tess."

"Don't apologize."

"I am, though."

"Okay, here, how about this. I forgive you, in advance, for anything and everything you may say or do."

"More," I say, shaking my glass at her.

"Fine, you lush. But this is the last of the un-punch."

"Good. I think I'm about pickled, by now."

"Can you even stand up?"

"I dunno. Standing is dumb. Who needs to stand up anymore? I'm not a stand-up kinda gal."

"Ohhhhh-kay. That answers that."

"Can I just pee in the un-punch bowl?"

"The physics of that are problematic."

"Shit."

"Nads?"

"Yeah?"

"You really need a shower."

"Just put me in the tub and leave me."

"That's not fucking funny, Nadia."

"It wasn't a joke."

"Don't talk like that."

"It'd be best."

"No, it wouldn't."

"He'd be angry."

"Huh? Who would be angry?"

"*He*. He would be. Because I promised him I'd live. I promised him...that I wouldn't just stay alive, but *live*. But I don't want to, Tess."

"Don't want to what?"

"Live." A bloody silence. "Not without...*him*."

Fuck. Here it comes.

Fourteen

day unknown

PEOPLE TALK JOKINGLY ABOUT HAVING A BREAKDOWN, BUT unless they've really experienced it, they don't know.

Imagine, or remember if you're that unfortunate, crying so hard every bone rattles inside your skin. Crying so hard you wonder if you've gone literally blind, because the salt of the river of tears has seared away your eyes. Crying so hard your chest feels like it's clamped in a white-hot vise.

Then multiply that by a thousand.

Crying so hard you can't physically function. You can't breathe. And when you do breathe, it's a hoarse scream.

Screaming until your throat bleeds.

And it doesn't end.

You've been expecting this for weeks.

Pent it up inside a vault of vodka and silence and denial.

Now, the interest is due on that grief.

It's come collecting, and it has no mercy.

This kind of sorrow is utterly savage.

It's the army that razes the city to the ground, raping and killing everyone within, but doesn't stop there. It burns the wreckage, and then salts the earth where the city once stood.

I've burned through the alcohol—my misery is entirely sober, now.

When I start clawing at my face and chest and arms until I bleed, just to feel anything besides this ravaging misery is when Tess sticks me with a needle.

❧

After that, the ferocity is spent. Now, I'm just merely paralyzed by grief. Literally. I cannot even get out of bed. I tried, but my legs wouldn't support me, and I fell to the floor and hit my head so hard I saw stars.

I lie in bed for an endless amount of time, crying, sobbing. The sound of it must be awful.

❧

I run out of tears, at some point. That's when I finally sleep, my first nonchemical-assisted sleep in almost a month.

When I wake up, an unknown amount of time later, I discover a renewed reservoir of tears.

Fifteen

day unknown

"Nadia?" Tess, hesitant, quiet. "Are you awake?"

"Yes." My voice is hoarse; I sound like a twenty-year pack-a-day smoker.

"Can I come sit with you?"

"Please."

Her weight dips the bed beside me. "I wish I knew what to ask besides if you're okay. I know that's not even a real question."

"I don't know." It's the only words that come to mind.

"The lawyer called. The executor of...of the estate."

"Estate." I repeat it, but it still has no meaning.

She's tiptoeing, for good reason.

"Say his name, Tess. I can't."

"Adrian."

"Adrian," I repeat, in a ragged whisper. "Adrian." Silence. "Adrian Robert Bell."

More tears, but quieter, now.

"*I miss him so much,*" I hiss.

"I know you do, I'm so sorry."

"What does the lawyer want?"

"I don't know. He says he's not allowed to share details with anyone but you. He says he only needs a few minutes. He can come here, or we can meet him at his office."

"Why."

"Adrian left a will. And he, the lawyer, has to read it to you, or however that works."

"Oh." I sniffle. "How long has it been?"

"Since…when?"

"Since Adrian…" I have to force myself to say it. So it will be real. "Since Adrian—died." The word is hissed, whispered, broken.

"It will be one month ago this Friday. That's in two days."

"Tell him we'll meet him at his office Friday afternoon."

"Okay."

"Tess?"

"Yup."

"Did I…did I hurt you?" I have fuzzy memories of a struggle when I was mad with grief. It was fury, too. The real deal. Complete loss of all control and coherency.

"It's fine."

"Tess."

She sighs. "Yeah, you did. You were kicking and screaming and clawing at yourself." Her voice is shaky. "You were in the tub because it was the only place I could get you that you wouldn't…hurt yourself on something. I was worried I'd have to, like, call for professional help. You were pretty out of your head. You left me with some bruises, but I'm fine."

I look at her, really look. She's my height, tall, but way curvier. Her mom was black, her dad white, so she's got skin somewhere in between, with curly black hair and hazel eyes. She's paler than usual, with bags under her eyes. She's lost weight, and not in a good way. She didn't need to.

She has the remains of a healing black eye, the awful purples and greens and yellows.

"Holy shit, Tess. I'm so sorry."

"Hey, you warned me."

"Doesn't make it okay."

She lies on the bed behind me and spoons me. "It's fine, boo. I love you. I'm here. I forgave you beforehand, remember?"

"I miss him so fucking much."

"I can't even begin to understand."

"I wonder what…what Adrian left in his will?" I say. "He handled all our finances, but as far as I'm aware, it's not like we had a lot of stuff or investments for him to leave."

"I guess we'll find out Friday."

"I guess so."

"I'm going to need a shower."

"Bitch, you're gonna need like four showers."

"I don't smell *that* bad."

"Oh yeah? Sniff your pit."

I do so. "Holy hell." I cough at my own stench. "You might be right."

"Why are you still here with me, Tess?"

"Because you're my best friend. And you'd do the same for me. We made a pact, remember? When we were in that Gaia, Mother Earth phase? We did this whole thing involving period blood and herbs and that godawful wine we made ourselves?"

I can't help but laugh. "God, I remember. That was so nuts."

"I meant that shit, Nads. Ride or die."

"I meant it too. I just…I guess I feel like I've really tested it, these last few weeks."

"You haven't tested anything, Nadia. There's no such thing as testing it. You need me, so I'm here. No matter what."

"What would I do without you?"

"You'll never find out."

A while of silence.

"You've been in here a week," Tess says, eventually. "I could barely get you to eat or drink. I had to force-feed you electrolytes. I was really worried about you getting dehydrated."

"Oh."

"You've lost a shitload of weight, Nads. Like, a *lot*. You're skin and bones."

"I'm not okay. This feels like the eye of the storm. I don't think I'm going to have another breakdown, but it's going to come in waves. Just…so you're aware. I'll have more bad days."

"I know."

"You can take a break from me, you know."

"I don't want one."

"Crazyhead." She ruffles my hair like I'm a child. "Try to rest."

"'Kay."

"Nadia?"

"Yeah."

"Do I have to worry about you? For real."

"Not like that."

"Promise?"

"I promise."

"Good enough. Now rest."

But rest doesn't come, though. Now that I've begun the process of grieving, I'm inundated with memories of Adrian.

Sixteen

30 days

"I, ADRIAN BELL, BEING OF SOUND MIND AND, OBVIOUSLY, failing body—"

"I'm sorry," I whisper, interrupting. "But can you just give me a copy to read on my own time, and give me the details as succinctly as possible?"

We're in the law offices of Levine, Levine, and Anton, in a glittery high-rise in the heart of Atlanta. It was the first time I had left the house after the funeral, but I barely remember the trip in—Tess drove. The lawyer Adrian chose to execute his estate, whose name is Tomas Anton, resembles the evil food critic from *Ratatouille*: extraordinarily tall, but stooped, hunched at the shoulders, with a dour face, silvering dark hair cropped short and balding. He wears an expensive dark charcoal suit with light pinstripes, a somber maroon tie, and slick, polished Italian leather loafers. His voice is sonorous, stentorian.

"That is not how these things are ordinarily done," he protests.

"I can't—I just can't handle this." I close my eyes. Hearing Adrian's words, read by someone else, is just too hard.

"Very well." He clears his throat, and then spends a moment thinking. "The details are thus: his automobile, a 2017 BMW M4 convertible, has been sold for a cash value of forty-five thousand dollars, which funds are currently available in the joint checking account. There were many investments made over the years, upon the advice and urging of his financial advisor, one Lewis McCleary, and those have been largely cashed out, all appropriate taxes paid upon cash-out. The sum total of these comes to…let's see…one million, seven hundred thousand, and forty-five dollars. And sixty-six cents, by way of precision."

I gulp. "Wait, what? We had a *million dollars* in investments?"

"It seems so."

I blink. "He told me he'd made some investments, but he made it sound like it was just…little stuff. Small amounts."

"You would have to speak to Mr. McCleary for details. The only information I'm privy to is what is contained here." He gestures with the will from which he is reading. "Shall I continue?"

"Yes. Thank you."

"Of course." He scans the document rapidly. "Ah, here we are. Further to the topic of investments, he retained several of the, and I quote, 'most stable, long-term investments,' for the purposes of securing your future interests, but these can be managed at your convenience, as you see fit. The value of these investments currently totals just over one million dollars. Again, Mr. McCleary can provide you with all the information you require."

"A million dollars in investments," I repeat. "Adrian, you absolute shitshow. Why didn't you tell me?" I clear my throat. "Is that all?"

"No, ma'am. Furthermore, he has a life insurance policy, purchased when you were first married, which he seems to have been aggressively funding. I've contacted them, and they are in the process of distributing the payout. Which totals, let's see...." He consults a yellow legal pad on his desk in front of him, peering down his nose through his readers. "Five million dollars."

I cough in shock. *"What?"*

"He specified payout terms. A lump sum of fifty percent, with the remainder paid as monthly installments. I can provide you with the breakdown, if you wish?"

"No, that's fine," I murmur. "Five million dollars in life insurance? You're sure you have that number correct?"

One corner of his mouth turns up in something like a near-smirk. "Yes, Mrs. Bell. I'm certain."

"Just making sure." I have to lean forward, elbows on my knees, face in my hands. "I had no idea."

"The only other pertinent item at this time is that he wanted you, upon the reading of this will, to be made aware that all outstanding debts have been paid. This part, I believe, I should read in his words."

I close my eyes, nod. "Okay."

"Ahem. 'Upon confirmation that my illness was terminal…' ummm…ah, here we are. 'The total cash value of our investments was actually considerably higher, but I paid the taxes on it and then used the proceeds to zero out our debts. My student loans and yours, low interest though they were, are gone. All credit cards are at zero as well, and mine have been canceled and cut up, as well as your car loan; and as specified above, I sold my car. Our mortgage as well is now paid—you own the home free and clear, my love.' His words, clearly. 'You owe nothing to anyone. I arranged everything for the funeral, and all costs there have been paid. I also created a separate account, in your name, which I funded and then created an auto-payment system for all utilities. You won't have to worry about paying utilities or the funding of that account for at least a year. Transfer a few grand into it at the start of each year and you'll never have to worry about it. I have instructed Lewis to take care of this for you, however. He has access to everything, and I trust him absolutely. Focus on yourself, Nadia. One day at a time.'"

Tomas Anton removes his reading glasses, sets the will down and his glasses upon it. "That is all."

"It's a lot to process," I whisper. "I had no idea he was doing all that. That we had…all that."

Tess rubs my shoulder. "He's taking care of you, even now."

I hiccup, attempting to hold back sobs. "I have to go now." I stand up, abruptly. "Is there anything I need to sign, or to do?"

"I do need a few signatures." He twists a stack of papers, marked with arrow-shaped sticky notes. "Here…and here…and here…one more…and last one. Thank you. As I've said, specific financial details are available through Mr. McCleary. His card is included in the folder, here. Some of this will take time to work out, payments and such. The life insurance in particular might take up to another thirty days before you see it. They are not swift to pay out, I'm afraid." He stands up, handing me a black folder containing the will and pertinent documents, with a business card attached to the inside flap via paper clip. "Your husband spent much of his last months preparing all of this. He has seen to your every need, as well as can possibly be done. You should be very proud, Mrs. Bell. It was an honor to have worked for him."

"Th-thank you, Mr. Anton."

"If there is anything else you need, please do not hesitate to contact me. My specialty is estate law, but if you should need legal representation or advice, I am but a phone call away."

"Thanks." I just need to get out of this building, away from people. I need to be alone.

Tess guides me out of the office, down to the parking garage under the high-rise. The inside of her car is silent for the first fifteen minutes of the drive home.

"Six million dollars, Nadia."

I shudder. "I'm having a hard time fathoming what that means."

"It means you don't need to do a damn thing for the rest of your life."

"So I'm supposed to do...what? Just sit around in our empty house and watch TV for the rest of my life?"

"Take the time you need, that's all."

"What I need to do is to get back to work."

"You don't *need* to, Nads. For real."

I shake my head. "Tess, I have to *do* something. If I just sit around that house, I'll go crazy. I have to go back to work."

"If that's what you need, then I support you. Just...you don't need the money."

"It's not about money. It's about my mental and emotional health. Even before...before, um. Yeah, even before all this, I had to work, to stay busy. You know this about me." I laugh. "Six million dollars." I laugh again, because it's better than crying. "What the hell am I going to do with it?"

"Live off it? Splurge?"

I can't stop the tears, now. "On what? What matters, anymore? Purses? Shoes? A new car? What the fuck am I supposed to want, or care about, Tess? My husband is dead. Everything else just seems… meaningless."

"Oh, I don't know. A Birkin bag might make you feel better for a while."

I cackle. "If you think I've *ever* been psychologically capable of spending that kind of money on a purse, you know nothing about me, woman."

"That's because you've never tried."

I sniffle. "Maybe. I guess it just…doesn't interest me."

A sigh. "Yeah, I guess I get that." She glances at me. "The hot tub is supposed to come later today. That'll be fun."

I barely hear her, though. I'm lost in thought. Imagining Adrian, sicker by the day, continuing to pay bills, to set me up financially for life. Thinking about *me* while *he* died.

I can't sob—it feels like that ability has been used up, worn out. Now, crying is a quiet, slow affair. Tears trickling down my nose, one at a time.

Adrian, god, you selfless man. I love you so much. I miss you. Fuck, I miss you.

Seventeen

33 days

"WHAT'S THIS?" TESS ASKS, ACCEPTING THE BOX from me.

It's large, wrapped in white tissue paper held in place by a blue silk ribbon I found in my closet.

"Just open it," I say.

She doesn't. Just holds it on her lap. We're sitting on the back porch, a fire going in the little firepit, a bottle of wine half finished. It's white wine, a dry white. I still can't drink red. It reminds me too much of Paris.

"Nads, I don't want anything from you."

"I know. But...I just...you've been here for me twenty-four hours a day, seven days a week. You take care of me when I can't function. You've literally kept me fed, kept me from getting dehydrated. You've cleaned my house. You've done more than the term 'friendship' can even begin to cover." I tap the box. "This is nothing. It's not even a thank-you, Tess. It's just...a token, I guess. Appreciation is the only word

I can come up with, but that doesn't cover it either." I sniffle a laugh. "Just open it, dammit."

She sighs in something very like frustration. She unties the ribbon, slides the layers of tissue paper off from around the box which is square and black, with a black ribbon tying it closed. The word "CHANEL" is written on the top of the box in large white letters.

"You didn't."

I just smile.

She gingerly slowly opens the box. Within is a signature Chanel purse, small, black, quilt-stitched leather, with a chain strap of gold woven through with leather, the clasp in that iconic twin C logo.

"Nadia, no."

"Nadia, yes."

"You wouldn't buy one for yourself, if I'm remembering correctly." She lifts the purse out. Sniffs it. "You said it was too extravagant for your taste."

"True."

"So, why...?"

"Because I wanted to," I say. "I wanted to find some way of showing you how much I appreciate you, and all you've done for me the last...however long it's been. It's for our whole friendship in general, but since all this started in particular." I touch her wrist. "I could never repay all you've done, Tess. Never."

"You're my best friend, Nads," she whispers, sniffling. "It's what we do."

"You've gone above and beyond, Tess. Way above, way beyond."

She sighs. "Is this your way of kicking me out?"

I laugh. "Hell no! This is your home now, too. For as long as you want it to be home. You move out when *you're* ready. Don't worry about me."

The laughter hurts. It feels wrong. I have to kind of force it. Because I know it's necessary, socially. She needs the social signifier that I mean what I'm saying. But I don't feel like laughing. Inside, there is nothing but sorrow. All other emotions have to be faked.

"I do worry about you," Tess says. "I see you putting on a brave face, Nads. You're not a good actress, I have to admit."

I sigh. Nod. "I'm not okay. But I have to...I have to do something. I can't just sit around feeling sorry for myself. Missing him." I blink hard. "I promised him I would try, so this is me trying. I'm going to call my boss tomorrow and have her put me on the schedule for as many hours as she can."

Tess sighs in frustration. "You can't bury your grief in work."

I shake my head. "Tess, I...I don't know if I know *how* to grieve any other way. Thinking about him hurts too much. I can't stop it, and it hurts. It's all I know how to do. The only way I can take care of myself is by taking care of my patients. It's what I do. It's the only part of me that I recognize anymore."

She handles the purse, opening it, pulling out the wad of stuffing, playing with the strap. "This is beyond amazing, Nadia. Thank you doesn't begin to cut it."

I cup her cheek. "You're not supposed to thank me for a thank-you gift, silly."

"You're impossible." She holds it up. "You seriously bought me a Chanel."

"I seriously did." I grin—my cheeks hurt from the effort. "I almost bought you a Birkin instead, but I felt like you wouldn't have accepted it."

"You felt correctly," she said. "That would've been too much."

"There's no such thing, in my mind. Not after—"

"Enough, Nadia. I'm your friend. We made an oath, remember? Ride or die, bitch."

"Ride or die."

Eighteen

90 days

THANK GOD FOR DOUBLE SHIFTS.

My boss tried to talk me out of it, but I insist on doubles, as many as possible. I throw myself into work. More hours than I've ever worked in my life. Eighty, a hundred hours a week. I take shifts in the ER, in L&D, wherever I can get work. Anything to keep me away from home.

Tess has stopped trying to tell me to slow down. She sees that I can't.

He was right.

He haunts that house.

I hear his voice reading to me in the living room.

I see him lying beside me, in that big empty bed. Hear him laboring to breathe.

His office is closed, always.

I keep half expecting to hear those barn-style sliding doors open, to see him come out, grinning tiredly after a long writing session.

I wonder what happened to that last story he was writing? Maybe it was all fake, a cover up for his illness and the preparations he made.

Nineteen

120 days

Ⅰ LIE IN BED, AT THREE THIRTY-THREE IN THE MORNING. Staring at the ceiling.

He died four months ago today. Four months ago, this very second, he breathed his last breath.

I can't cry. It hurts too deeply to cry anymore. Something inside me is deeply, irreparably broken. Shattered into a million, trillion pieces. Into dust.

I'm good at faking. I have my work smile down pat. *Hi, Mrs. Murphy, how are we feeling, today?* Easy.

Inside, I'm hollow.

I can't bear to look at photographs of him. Not yet. But...the details of his face are beginning to blur in my mind. The sound of his voice. His scent.

I haven't cleaned out his drawers, or his side of the closet.

I open his shirt drawer, sometimes, just to get a whiff of his scent. Briefly, so the smell that is part of *him* doesn't fade.

I wear his silver Citizen Eco-Drive watch to work. I had a few links taken out so it wouldn't be so loose around my wrist. It's still massive on me, which reminds me of him.

Twenty

210 days

FUCK, I MISS HIM.

    I finally looked through my photos on my phone. I'd started to forget what he looked like.

I watched a few videos of us: in the park, running together. Laughing at the old man in the grass behind us, hand shoved in a plastic grocery bag, trying to catch poop as it fell out of his dog's butt.

Christmas, two years ago. We gave each other fleece onesies and nothing else. Or at least, that was the agreement. We both broke it, though. I bought him the watch I now wear all the time, and he bought me a Pandora bracelet and a pair of earrings.

I made it through maybe fifty photos and two videos, and then I was crying so hard I couldn't see and my heart felt like it was going to crack into pieces. Or maybe I just felt the cracks more acutely.

I've worked eighty hours a week minimum since I went back to work. I haven't cooked myself food once in that time—I live on coffee, takeout, fast food, and protein bars.

Tess moved out a few weeks ago, to her sleek top-floor condo downtown. She quit her job—she's now doing something technical involving computers from home; she's freelancing, doing her own thing instead of working remotely for some Silicon Valley megacorporation. She's happy. Sowing her wild oats, she says. And still worrying about me.

Don't, I tell her. I'm fine, I tell her.

But I'm a shitty liar, which she's well aware of. I'm not fine. Not at all.

But hell, my husband died. I'll never be fine again.

Part Three

Redemption's Song

Twenty-One

Letters From The Dead, Part One

*D*ING....DONGGGGGG...

The doorbell rings, surprising me, and I nick my thumb with the whittling knife.

"Shit," I hiss. "Ouch—motherfucker!"

I stick my bleeding thumb in my mouth and taste pennies as I head for the front door. It's 8 p.m., and I can't even begin to fathom who the fuck could be at my door, let alone at 8 p.m. on a Saturday night.

Whoever the hell this is, he's even taller than me, which is saying something, and he's hunched at the shoulders, with droopy but intelligent eyes, and I'm reminded of a vampire from an old black-and-white movie.

"Nathan Fischer?" he asks, in a slow, deep, syrupy Southern voice.

"Yeah, that's me. Who are you and you what d'you want?"

"May I come in? I shall be brief."

"Not until I know who you are, and what you want."

"Understandable. First, let me apologize for the late hour on a weekend." He withdraws a business card; it's thick, expensive card stock, ivory in color and printed in navy blue ink trimmed with gold leaf. This is the business card of a *serious* attorney.

Tomas Anton, Esq., specializing in estate law. Levine, Levine, & Anton, attorneys at law.

"What do I want with an estate lawyer?"

"It's more what I want with you. I represent the estate of the late Adrian Bell."

"Adrian…" I swallow. "Okay. Still not following what you want with me."

He nods. "I understand your confusion, Mr. Fischer. Please, may I come in? What I have to say is private, and sensitive."

I nod, open the door and admit him. My kitchen table is my makeshift workbench, so it's littered with curled bits of shavings, and the piece I'm working on sits in the midst of the largest pile of shavings. It's a bird, a life-size rendering of a raven caught mid-caw, wings ruffling.

Mr. Tomas Anton, estate attorney, ambles to the table, bends at the waist and peers at the nearly finished carving. "That is remarkable, Mr. Fischer. You are a true artisan."

"Thanks. It's a hobby."

He has a briefcase, a slim leather thing that's probably more accurately called an *attaché*. He pulls a chair away from the table, sweeps the pine shavings off with a long, elegant hand, and sits down. Props the case on his knees and pops the latches. Lifts the lid. Removes a manila folder, marked with my last name in calligraphic handwriting on the tab. Closes the lid and sets the folder on top of the case. Each movement is precise, considered.

His eyes lift to mine. I'm standing, arms crossed, hands tucked under my armpits. "Perhaps you would like to sit down."

"You're recommending?"

He nods. "Indeed."

I sling a chair around, perch on it backward, arms folded over the back. "I'm listening, Mr. Anton."

"I will get right to the point. Mr. Bell, with whom you were friends, made rather extensive arrangements prior to his tragic passing."

"Extensive arrangements," I repeat. "You said you'd get to the point. It's been a year—like, almost exactly. So I'll ask again—what's this got to do with me?"

He opens the folder. "This letter will, I believe, explain everything. But I shall provide you with a brief summary. His last wishes, which he arranged as part of his will, included the transference of ownership of a small piece of property with two cabins some ways north of here in the Appalachian Mountains. He has divided the property and deeded a portion of it to you. Lake frontage, a cabin, and a few acres."

I feel my brow wrinkling in shock. "Adrian gave me a cabin on a lake in the mountains?"

"Yes, Mr. Fischer."

"Why now?" I shake my head. "Wills are read shortly after death, not a year later."

"It was part of his wishes."

"That I get the cabin *now*, a year after he died?"

"Yes."

"Why?"

"It would be inappropriate for me to speculate on that, but all shall be made clear in time." He hands me the folder. Opens his case again and withdraws another stack of papers. "Sign, please. It is the deed, assuming ownership."

I sign.

"He left me a cabin in the woods," I repeat.

"Indeed, he did."

"And you can't tell me why?"

"More accurately, I will not. It would go against the nature of his final wishes, which he contracted me to carry out."

"Okay, then."

"Read the letter, Mr. Fischer. It will clear up much, if not everything." He latches his briefcase. "I will mail you a copy of the deed."

"Are there keys? An address?"

He indicates the folder in my hands. "Everything you need is in that folder."

"Okay. Thanks, I guess."

He hesitates. "I said it would be inappropriate for me to speculate. And that is true. But this much I can say that is not speculation: Mr. Bell's final wishes were elaborately and carefully thought out. It may feel random to you, but I assure you it is not."

"Okay." I'm not sure what to say to that.

He stands and inclines his head to me. "Thanks for seeing me this evening, Mr. Fischer. Call me if you have any questions. "

It's not until after he's gone that I think of a question. Who owns the other half, the other cabin? Well, all shall be made clear, he said. I guess we'll see.

I take the folder to the couch.

Inside is a letter, handwritten in a fountain pen on linen stationary, with Adrian's name across the top.

Nathan,

Out of the blue, I know. On purpose.

You're still mourning Lisa. I could see it on your face, hear it in your voice, when we sat down to drinks that last time. And yeah, buddy, I knew then that I was dying. I was in denial still, to a point, but I knew. I was picking your brain, that day. I hope I didn't cause you pain with my questions, but I needed to hear the answers from someone who knew.

I was coming to grips with understanding that I'd be

leaving Nadia behind. How could I prepare her for it? What would it be like, for her, after I'm gone? Will she be okay?

I'm gonna say some stuff now that might piss you off, and I'm sorry in advance. Know I'm coming from a place of love, here, okay?

I wanted better for her than I saw in you. You were bitter. Lonely. Angry. Sad. You spent more time working than you did anything else, because it was easier. And then that became a habit, became your life. Your new normal. You've been on, from what you've told me, one date. Maybe two, since she passed? I don't know, and it doesn't matter. It's a question of moving on, Nate. I asked you, that day over scotch, if you'd moved on. If you could. And you said, boiling it all down, no.

Fuck, dude. Hit me with a hammer from the grave, why don't you. My eyes sting, my chest hurts, my heart sits heavy in my stomach. I haven't moved on. I can't. I don't know how.

Nate, I need your help. And hopefully, in helping me, you'll help yourself. Or I'll help you. It's hard to know how to phrase all this. I'm writing this at my desk, and I know I've got weeks, months at most to live, and I'm just...frantic. Desperate to do something for her.

For my Nadia.

She's going to be worse than you. I wasn't there when your wife died, but I can imagine you took it pretty hard.

Spent a while at the bottom of a bottle, and then dragged your pieces together such that you could go back to work, and eventually just found enough distance from the whole thing that you feel like you've healed as much as you ever will.

And, like I said, I want better for Nadia.

She deserves life. Real LIFE, not just a macabre, zombie half-life. Not just working till exhaustion kills emotion, not just trudging one grief-stricken step after another through a cardboard approximation of life, from workday to workday.

I want her to live, Nathan. But she won't know how. Like you, she'll be stuck in her grief.

She'll mourn me, and her mourning will consume her. She won't see the stars at night. She won't see a sunrise, or a sunset.

She won't know the comfort of an embrace.

She will go into mourning, and never return from that dark land.

What does this have to do with Tomas Anton whom I assume just left your home? What does this have to do with a cabin in the woods?

Go fishing, Nathan.

Pack some clothing, turn down the job offer you have waiting. Bring your carving and whittling tools. Drive to the address below, and stay there. Fish. Whittle. Watch sunrises. Drink coffee and watch fish jump.

Live.

Take the time for you. You need it. You deserve it.

You're a damn good man, Nathan Fischer. The best. I enjoyed our talks over Scotch more than I think I ever really let on.

But as you fish and whittle and live, ask yourself one question. Would Lisa, your dear departed wife, want you to live as you've been living? Alone, and lonely? Or would she want you to find happiness?

Really ask yourself that question.

When you get to the cabin, you'll find something else I've left for you. Something even more important than the cabin or this letter.

Try to trust me.

Yours,
The Ghost of Adrian Bell

P.S.: Sorry. Gallows humor. I couldn't resist.

I look at a five-by-eight notecard with two keys taped to it, one a house key, the other I'm not sure of—it's small, with a round head and a simple cut. For a lockbox, maybe. Below the keys is an address, which a Google search shows is, as Mr. Anton indicated, way up in the Appalachians.

I consider.

But not for long.

Because goddamn it, but he's right. I've not been

living, just staying alive. Moping through one day after another. Waiting to age out of life, maybe.

I don't need to sit on a lake to know the answer to his question, either. I can hear Lisa in my head right now, and I think she's been screaming this at me for years.

Quit moping, ya dumb lunk! Yeah, I loved you, you loved me. Yeah, I fuckin' died. She had a potty mouth, my Lisa. *If I was alive, I'd expect to be your one and only. But I ain't. I'm dead. Dead and gone, and you buried me, and now you gotta live. LIVE, motherfucker. Be happy.*

Fuck.

I pack—I don't need much. Some jeans, some T-shirts, some sweaters, some underwear and socks, the usual. My old leather roll-up case of antique woodworking tools. My fishing supplies—tackle box, a few fishing rods, waders, net, all that stuff. I toss it all in the backseat of my truck, along with a few things in a cooler, and I head out.

This cabin is hours away; it's just now ten at night, but fuck it. I don't sleep much anymore anyway.

My tires crunch on gravel, and then the gravel gives way to grass. I pull to a stop, and my headlights illuminate cattails waving in a breeze, dark water rippling against the shore, a small dock, wood planks and four posts, with a tin fishing boat tied to the post at the end of the dock.

Moths swirl madly in the twin spears of my headlights.

To my left, I can make out the small bulk of a building. My headlights only cast the dimmest glow on it, but I know it is made of logs, and I can see a few steps leading up to a porch. The rest is in shadow.

I shut off my engine, step out. Stand in the cool of a late summer night in the Georgia mountains. Crickets sing. A frog goes *rrrrrrUPP* in the distance. I look up—stars in an endless multitude, outshone only by a bright silver half-moon.

A bat flitters across the moon, chasing moths.

I take a long, slow, deep breath. My chest aches—I don't know why.

Now that I've opened my mind to it—or maybe my heart—all I can hear is Lisa's voice.

Now you're ready to heal, ain'tcha. Boy, you been wallowing in some fake-ass shit, and you know it. Time to move on, big ol' lover boy.

"Okay, Lisa," I whisper, my voice harsh and loud in the silence. "Okay. I hear you. I'll try."

The automatic headlights of my truck shut off, and I'm wrapped up in darkness. Now only the moon and stars shed light, and after a moment of standing in the darkness the night songs grow louder.

The sky is mammoth. Out here, in the mountains, an hour from the nearest real town, there are more stars than dark space between. Down low, the trees on the far end of the lake obscure the stars in spires and clumps, and there's the faint *chooonk-clop* of waves against the dock posts.

I have the key in my pocket, and I fish it out. My shoes plonk on the old wooden steps, two of them. I click on the flashlight on my phone, a sudden burst of white light revealing an old brass door handle, the area around the lock scratched into faded graphite scribbles. The door is pine, with four panes of leaded glass, dust-clouded. My cell phone light reflects garishly off the glass. I unlock the door and twist the knob, push in. I fumble along the wall next to the door and find a light switch; a handmade chandelier turns on, made from braided silver strands and sections of stained glass. It's an odd choice for lighting in a rustic fishing cabin, but it's pretty, and a work of art, lovingly crafted.

I turn in a slow circle taking everything in.

On the back wall there's an avocado-colored refrigerator and an antique gas range in a darker forest green. The counters, a few feet of them on either side of a porcelain farm sink, to the right of the door are slate, rough-hewn, probably locally quarried and handmade. The floors underneath are pine—they're solid, squeak-free, restained within the past ten years and well cared for, but old, very old. Like much else I'm seeing, the floors are handcrafted, and by someone skilled in woodworking well before the time of electric saws and sanders.

The walls are bare log, with a few antique decorations: a Coca-Cola sign, some snowshoes, a two-man saw, an old fishing net. Over the door hangs a muzzleloader, the barrel octagonal, the stock made from a dark, polished hardwood.

"Nice," I murmur. Not so much to myself as to the spirit of Adrian.

It's clean, so someone's been here to freshen up.

There's a door on the back wall, left of the range, leading to the bedroom. The wall left of the front door is dominated by the fireplace, made from giant river stones and boulders, with a thick pine mantle over it. On the mantle is a small envelope, and within, a sheet from a legal pad, in Adrian's handwriting.

I open it; it's from Adrian.

Welcome home, Nathan.

This place was built in 1899 by a man named Roger Klupinsky. He was a craftsman, as I'm sure you can see. He built the whole place, top to bottom, with his own two hands. Quarried the stone for the counters, cut down and worked the trees for the walls and the floors, everything. His great-grandson did some retouching a decade or so ago, refinished the floor, put on the metal roof, updated the wiring and plumbing. The appliances are genuine antiques, but refurbished. The muzzleloader works, there's powder and shot and all that stuff in the closet in the bedroom, I'm told.

The other key is for a lockbox at the bank in town. It's

in your name. Go get the contents of that box. Meet you there, partner!

Unsigned.

It's like a scavenger hunt, eh, Adrian? All right, I'm game. I lost track of the hours it took to get here, and I'm wiped. Maybe I'll even sleep.

The bedroom is tiny, just big enough for a queen bed, again handmade by the same hands. A newer mattress, though, and I spy bedding in a large zippered bag in the closet on the shelf. I make the bed, and then check out the bathroom. Tinier yet. Toilet, pedestal sink, mirrored medicine cabinet. Subway tile shower, a glass door, the enclosure barely big enough for someone my size. Thank god, though, the showerhead is hung high enough I won't have to do the limbo to get under it.

Home.

Huh.

I collapse on the bed, barely kick off my shoes and climb under the blankets, fully dressed, before falling asleep.

I dream of Lisa.

She's standing in a pool of light, as if she's on a stage under a spotlight. She's wearing the dress I last saw her in, lying in the coffin in the church. It's her favorite dress, she called it her LBD. She wore it whenever we went on dates, because the sight of her in that dress made me plumb nuts. It just hugged her curves exactly right, wasn't revealing but was certainly sexy. In death, it hurt to look at her in it.

In the dream, it hits me like every other time I saw her wear it on date night—a punch to the gut.

Skin is fair, a freckle here and there. The spotlight seems to illuminate those fine hairs on her forearms, which she hated but which for some odd reason were just so damned cute and endearing to me.

I take a step toward her, wanting to hold her. My feet are stuck to the floor, like I'm sunk to the calves in rubber cement. I can pull at them and they move a little but won't come free.

"Lisa," I say. "Wait."

She smiles sadly at me. "Time to let me go, lover boy." That was her pet name for me.

"No, I can't."

"You gotta, babe. Time to live."

"I'm living."

"Hell no, you ain't. You've been living for me, lover boy. I'm dead. Time to live for you."

She's fading. Takes a step back. The pool of light fades.

"Lisa! Don't go." I want to cry, but I can't. I never could.

She blows a kiss at me, from the shadows beyond the dimming pool of light. "I'll always love you."

"Lisa!"

"Time to let go, lover boy."

Her words echo.

I wake up sweating, thirsty. Shaking. I haven't dreamed of Lisa since right after she died. I used to have a recurring nightmare of her accident. I didn't see it happen, but I saw one like it, once, before I met Lisa. A semi swerved, crossed the centerline, and hit a minivan head-on. I'd been a volunteer firefighter at the time, so I went to help. Wasn't anything to help—and that sight stayed with me. My brain used that to supply a recurring nightmare of having been there when Lisa died, being on scene. Seeing her crushed and broken body…

Eventually those dreams stopped, and if I've dreamed anything since I haven't remembered them. Now this.

Lisa, telling me to move on.

I stumble to the bathroom, turn on the faucet—the pipes jangle and pop and bang, and rust-colored water spurts out and then runs clear. Tastes like well water, but I grew up on well water so that's fine.

I rinse my mouth, sip some. Shuffle outside. It's just dawn, the sun peeking up red-orange over the top of the trees—all pines. Tall, green-boughed. The lake is glass-smooth, and the air smells like dawn, like dew and fresh sunlight.

Thank god, I brought my Brita pitcher, electric kettle, Chemex, coffee beans, and grinder. I set the Brita to trickling clean water for me, because well water makes shitty coffee, I can tell you. Plug in the burr grinder and grind some beans. Heat the water, and when it's just off the boil, I slowly pour it over the grounds. Once it's done, I pour myself a mug—I also brought my favorite mug, a hand-thrown piece Lisa made for me. Pottery was her passion and her profession, and part of what brought us together—making things by hand. That feeling of crafting something with your hands—there's nothing like it.

For the first time in years, I sit and sip coffee and do…not a damn thing else. No cell phone—it's off, in the glove box of my truck. No TV, no radio, no set to build. Just sit here and drink my coffee.

Off to my right a few hundred feet is another cabin—close enough to be considered neighbors, but far enough that you have privacy. Slightly larger than mine, but something in the craftsmanship I can see even from here says it was built by that same guy, Roger. Looks dark, to me. Either no one there, or no one is up yet. There's a dock, as well. No boat at that one, but unlike mine, there's an Adirondack chair at the end, and a little round table. Perfect for sitting and sipping something and watching the sunset; the cabins are at the south end of the lake and face north, so you'll get the sunrise on the right and sunset on the left.

There's no car visible at the other cabin, so I figure it's empty for now. Whoever owns the rest of this property is not here. It's natural to assume his wife would own it, but seeing as he gave this part to me, and a year after his death, I don't like to hold on to that assumption. No matter, either way. I'm here for me.

I see no other cabins on the lake, just these two.

Finally, it's late enough in the morning that the bank ought to be open, so I head into town with the lockbox key in my pocket. The town is minuscule—a crossing of two local highways, with a gas station, a church, a bank, a post office, a bait and tackle shop, an army and navy surplus, a tiny supermarket, a general store, a couple cafes, a couple bars, and one sit-down restaurant a quarter mile outside town on a different little lake. I don't even know the name of the town, as the address of the cabin is not the same as the nearby town. Doesn't matter.

I head into the bank. The teller is an elderly woman with bouffant white hair, half-moon glasses, and a necklace made from chunky beads of red plastic.

She smiles maternally at me. "Hello, dear. I don't recognize you, which means you must be new here." She extends her hand, and I shake her hand gently; her fingers are tiny and cold and wrinkled. "I'm Mrs. Forniss."

"Nathan Fischer," I say, offering her a smile. "I am new. Just got in last night. One of those two cabins down on the lake, about fifteen minutes from here."

Her eyes widen. "Oh. Oh my. I heard someone bought the old Rupinksy property. Glad of it, as we all are. The Rupinsky family partly founded this town, but when Michael passed away back in, oh, twenty-ten, twenty-eleven? The property went into the care of an estate run by some cousin out in California, I guess, and those beautiful cabins were left empty for years. There was talk about the man who bought it. He's a writer, I heard. Is that you?"

I shake my head. "No, I'm a carpenter."

"Oh, I see." She's clearly waiting for me to elaborate, but when I don't, she clears her throat. "Well. What can I do for you, Nathan? Open an account?"

I set the key on the counter between us. "I've been told there's a lockbox here in my name."

She pushes away from the counter, stands up. "I'll go look."

She's gone about five minutes or so, and returns with a lockbox. "Can I see your ID, please?" I show it to her, and she sets the box on the counter. "Would you like a private room?"

I shake my head. Unlock the lockbox. Within is a single paperback book.

The title is *Redemption's Song*, by Adrian Bell.

Huh. That's not a title I've ever seen. I pull out my phone and search; no book by that name by Adrian Bell exists.

I lift the book out—there's nothing else. Just the book. Oh, wait…there's another note on that legal pad paper, tucked into the first page.

I close the box, slide it toward the teller, smiling. "Thanks."

"Will that be all, Mr. Fischer?"

"Yeah, that's it. Thanks."

I tuck the book under my arm and head out to my truck.

Drive back to the cabin—back home.

Sit on the front porch with the book in hand.

Finally, I take out the note.

Nathan,

This is the last one. The last note you'll get from me. No point dragging this out anymore.

This book is my final story. No one has ever read it. It will never be published. It will make zero dollars.

I wrote it for you.

And for Nadia.

It's a story about moving on. About finding love after loss. It's me asking the question, how do you move on when your heart's true love has died? And then attempting to answer that question.

I'm no Great American Novelist—I just tell romance stories. But I think this is my best work. My opus.

Read it. Please read it, Nathan. Read it, and hear the song in it. Hear what I'm trying to say to you. To Nadia.

Don't show it to her. Not yet. She's not ready.

You're here for her, Nathan. I'm sorry if this feels presumptuous of me. But it's the only thing I can do.

These are my last words, the final words I shall ever write. This is where I write THE END on my life. I have a few more weeks yet, perhaps months, but I shall spend them with her.

I wish I had time to tell you about her, Nathan. How she has a dry, wry sense of humor. How she's silly when she's drunk. How she sleeps splayed out like a starfish. So many things. But there isn't time. And, that's what the story is for. What the cabins are for.

Redemption's Song is for you, Nathan. Read it, and hear my final song.

The End,
Adrian

I open the book. No copyright page, no contents, no dedication. Just...chapter one, page one. He had this printed himself, just one copy.

I shut the book and hold it, stare at the cover.

I wonder what Adrian's game was. A cabin in the woods, a book, and a few somewhat cryptic notes.

We were friends, yes. Even good friends.

But what any of it means, I don't know.

I suppose I'll find out.

Twenty-Two

Letters From the Dead, Part Two

"NADIA, CAN I SEE YOU IN MY OFFICE, PLEASE?" DR. Wilson breezes past me as he speaks, white coat flapping behind him, green scrubs flashing under it, stethoscope and pens and pager and ID badge arranged on his person like armor.

"Uh, yes, sir. Right now?"

"Yeah." His office is around the corner, and I follow him there. We enter, he takes his chair and I perch on the edge of one of the hard plastic ones stolen from the waiting room. "Would you like some coffee?" He gestures to a Keurig on a filing cabinet.

"No, thank you."

"Sure? You look tired."

I laugh. "I'm off soon. If I have coffee now, I won't sleep."

He snorts. "After enough years of pulling crazy hours, you get to the point where coffee stops affecting you that way."

I nod. "I know." I pause. "So, what's up, Doc?"

He rolls his eyes. "Didn't take you for a Bugs Bunny fan." He leans back in his chair, eyes on mine. "I'm worried about you, to be blunt."

"I'm fine, sir."

He shakes his head. "Don't 'sir' me, Nadia. I've been your boss for how many years now? And, I hope, something like a friend. You've worked seven days a week for a year now. I've let it go, because your work speaks for itself. I can't stop you from working too much. Hell, I work too much myself. But…I am growing concerned."

"Did Tess put you up to this?"

"No, she didn't. I am putting myself up to this." He hesitates. "I can't presume to know what you've gone through—"

"Then don't," I interrupt. "I'm fine."

"You're not." He sighs, leans forward. "You know, before I went into medicine, I almost became a psychiatrist. I'm also an astute judge of people. You have to be, running a department like this. I know you need a distraction. I know you need to keep busy. I know. I get it as well as anyone who hasn't been through what you've been through can understand."

I clench my jaw. I have to bite back words—all of them bitter, four-lettered. I'm short-tempered, bitter. I know it's from working too much. But it's not just that. It's me, now.

"What are you saying, Alan?"

He shrugs. "I don't know, honestly. You need more than a day off. I could cut your hours, I could do a lot of things. I *am* your boss. But…I suppose I wanted to express my concern. You're pushing yourself to exhaustion, Nadia. Beyond it." He wipes his face. "You nearly overdosed a patient, Nadia. Lydia caught it. A couple milligrams too much, nothing fatal, but still."

I feel the blood run out of my face. "I…what? Who?"

"Deckard, 217."

I think back. I'd been in a hurry, rushing to get the medication dosed so I could get to 214—and then an alarm had gone off, someone had coded. I must have…

Shit.

And suddenly, I'm not angry.

I'm scared.

"Don't come in tomorrow. Not this department, not any department."

"Am I…are you firing me?"

"No. I'm not doing anything official. It was caught before the dose left the nursing station. It's not going on your record, which is up until now, perfect. And it's going to stay that way. You're going home, *now*. And you're going to think very hard about what's best for your patients. Because what you're doing is…deeply unhealthy. As your friend and coworker, I'm concerned, and as your boss, I'm concerned. Just on a human level. Everyone sees it. We're all worried."

I nod. Put my face in my hands. "I'm sorry." I heave a sigh. Work to contain myself. "Tell…tell Lydia I'm sorry."

He looks like he's going to say something else, but his jaw clicks closed. Opens again. "Go home, Nadia. Rest. Do some soul searching."

I nod again. Rise. Feeling like a zombie, I don't even say goodbye. I shuffle to my locker, collect my purse and sweatshirt. I barely remember the walk to my car or the drive home. I remember stoplights, the half-moon peeking behind the high rises and then hovering over strip malls and then ducking behind suburban homes.

I don't pause at the top of the driveway anymore. I open the garage door as soon as I hit the driveway and pull right in.

I toss my keys on the island. Did I even close the doors? I don't know. Don't care.

I almost OD'd a patient.

I flop onto the couch.

I haven't slept in my bed in months. There's a blanket here. It's easier.

He was right, I now realize. He haunts that bed. I changed the sheets but I still smelled him. All the sheets smell like him. New sheets make no difference, I tried that. He's in the shape of the bed, the way the mattress is molded to where he slept. He's on the walls.

He haunts that room.

"Mrs. Bell."

…

"Mrs. Bell."

…

I blink. Sunlight. A face.

"Huh?"

"Mrs. Bell, are you all right?" It's…Tomas Anton? I'm confused. "Your garage door and the door to your house were wide open. I saw you on the couch and I was concerned something had happened to you."

I try to sit up—I'm on the floor. Drool is crusted to my cheek. I'm in my scrubs, hair braided. Shoes on. Sweatshirt on. Stethoscope around my neck. "I…I worked late."

He backs away as I get upright, scoot up onto the couch. "I feared the worst when I saw you lying there, I do confess, what with your doors behind left open."

I wipe my face, trying to scrub the sleep off. "I must've not closed them all the way last night. It was a long shift, I was delirious." I groan. "I need coffee before I can even begin to wonder why you're in my house."

Adrian used to make the coffee. He bought special beans from obscure roasters, hand-ground them in this antique thing. He was a coffee snob. I miss his coffee. I make off-brand, bottom shelf garbage, and it tastes like shoe leather and cat shit.

Once the coffeemaker has brewed enough for me

to steal a cup, I pour some and bring it back to the couch. I'm sipping it, eyes closed. "I know this is where I'm supposed to offer you some, Mr. Anton, but I—"

"No, please. I require nothing." He clears his throat. "Take your time, please."

I take him at his word. Sip, breathe, and try to gather the strength to deal with my dead husband's estate executor.

Finally, I meet his gaze. "I'm not sure why you're here. His will was executed a year ago."

"Well, a portion of it was, yes."

"A...a portion?"

"He made rather extensive arrangements, you see."

"Extensive arrangements."

"I'm making rather a muddle of this, I'm afraid." He inhales softly through his nose, lets it out. "He gave me instructions to come to you, here, on the one year anniversary of his passing."

I don't have to consult a phone or calendar. I know. My heart knows.

"Come here today, why?"

He opens a briefcase. Removes a pair of envelopes. Both have my name written on them in Adrian's handwriting—in the deep black ink of that fancy fountain pen I bought him for our seventh anniversary.

One seems to contain only paper, but the other is heavier, as if it contains something metal. I feel it—a key?

"What is this, Mr. Anton?"

"His final wishes, Mrs. Bell."

Something about the way he says that seems funny.

"You remind me of the Hollywood stereotype of an English butler."

"Most people say Nosferatu. A vampire."

I snort. "That too."

"It's the boarding school education and the elocution lessons. And the hunch."

"His final wishes," I say, gripping the envelopes. "You mean, the insurance and the other money weren't his final wishes?"

"No. Those were his…affairs, you might say."

"Oh."

"Would you like me to stay, while you read the letter? In case you have questions?"

"I have a million questions. But…just…just summarize. What is this?"

"It is a letter from him, to you, to be delivered in person on the one year anniversary of his passing. The other envelope contains an address and a key."

"Address and key? For what?"

"He left you property, Mrs. Bell. Anything else I could say, I think, would detract from the message."

"Why…" I feel the tears. Fight them tooth and nail. "Why now? Why a year later? What property?"

He shakes his head. "I think the letter will say

more, and say it better, than any meager words of mine, Mrs. Bell. I think you would like to be alone, now."

"Yes, I think I would."

"You have my card?" he asks, rising, briefcase in hand.

"Yes."

"I shall see myself out, so please do not disturb yourself on my account." His smile is somber. "Be well, Mrs. Bell."

"Th-thank you, Mr. Anton."

I am trembling. Quivering all over. My breath shakes in my lungs. My hands flutter like papery orange maple leaves in a stiff autumn wind. My eyes burn, sting with hot salt tears. You think you've wept all the tears a human could contain, wept enough for a lifetime, and yet there you go, weeping even more. Apparently, sorrow is an endless wellspring.

Easy one first. I open the second envelope. It contains, as Tomas indicated, a notecard, five-by-eight, white with blue lines—I recognize it as being from a stack he kept in a desk drawer, for scribbling ideas and research notes and plot points. There is an address in his handwriting on the card—a Georgia address, which I do not otherwise recognize. There is a key, as well. It is not new, the key. Old, tarnished brass. Taped to the notecard underneath is the address.

Hands trembling, I work with ginger delicacy to open the flap of the last envelope. Within are several pages, folded thrice into a compact, flat bundle. The pages are ripped from his legal pad, the one he used for outlining and plotting and researching his stories. He would go through several of them for each book.

Immediately, I recognize the shakiness of his handwriting. He wrote this toward the end. When he could barely sit upright on his own, when he couldn't keep food or water down, when his hands shook like mine do now, but all the time, sometimes even in sleep. When he should have been in a hospital, on an IV pushing fluids and painkillers. Instead, he was at home, making "extensive arrangements." Whatever the fuck that means.

God, Adrian. You never did anything the easy way, did you?

I am putting off reading the letter. It represents his last words to me, when I thought his final words had been heard a year ago.

I'm tempted to have a drink before reading it. Slam vodka till I'm dizzy rather than read this.

What could he have to say? Why make Tomas— and me, more to the point—wait a whole year?

Why now?

I was just starting to find something equilibrium.

I can almost hear his sarcastic laugh, when that thought runs through my brain. Because no, I am not finding anything like equilibrium. I nearly overdosed a patient. I should tear up my RN certification. I am not okay. I sleep three, four hours a night. Sometimes up to five. Sometimes less.

I barely eat. I've dropped to about a hundred pounds, on a five-foot-ten frame. I'm a stick, nearly skeletal. My cheekbones could cut you. My hipbones, my pelvic bones protrude. You can count my ribs. I have no energy. I'm sick all the time. I snap at everyone. I am filled with rage and sorrow and bitterness. I have moved beyond grief. This is something else.

This is the Valley of the Shadow of Death.

I am not anything like fucking all right.

The letter shakes noisily in my hands, and I know I need backup for this.

My purse is on the counter, and it feels very, very far away. My legs struggle to support me, and I wobble like a newborn fawn. Brace myself on the counter with one hand and paw through my purse until I find my cell. Drop it on the counter from nerveless fingers. Swipe clumsily to open it. Find Tess's speed dial, and it rings on speakerphone.

"Nads, babe, hi." She's in the car, I can tell. "What up?"

"I…I need you."

"I'm there. Give me…seven minutes, tops. Don't…don't do anything."

"It's not like that. I just need you."

It nearly *was* like that several times. I sat in the tub, once, a month ago, bubbles up to my neck, and contemplated dropping the plugged-in curling iron in with me. I contemplated it like one would contemplate having a fourth glass of wine, or that last bite of chocolate mousse cake.

I didn't. Some fucked-up part of my soul told me that Adrian would be so angry if I did. And for some reason, that stopped me. A dead man would be mad at me if I committed suicide.

Okay, Nadia.

Another time, looking for Tylenol because I had a headache, I found a bottle of leftover Nuclear Option painkillers. I had a bottle of vodka downstairs. A handful of these, a few long slugs from the Goose. Bye-bye, cruel world.

Again, I didn't. I took one Tylenol, put away the vodka, and binged on a season of *Dexter* until my next shift.

Two days ago, driving home from work. I'd spaced out and found myself drifting into oncoming traffic lanes. Fortunately, for me, it was three in the morning and the road was empty except for me. But I'd thought, it would be so easy. Find a semi, swerve in front of it.

But then I realized I'd be dragging that poor innocent driver along with me, and having cared for head-on collision victims, I couldn't do that to anyone.

The thoughts occurred, is the point. Tess's worry is not unfounded.

I hear the front door, Tess's heels clicking rapidly. She smells like Chanel perfume, and looks like she just came from the boardroom of a multimillion-dollar company.

"Where were you?" I asked, by way of greeting.

"An interview. I accepted a position as the head of an IT department downtown. I've been working from home for so long, I was getting bored with it. I'm alone at home like all the time. So I figured, fuck it. Take a nine-to-five. It's so close to my condo that I can walk to work, and it's a stone's throw to my favorite bar and a nice steakhouse. I'm going to love it."

"Congratulations," I say, summoning a genuine smile of happiness for my friend. "I'm proud of you for taking your life back. You're reinventing yourself."

She sighs, smiles, nods. "I really am, aren't I? Honestly, Clint divorcing me is the best thing that's ever happened to me. I'm a new woman." She grins lasciviously. "I'm getting so much good dick, Nads, you don't even know."

I snort. "I don't need or want to know, Tess-icles. But good for you. I'm glad you're happy. I mean that, hon. I really, really am."

"I know," she says, setting her purse on the island next to mine.

She shucks her power suit jacket, wearing the

matching maroon pencil skirt and white silk blouse, unbuttoned to reveal a provocative but not totally immodest amount of cleavage. Kicks off her nude pumps—Louboutin, judging by the signature red bottoms.

She then comes to sit beside me, sees the envelopes. "What are those?"

"Letters. From Adrian."

She blinks. "Um...come again?"

"Tomas Anton came to visit just now. He delivered these. They're from Adrian. He gave Tomas instructions to deliver them today."

"Today?"

I nod. "He died one year ago today. At three thirty-three." I glance at the clock—it's 9:15. "Five hours and forty-two minutes ago."

"Today is the one year anniversary." She glances at the ceiling. Blinks. "I should have been here sooner, Nadia. I'm sorry."

"Don't be. You have your life to live."

She shakes her head. "It's a major milestone."

I heave a shaky sigh. "I haven't read it yet. I don't want to. I'm scared."

"I can only imagine." She touches my forearm. "Want me to read it to you?"

I shake my head. "I just...I need you here with me when I do." I sniffle. "I'm...I'm not fine, Tess. I say I am, but I'm not."

"I know. No one expects to you to be."

"I almost dosed a patient with too much medication yesterday. Not a lot. The patient likely wouldn't have even noticed. But my coworker did, and told Dr. Wilson."

"Nadia, god."

"I know." I swallow hard. "I think...I think I have to resign. I'm clearly losing my competency."

She side-hugs me. "Nadia, the problem is you're not taking care of yourself. You're so skinny now I could put you in my purse. You look like you're not sleeping."

I lift my scrub top to show her my torso. She inhales sharply. "Yeah, that might be part of the issue."

"Nadia..." she breathes. "You're a skeleton."

"I know," I whisper.

"When was the last time you ate anything?"

"I..." I try to think. "I don't know. Before work yesterday, I think? I had half a bagel."

"Jesus, Nads. You're the nurse here, not me, but I almost think you might need hospitalization."

"Possibly."

"This is officially an intervention," she says. "From now on, I'm not leaving you alone until I know you're healthy enough to be left alone."

I want to deny the need. But I can't. "Okay," I whisper. "I think that might be a good idea."

She flicks a finger at the envelopes on the coffee table. "So...what's the deal with the key?"

The notecard with the key sits on top of the envelope.

"I don't know yet. I haven't read the letter, which I'm guessing explains it. There's an address, but I don't recognize it."

Tess plugs the address into her phone. "It's... several hours north of here. Near the border, in the mountains. Looks like it's on a lake."

I lift the letter and unfold the pages onto my lap. "Okay. Here we go."

I begin reading.

Dearest, beloved, darling Nadia,

I have put off the writing of this for too long, I fear. Everything else has been arranged. It's all ready. I know without a shadow of doubt that I'm nearing the end of my time on this planet. I want to deny it, I want to pretend otherwise—continue to pretend otherwise, I mean. But I can't. I have waited too long and now my hands shake so badly I can barely make this legible. I'm sorry if it is not.

Ye gods, what a morbid opening to this letter those words are. I do not have either strength or courage to begin again, however, so...onward.

Firstly, and most important: I love you. You know this. I hope I have—and believe I have—shown you with my life and my actions in our marriage how deeply and truly I love you. I know you are likely still struggling with anger toward me over having hidden my illness. But I also think you probably understand, because you know me. Better than I know myself, I think.

It bears repeating, in writing: I love you, Nadia Bell.

All I have done, I have done because I love you. Because love is not a feeling, but an action. My life is ending, but yours is not. That's the most salient fact, for me. I am going to die, and you will remain living after I am gone.

By the time you read this, I will have been a year in my grave. I hope, I pray—and I am not a religious man, as well you know—that you are healing. That you have grieved, and mourned, and found strength to...be okay.

But I know you, Nadia. I know you better than you know yourself.

Here is what I know. You will have spent the past year working yourself to the bone. Worse, I fear. I am afraid that you are not sleeping. That you are not eating. That you have thrown yourself into a killing number of hours at the hospital. I have nightmare visions of you collapsing from exhaustion, hunger, and sorrow. I lay awake at night, yes, in physical pain, but in metaphysical pain. In worry for you.

You will not do anything so rash as outright, direct self-harm. That is not your way. You will be indirect about it. You will attempt to work yourself to death.

I don't know how else to put this, my love, except bluntly: I do not want to meet you in Heaven for many, many years yet. You are too beautiful, too wonderful, too mesmerizing and talented and funny and sexy to leave this world prematurely. While I live, I am selfish with you. I hoard you. I gather the glittering treasure that is you unto myself and I protect it greedily, refusing to share it, like a dragon. Do you know, when we go to the beach and you're flaunting your body in that little blue bikini you wear so well, a part of me, a caveman part of me clamors to cover you, so no one else can even have the gift of seeing even that much of you? I never say anything, because I am not so boorish as all that. You would not tolerate such behavior from me. But it's here, inside me.

I suppose I should apologize for the floridity of my writing, but delirium and exhaustion and pain and the narcotics conspire to make me verbose. You know how I am. I love the feel and the taste of my own writing. I have always been guilty of lapsing into purple prose, as my editor likes to say.

What was my point? Oh, yes. Now that I am going to die, I know I must let you go. I cannot hoard you to myself any longer. Beauty like yours, love like yours...it deserves to be shared. Someone out there needs you, and you need them.

You will sicken from an excess of grieving, Nadia. You will shut down and the processes that generate your energy and your love and your affection will atrophy, and all that makes you YOU will shrivel. And that is a tragedy I cannot countenance.

I Will Not Allow It.

So. I have given you a year. 365 days from the day of my death. A year in which to grieve. A year in which to mourn. To let yourself drown in your sorrow, however you see fit.

Now, though, my love, it is time to move on.

I am gone.

You must LIVE. You promised, remember? I say this proactively, because when I feel the end approaching, I will make you promise. I will exact an oath from you to Live. And you WILL promise, Nadia. I know you.

So. You promised, remember?

Live.

That means moving on.

You have not been living. You have been surviving, and probably barely even that. Now it is time to let go of my ghost, to resume breathing. To look ahead and see the coming march of years of your life, and see them not as decades in a gulag of despair, but as years which can and should and will be full of joy and happiness.

You have to let me go, Nadia.

Please.

But I know you cannot and will not do this—not on your own, so I am going to help you.

The second envelope, which I imagine you opened first, contains a key and an address. There is a lovely little cabin on a picturesque little lake, up in the mountains. I had a realtor take me on a virtual tour, as I could not travel to see it in person, but it is amazing. It's a snug little place, cute and quaint. Rustic, perhaps, but there is electricity and plumbing.

I want you to listen to me now, Nadia, and do exactly as I tell you. You just have to trust me. Pack your things. Just clothes. Bathing suits, yoga pants, sweat pants, jeans, your favorite hoodies. Bring your whole closet, if you want. You will be staying there for some time.

Leave the house as it is. Just leave it. I have made arrangements through Tomas to have it taken care of in your absence. Bring only your personal effects, clothing, toiletries, etc.

Just go. Put the address into your nav, and go. Right now. The moment you finish this letter, go.

Tess: I know you're sitting with her, and first, thank you, thank you a million times for the care and the love I know you will have shown my wife. See that she follows these instructions. Help her pack. Send her on her way.

When you get there, Nadia, I want you to unpack. Put your things in the drawers and the closet. I have made arrangements so that you will not have to do anything but unpack. And then, after you've unpacked, I want you to take a glass of red wine—your first in some time, I imagine, if I know you at all. And I want you to sit on the porch and sip it slowly, and just...BREATHE.

Feel what you feel. In the words of those yoga instructors you like, let the emotions flow through you, notice them, and let them go on their way.

Take up yoga again. There's an adorable little dock— take your yoga mat and do some sun salutations out there at sunrise.

Just learn to BE, Nadia. You'll have forgotten. Now it's time to relearn.

There will be more for you to do in learning to live again, but the important thing for you to hold foremost in your mind, my love, is this: I WANT you to move on. In every way. Please. When I made you promise to live, this is what I meant. Move on.

Love again, Nadia.

Yes, even that.

It hurts to say this, I admit. You're mine.

But I'm gone, now. And it's time for you to live again. You have too much love to keep hidden inside. To keep buried under my skeleton.

Dig it up, that love. Dust it off. Try it on, and then, before you feel ready, use it again.

I want you to. I expect you to.

If we meet in heaven and you have spent the rest of your life alone, I shall be angry with you, my love.

Life is for the living. So live.

I want to keep writing. I have so much I wish I could say to you. But this letter must serve a purpose, and that purpose is to help you live again, and to tell you that I love you, and that I want you to move on.

I love you. I am grateful beyond the capacity of human language to express for every single second I have had the privilege of spending in your presence. You have loved me well, more than I deserve and more yet. You have made my life a more beautiful place, my love. And even in this harrowing experience of dying, you have continued to love me with understanding and grace and gentleness and affection. I hope you look back on our life together with joy, Nadia. Remember me as I was—alive, and loving you. Remember all the good times we had, and hold on to them. They're yours forever.

And now, my darling Nadia, I must say goodbye.

This is not the last goodbye for me, for I have some time yet, but for you, these will be the final words from me:

I love you.

Thank you.

Live again.

Yours in life, in death, and beyond,
Adrian

It is a long, long time before I am able to stop crying.

When I can see, albeit with stinging eyes and a plugged nose, I realize I am alone, curled up on the couch, clutching Adrian's now tear-stained letter. I hear a noise: *thump, thud, thudthudthud, thump...*

I look, and Tess has already packed all of my belongings. There are four suitcases by the front door, and she's hauling down a fifth, along with a smaller duffel bag.

She's sweated through her blouse. She wipes at her forehead with the back of her wrist, blows a curly tendril of hair aside. "Okay. This one, with the stripes, is all your athleisure wear, so leggings, yoga pants, booty shorts, tank tops, long-sleeve running...things, headbands, all that. Next, in the plain black Swiss Gear, is your more formal, dress-up stuff. This will have all your skirts, hang-up blouses, sundresses, and your little black dresses of all colors—because a little black dress, as we all know, is a particular style not just a color. You have some power suits in here, but I don't see why you'd need them, number one, and number two you'll have to put on, like, thirty pounds for them to fit. But they're in here." She's pointing at each suitcase in turn. "This puppy, mister ugly ass turd-brown whatever the fuck this is, has sweaters, sweatshirts, hoodies, cardigans, one heavy coat, one leather jacket—your best one—your best jean jacket, a windbreaker-slash-raincoat, and...I think that's it in there. Oh! Your big fuzzy purple guy, you love that coat."

Her voice takes on the tone of a game show host.

"And in the hard-sided red suitcase, I've packed your shoes. Sneakers, running shoes, TOMs, three pair of heels—red, black, and nude—slippers, rain boots, hiking boots...leather knee-high shit-kicker boots, pretty much one of everything." She taps the last suitcase. "And in here, jeans and T-shirts, and that's pretty much it." The duffel bag, then. "This is bare essentials makeup—not the full set up, just the basics—your hairbrush, all that good stuff. Your cell phone charger. Your Kindle and a charger cord and block for that."

She winks at me.

"Also in the duffel are a couple of your, ahem, rather dusty lady happy time buzzy fun helpers."

I blush. "Tess, really?"

"I was being circumspect in consideration of your delicate sensibilities."

"Lady happy time buzzy fun helpers. That's your idea of being considerate?"

She snickers. "NO, but it's fun to say, isn't it?" She has the duffel on her shoulder, still. "You need them. You need to *use* them, Nadia. You are still a sexual being."

I shake my head. "I'm broken, Tess."

A sad smile, her hand on my cheek. "I know. He knew you would be, too. That's why you're going."

I can't fathom leaving this house. "Tess, I...I don't know if I can."

"You are."

"Tess."

She points at the letter still clutched in my fingers. "Nadia, you have to. You know you do."

"Yeah, I..." I scrub my face with one hand. "I know. I know I do." I look up at her. "But I don't want to be that far from you."

She laughs. "You can't get rid of me. I'll come visit. But I think you need this." Sober and serious, then. "You need time alone. You need to...well, exactly as he put it. You need to relearn how to live. This is how you do it."

I sigh. "I guess there's really nothing else left to do but just...go."

She nods, points at the kitchen. "Your marching orders are to first make yourself coffee. Second, as big a breakfast as you can manage. You've been starving yourself so long it may not be much, but you need to eat. Third, you have to call Doc Wilson and tell him you're taking an extended, open-ended leave of absence, starting immediately. For health reasons."

"Okay." I blow out a nervous breath. "Tess?"

"Nads?"

"Thank you."

"Anything, anytime, always."

An hour and a half later, I was behind the wheel of my car, fed, caffeinated, jobless, with all my clothes packed in the trunk and back seat of my little red A5. All the lights in my house were off. The garage was empty. The doors were locked.

It felt like I was going on a vacation…alone. It felt weird.

I'd said goodbye to Tess, hugged her at least four times, and then she physically shoved me in the car, leaned into the passenger door and input the address for me in the nav system, pressed "GO," and kissed me on the temple.

"Next time I see you, you're gonna be a different person, right?" She palmed my cheek.

"Yeah."

"You have to invest in the process, Nads. Okay?"

"I will." I booped her nose. "Get some good dick for me."

"Oh, I'm getting *all* the good dick. I might even keep one, someday."

I laughed. "And the rest of the man attached to it, I hope."

"Maybe. If he's nice enough."

"You're a dork."

"Bye, Nads. Drive safe."

"Bye, Tess-icles, I will. Thank you."

"Don't call me when you get there. Don't text. Just turn your phone off, leave it in the car. If I hear from you, it's because something went horribly wrong. So I don't want to hear from you. Okay?"

"I can't promise, but I'll try."

She exited the car, closed the door, and stepped back onto my lawn. Waved.

And I drove away.

Next stop?

The cabin.

Twenty-Three

Resurrection

I'VE BEEN HERE TWO WEEKS. IT'S BORING, SOMETIMES, BUT that's good. Boring is good. I've carved a bunch of new pieces, a squirrel, a raccoon, a cardinal, a moose, a little clutch of field mice. I sit and drink coffee on the porch in the morning, sip whiskey at night. Never more than one, because for once I'm not trying to escape.

I've cried a bunch. It was embarrassing at first. I'm a man's man, raised by a man's man. I drink whiskey and punch sissies, and only sissies cry. But Dad died lonely and bitter, of cirrhosis and misery.

Fuck that noise.

The first time I was sitting on the dock, toes in the water, drinking a beer, it just…hit me. I missed Lisa. Missed her laugh and her voice and her soft curves. And my eyes stung, my nose itched, and then I just couldn't stop it. And hell, I was alone, right? No one to see, so I just let it go.

And you know what? It felt *good*, in a weird way. Like I'd been holding it in all these years.

After that, I was as emotional as…well, the only comparisons that come to mind are probably sexist and shitty, so skip 'em. I cried a lot. Just sat around and let myself cry for…me.

I've fished. Caught a few lake trout, mostly just tossed 'em back.

Read books—turns out there's a library next town over, and I got myself a card and checked out some fiction. Westerns, mostly. Zane Grey, Louis L'Amour, Larry McMurtry. Some historical stuff, a couple biographies.

Mostly, though, I whittle and I carve.

And I wonder about that cabin down the way.

Just sitting there empty, and it feels ominous.

I know I should be reading Adrian's book, but I just can't. I dunno why. I'm not ready for it. I have to… let the bats in the belfry of my soul air out a bit, so to speak.

I can't fathom why Adrian gave me this place, what his greater purpose was, but I'm goddamn thankful. I was suffocating, I'm starting to realize. Wearing a path in the floor of life, pacing back and forth from work to the bottle to work to the bottle, rarely even engaging in conversation with anyone beyond idle chitchat, and I ain't got time for that most of the time. Well, patience is what I lack, more than time, but still.

I needed this.

I'm starting to breathe, a little, finally.

Four in the afternoon. I'm on the porch, sipping an IPA, reading *Lonesome Gods*. I hear tires on gravel, a car motor. Squeal of brakes that need a tune-up. Glance left, and there's a little red convertible pulling up on the far side of the other cabin. The top is back, and I get a glimpse of black hair.

The engine shuts off, and there's a while of silence, followed by the car door opening...closing. I can make out the nose of the car, some of the windshield, and some of the front seat. A tall, slender figure emerges around the front of the cabin. A woman.

She's wearing black leggings, colorful sneakers, and a baggy gray sweatshirt hanging low on one shoulder. Her hair is long and black, loose around her shoulders. A purse hangs from her left elbow; sunglasses perched up on the top of her head.

You know how sometimes, even though you can't make out someone's features, you can tell just by seeing them from a distance that they're good-looking? I get that feeling with her. She's gonna be beautiful.

It's weird to even think that. I haven't really noticed women, not for years. I tried, too. But it just went...nowhere. I couldn't make my heart less of an ice block, couldn't make my brain interested, nor my body. It's like I just shut down when Lisa died, and not all the systems came up online again.

So to even think about a woman as being beautiful, worth noticing, is in itself weird.

She just stands on the porch, staring at something in her hand—a key, I imagine. Something about the way she's just standing there feels familiar. Like she's getting up the nerve to go in. Like I did, the first time.

Whoever she is, she was given that key by Adrian. Or this is whoever he sold the other part of the property to. But somehow, my gut tells me he didn't sell it. He bought it at the end of his life, with a particular purpose in mind.

Maybe it's his wife.

Nadine? No, I always think it's that, but it's not. Nadia? I think that's her name. Maybe it's her.

I just sit on my porch, the sweating bottle cold in my hands, and watch. Eventually, I see her sigh. Even from here, it feels heavy, that sigh. She unlocks the door, and vanishes inside.

She's in there a while. An hour, maybe. When it's clear she's not coming back out right away, I go back to reading, but now my mind is on her. Wondering who she is, if my—not assumption, nor a guess; my feeling, I suppose it is—if my feeling that the woman is Adrian's widow, is correct.

It feels right. Who else would it be? Showing up now, on the anniversary of his death. When I was in town getting library books, I looked up the obituaries around the time I know he died, and today is the one year anniversary; the funeral was immediate family only, so I wasn't there, and I was out of town for work anyway. So...yeah. Who the hell else would show up, here, today, and stand there as if summoning the nerve to go in?

What does it mean for me?

In light of the note and the letter he left me, the book I have yet to read...what does it mean that she's here?

The math of Adrian's arrangements seems obvious. But...I recoil mentally from going down that road. I haven't even met the woman. She's grieving. Hell, *I'm* grieving—and I'm realizing I never did that. I just shut down, and then went about shuffling zombie-like through a muddy, miserable half-life.

I keep reading.

When she comes out again, it's to unload her suitcases. I count five, and a duffel bag, plus her purse. Looks like she's planning on staying a while. But so am I; on my last trip into town I brought a few of my carvings, showed them to the owner of the little shop that sells knickknacks and local art, and he agreed to try to sell them, for a few bucks off the top. I don't need the money, but if I'm going to be sitting around carving, and the pieces don't go anywhere, I'll be up to my neck in them in a month.

Once all her suitcases are inside, she's in there again for another hour, closer to two. I'm getting hungry, but my dinner isn't ready yet. I found a second-hand crock-pot in town the other day, and I've been playing around with pot roasts and such. Ain't much for cooking, but you gotta learn sometime, right? Out here, living off fast food and pizza delivery ain't an option. Which is probably a good thing for the diameter of my midsection.

She comes back out, a third time. This time, with a glass of wine in one hand, and the bottle in the other. It's sunset, and a marvelous one. Lots of purple and crimson and orange reflected in the gently rippling lake. She sits in the Adirondack, sips her wine. Sighs, now and then.

I have no impulse to go over there. Not yet.

I go back to Louis L'Amour. Johannes Vern is talking to a giant—one of my favorite parts.

But really, I'm watching her. She's uncomfortable just sitting there, doing nothing. She crosses and un-crosses her legs. Sips too fast, then sets it down as if to slow herself down. Rakes her hand through her hair, then realizes she's fidgeting, and tries to still herself again.

I want to tell her she's trying too hard to relax. It won't come right away, the ability to slow down. If you try to force it, you'll just stress yourself out even worse. For a go-go-go type of person, like me, like Lisa was, it takes some practice.

I think, too, she's just too sad to be able to enjoy anything.

And that, now, *that* I get.

I'll bide my time. I don't really understand anything, but I feel like this is what Adrian intended. What *this* even is, I don't know. Maybe I'm crazy.

I put a receipt into the book to mark my place, take it inside, and set it on the little shelf next to the bed. On top of the shelf is Adrian's book.

It's time to read it, I think.

I open it up, and turn to chapter one, page one.

When my wife died, I died with her.

Okay, a doozy of a first line.

When my wife died, I died with her. It wasn't supposed to happen. Or, if it was, it should have been me. I should have been driving. I shouldn't have had so much to drink. I wasn't drunk, but she'd had less than me and it was just safer to let her drive. It was just ten minutes to home, and we had a back route we knew, no main roads, no highways.

There was a deer. She swerved and hit the brakes. We spun out on a patch of ice, and ended up wrapped sideways around a tree. Driver's side impact. I broke some bones, cut my head open, whiplash, bruises. But her? She died. Not instantly, either. There was time for her to look at me, goodbye in her eyes, and then the life drained out of her, onto the seat belt buckle. Drip, drip, drip, crimson life pooling slowly on plastic and leather.

She died, and I died with her.

But it was the worst kind of death, for me. The kind where your body stays alive, but your heart and mind and soul go down into the grave with her.

But, this is only the prologue, so I can tell you the good news, too.

I was resurrected. It took time. There was pain—don't ever let anyone tell you that coming back from the dead doesn't hurt, because it does. A fucking lot.

Sorry, that was supposed to be good news. Let's try that again: I was resurrected.

Her name is Nadia, and she brought me back to life.

This is the story of how.

I close the book around my index finger, head lolling back on the couch. Holy shit, Adrian. You're gonna hit me over the head with a hammer, aren't you?

I open the book again and keep reading. I hear Adrian's voice in it. Feel him speaking to me.

"*Redemption's Song* is for you, Nathan. Read it, and hear my final song."

I hear you, buddy. Not sure what you're trying to tell me just yet, but I hear you. I'm listening.

I'm listening.

Twenty-Four

Stars

NOT WHAT I EXPECT, WHEN I PULL UP. OR MAYBE IT'S exactly what I expect. It's like something out of a Thomas Kincaid painting, late afternoon sunlight golden-yellow on pine trees crusted thickly around the banks of a placid lake. Private. The only cabins on the lake are the one I pull up to, and another one next to it. My hindbrain registers the pickup truck pulled forward at angle in front of the other cabin—it's steel gray, enormous, with a silver toolbox across the bed behind the two-door cab. A thick black brush guard protects the headlights and grille, and black running boards stretch from front tire to back. It's a macho truck, but not so over the top as to be unusual.

The truck means the next-door cabin must be occupied; that's all I have mental or emotional room for, that observation.

The cabin is incredible. Thick pine logs, a dark green metal roof, covered porch, a chimney made from big stones and boulders. The two cabins are twins, not identical, but alike. The other one looks a little smaller and the roof is red rather than green.

The covered porch is homey, cozy. A rocking chair that looks antique and handmade sits at an angle near the door, with a short, thick section of tree trunk denuded of bark beside it for a table. I am standing beside my car, just taking in the fact that I'm here and that Adrian chose this place for me. He let me spend a year alone, mourning, before telling me about it. But he knew me. He knew I wouldn't have come before now. He knew I'd need this *now*.

I mount the steps to the porch, which is bordered by crooked lengths of tree limbs in two rows fastened to the upright posts, with two small steps up. You could sit out here at sunset, lean on the top rail…stare out at the lake as the sun stains it on the way down behind the trees.

On the porch, I feel my heart start hammering. He's not in there, I know that. It will be empty. A simple rustic cabin in the woods, a place to get away for a while. To rest. To try and heal. To do as he said—start learning how to move on.

The door is made of wide, rough-hewn planks secured with black wrought-iron straps at top and bottom, and another plank running diagonally from top left to bottom right. Brass doorknob, tarnished, key-scratched. Leaded panes of glass, four-square, old glass, bubbled and distorted. I can't really see inside through the glass, other than vague shapes and patches of darkness.

My hand shakes as I stare at the small brass key nestled in the palm of my hand and just stare at it. As if something momentous will happen when I put the key in the lock.

What do you want from me, Adrian?

Why am I here?

How am I supposed to move on? How am I supposed to…to live, without you?

He wants me to try. So…try I will.

I unlock the door, push it open. The hinges squeak softly. I step in. I'm prepared for, well, the kind of thing you'd expect from a hundred-plus-year-old cabin on a lake an hour from anything like real civilization. Dusty, rustic at best. Old and uncomfortable and plain. Colorless, everything decorated with animal heads and horns and the iconography of the nineteenth century.

But what I find is inside is not that…at all.

I find Adrian's fingerprints all over the inside. His knowledge of *me*.

Not an animal head to be found, not a single set of antlers, no stuffed fish or raccoons or foxes, much less those stupid "jackalope" things. I close the door behind me and put my back against it, hand over my mouth as I struggle with an onslaught of emotion at what Adrian has given me.

There are large windows on either side of the

door, letting in buckets of natural light, making the cabin feel airy and light. The fireplace is on the right-hand wall, a towering expanse of round stones each roughly the size of my head. A thick mantle runs over top, deep, square, stained dark.

On the mantle is a single framed photo: my favorite of him—he's at his desk, leaned precariously backward with his feet up on the corner of the desk, his laptop on his thighs, a mug in one hand, his favorite mug, with levels marked ranging from "don't even THINK about talking to me" at the top, "nope, not yet" below that, "still shushy time" below that, and at the very bottom "okay, NOW you can talk." He's wearing his blue-light-blocking glasses, and he's grinning at me, laughing at some dumb joke I told him to break his concentration. It's my favorite photo of him because it captures the essence of everything that is my Adrian. His joy, his humor, his deep, abiding addiction to strong, bold, single-origin coffee, his dedication to his craft.

There is a couch facing the fireplace, and it's bohemian and chaotic and colorful. White cloth cushions, wood armrests, covered in knit throw blankets and a one-of-a-kind pillows: one made from an old flannel shirt with a single huge wooden button in the middle, and one made from thick pile purple shag carpet, and another with a wild red and yellow and green zebra stripe pattern. Rugs line the polished wood floors, a profusion of various patterns and styles all overlapping. An industrial-style floor lamp stands beside the couch and it's made from old copper piping decorated at sporadic intervals with antique hosepipe knobs, the lampshade a bowl of hammered copper, with a long, dangling pull chain and an Edison bulb. Overhead is a chandelier that is clearly a handmade work of art, crafted from sections of stained glass in a brilliant explosion of colors, almost an imitation of a Tiffany lamp.

Left of the front door is the kitchen. The counters are thick butcher block, with a deep porcelain farm sink. The cabinets under the sink are painted a bohemian array of bright colors, no two colors or shades repeated, and no two cabinet pulls are the same, some being cut crystals, others brass knobs and others ceramic butterflies and delicately wrought designs of filigreed metal or oiled bronze. The cabinets above are white, open face, floating. On the shelves are blue-and-white china dishes. The faucet is oiled bronze, a high elegant arch with antique knobs on either side of the base. The stove is also an antique piece, while the refrigerator is stainless steel, French-doors over the freezer drawer, ultramodern.

The rear wall features a single open doorway, with a sliding barn door stained a dark reddish brown. Beyond, the bedroom. A king-size bed, four-poster, handmade. A tall bureau on one wall, heavy and dark wood with thick bronze pulls; a small, delicate white vanity opposite the bed, lined with Edison bulbs. A bathroom, all white subway tile and industrial fixtures and exposed piping, and a deep hammered-copper soaking tub.

The real draw, though, is the loft. It's over the back of the cabin, accessible by a ladder-like stair. The space is deep, taking up the entire rear half of the cabin's footprint, it's been turned into a library. Shelves line the walls, worked into every little nook and angle, and there's a large skylight in the metal roof to let in daylight. Instead of a couch or recliner is the largest beanbag chair I've ever seen, so big I could curl up on it. There's a wicker basket beside the beanbag, filled with fleece blankets. The bookshelves are lined with books of all variety, everything from sweet romance and women's lit and thrillers and horror to biographies and classics and collections of essays. Another floor lamp stands beside the beanbag chair, this one steampunk clockwork.

Every inch of this cabin was designed for me. It's everything I've dreamed of remodeling our home into one day. I've talked about it for years; from the moment we bought the house, I talked about knocking out all the interior walls and installing thick exposed beams and making it a boho, industrial-chic wonderland of coziness and color and warmth. I talked about it, but we never got around to it. There was always another book to write, another signing tour, another book-to-movie project for him to oversee, another week of double shifts at the hospital and then vacations to Italy or Spain or Iceland, where we'd spend a week playing tourist in exchange for twelve hours of him signing books and taking photographs.

It makes my eyes sting. Did he have this cabin remodeled into this, for me? Or did he find it like this and know it was meant for me, perfect for me?

My knees wobble as I explore.

The fridge is stocked—everything is straight from my personal grocery list. Everything he knew I would buy is here, from my favorite brand of ice cream to my favorite cans of flavored sparkling water, low-GI pasta, no sugar added condiments. Our own pantry, fridge, and freezer back home have been, in effect, lifted and transported here.

I browse the cabinets: Le Creuset pots and pans, cast iron skillets, deep pasta boiling pots, stoneware omelet pans. Even my preferred brand of kitchen utensils are here. A cabinet full of hand-thrown mugs which he knew I'd love. One cabinet near the fridge opens up to reveal a hidden wine rack—filled with my favorite brands of red wine.

Another cabinet reveals dozens of bars of my favorite chocolate, Stevia sweetened and ultra-dark, sea-salt almond.

Adrian, god.

He did this for me.

How? When?

I head into the bedroom. The comforter is the exact same as the one we have at home, one I had imported from France at great expense, a rare indulgence for me. Thick, heavy, but breathable, velvety soft on the underside and wild with colorful arabesques on top. I run my hand over the comforter, and feel a million joyful, happy memories of Adrian and myself under this comforter bubble up inside. Folded on the foot end of the bed is my favorite blanket, a thick, fleecy, stretchy, soft, warm thing that I was only ever able to find on an obscure Etsy site. He found a duplicate, somehow. He knew how much I loved to wrap up in it and read, or watch TV with him. It's a comfort item, that blanket. And here it is.

My eyes sting.

But there's more.

On the tall bureau is a handmade wooden tray, on which is a clutch of my favorite essential oils and a small diffuser. He made fun of me for my weird obsession with essential oils, but they just make things homey for me. Scent is a vital element of home, and I just love a diffuser gently bubbling with some thieves' oil, or an orange peel cinnamon.

On the vanity, a Jonathan Adler candle, another of my favorites. In the drawers, my favorite brands of makeup. Eye shadows, foundations, lip gloss and lipstick and lip stain, lip pencils, eyes pencils, contouring sponges, everything you'd find in my makeup kit back home, is here.

In the bathroom, there is more of everything *me*. In the medicine cabinet is my favorite mouthwash, face wash, hand lotion, body butter, moisturizer, razor, shaving cream, everything. Even the damn towels folded on a floating shelf over the toilet are my favorite kind, the thick, soft, enormous bath sheets. My shampoos and conditioners and everything, it's all here.

It hits me, there, in the bathroom.

Adrian just *knew me*.

I'll never find that again. No one could ever know me the way he did. He knew every single thing there was to know about me, from my absurd but paralyzing fear of wasps to my deep, abiding, passionate love affair with mint chocolate chip ice cream. My most embarrassing moments, he knew—including that mortifying wardrobe malfunction in high school, every teenager's worst nightmare come true, when my skirt literally fell off in the middle of an end-of-the-year speech in front of the entire school, leaving me in front of a microphone stand in my white granny panties, complete with visible maxi pad. Oh yeah. That bad. He knew about it. He knew my sexual peccadilloes, my hatred of lima beans, my obsession with New Kids on the Block, my "celebrity hall pass" list that consisted exclusively of Justin Timberlake and Hugh Jackman.

He knew it all.

He knew my makeup.

I fall to the floor in the bathroom, sobbing. I have a tube of lotion still clutched in one hand; the subway tile under me is cold and hard. I cry harder than I have since right after he died.

God, I miss you, Adrian.

I miss you so fucking bad.

This cabin is a love letter from Adrian. It said everything that language could not possibly begin to express. His intimate knowledge of everything I am as a person, as a woman. It's him telling me, *I know you, Nadia. I know you, and I love you. This is my gift to you.*

I sob on the floor for a long, long time. Missing him. Hating him for leaving. Hating the world for taking him. Hating myself for needing him so badly I can't figure out how to exist without him.

It's there, lying with my cheek squashed against the icy tile floor, that I realize how angry I am. I hadn't understood that until now. It's a white-hot rage. At *him*. For leaving. He promised he wouldn't leave me, and he fucking left me.

My intellect understands that he died, that he didn't walk away from me. But my emotions know only one thing: he *left*.

God help me, I'm so angry. I've been avoiding and denying that anger for so long, now. The anger is there, simmering, boiling under the surface, and I've been ignoring it. It's why I can't sleep. Why I can't eat—I have no appetite, and when I do eat, food is tasteless.

It's not just sadness, not just missing him.

I'm so angry at him for dying that it's been poisoning me.

This cabin is the antitoxin I need, apparently. How he knew, I'll never know. But he did.

I eventually manage to scrape myself off the bathroom floor. When I do, I have an imprint of tiles on my reddened cheek. I go out and haul my bags inside and I unpack every damn thing Tess packed for me, which is just about my entire wardrobe. I put everything away; fill all the drawers with my clothes and the shallow but wide closet with my dresses and my shoes and my boots.

I make myself at home.

Because somehow, I realize I won't be leaving here any time soon. I can't leave here until I'm whole again, and that will take a long, long time.

When I'm unpacked and my suitcases are shoved under the bed and on the shelf in the closet, I go over to the wine rack in the kitchen. Withdraw a bottle of Josh, slowly uncork it. I haven't had red wine since before Adrian died—it was our thing. He liked whiskey and I hate it; I like vodka and he hated it. The one thing we could agree on was red wine.

I pour a glass, swirl it, watching the ruby liquid

smear down the glass in receding waveforms. Take a tentative sip.

I'm hit with a tidal wave of memories. Sitting on our couch, two bottles in, a giant bowl of popcorn on his lap, marathoning LOTR, which was a yearly thing for him. It bored me to tears, so he'd get me tipsy and then I'd fall asleep. Or, sitting in bed with the iPad and a bar of chocolate, him reading while I binged *Vanderpump Rules*. Italy, getting drunk on red wine in a street-side cafe in Florence, telling the server to choose the wine for us because who the hell knows anything about all those weird, obscure, Italian name wines anyway? It's all good, especially once you're four glasses in and the world is topsy-turvy and beautiful with that golden Italian sunshine.

All that, in one sip.

I take the bottle with me as I head outside to the little dock. It's maybe twenty feet long, with four shoulder-high posts weathered gray and stained with bird poop. There's an Adirondack chair and a small table, handmade by whoever built the cabin and a lot of the stuff in it. It's deep, and comfortable.

The sunset is breathtaking.

I hurt, all over. Grief and anger are physical. I can taste them. Feel them in the tension in my shoulders. Relax? Ha. I have to think about breathing. Each breath, I have to tell myself to suck it in, and let it out. Take another breath. Keep breathing.

The wine rolls in my mouth, tumbles in my belly. I should have eaten first. But then, I haven't been properly drunk since my bender after the funeral. I know I should go slow, take it easy. But…how?

I think the alcohol does something to the anger. Metabolizes it, somehow. Half a glass, and I'm feeling it. I've not been a teetotaler the past year, but I've not gotten drunk. I'd rather work. If I were to get drunk, I think I feared I'd end up feeling things I was trying to hide from.

Well? Here we go.

The bottle lightens, and so does the pressure in my skull.

I miss you, Adrian.

I hate you for leaving.

Come back, goddamn you.

Hold me.

I've cried myself out, I think. I don't weep. I sit on the dock and slowly get drunk, watching the sun impale itself on the pines. A fish leaps, sending ripples skidding across the surface. I think about him. The good times, for now. I can't go back to the horrors of his death, not yet. For now, I just have to let myself remember him.

Start there.

The sunset fades into a purple sky, and the air cools. My feet are bare, and my toes are cold.

The bottle is empty, and the stars are making their first appearance.

I think of our one and only attempt at camping.

We took a weekend trip...actually, probably not far from here. It was early in our marriage. He wasn't a camper, and neither was I; he was more of a road trip person, and I was a homebody who rarely left my hometown. He went out and bought all the gear, the tent, the cooler, the lantern, the bug spray, the camp stove, all of it. He had enough gear for us to camp out for a month. It was a disaster. He pitched the tent in the most uneven, rocky area he could find. Mosquitoes ate us alive, rabid, bird-sized swarms of them. He couldn't get the fire going, and by the time he did, it was nearly midnight and we were snapping at each other. He brought a bunch of canned beans and fruit, but no can opener. A camp stove, but no propane. One sleeping bag each, and it was the coldest weekend of the entire summer, and we froze all night.

The most magical part of it was the last night. We were cold, miserable, hungry, and ready to go home and live like civilized people. We couldn't sleep. We were too frigid and miserable to even fuck, which says something. So, we abandoned the notion of sleeping and left the tent. Wandered down by the lake, where the moon was high and full and silver and bright, and we sat on a big boulder with our sleeping bags zipped together and wrapped around us both, huddling together, watching our breath huff out in a white fog, staring up at the sky full of stars.

We sat there all night long, just staring up. Holding each other. Not talking, just…being. Together under the stars.

I haven't seen stars like that since.

Until now.

I lose my breath, staring up at them. My chest aches. I feel him in their twinkling countless millions, feel him watching over me from somewhere behind them.

I'm not okay.

But for the first time since he died, I feel like maybe, someday, I *could* be.

Twenty-Five

Coffee & Home Cooking

Dawn—I've woken at 6 a.m. on the dot without an alarm since I was sixteen, and by now it's an unbreakable habit. I've been letting—sometimes forcing—myself to lounge in bed for an hour, dozing off, thinking, just enjoying being warm and in bed. Finally, around seven, just after sunrise, I take my cup of coffee out onto the porch—it's not quite truly cold outside, chilly enough to require a jacket, but it's bracing. The mug is hot against my palms, steam rising from the black liquid.

I sit with the book. In it, the narrator has met the heroine—like him, she's a widow who recently lost her husband. They're both closed off and bitter and hesitant to let anyone in—sounds familiar.

The heroine in the story is tall and slender with jet-black hair and green eyes.

The hero is tall, strongly built, and a carpenter.

A little on the nose, buddy.

I read on:

...I couldn't make coffee for shit. This is from the heroine's POV. *I worked early and stopped for coffee on the way, and so rarely make my own coffee. On the weekends, my husband used to make it for me, but now, it was just me. And I couldn't and wouldn't make it for myself. It's not like making coffee was hard or complicated. It was the principle of the thing, really.*

I think about my pour-over inside. I wonder if she's had coffee, yet. If she's awake. A cup of fresh coffee would be a nice way to introduce yourself as a neighbor.

I'm considering this when I hear her front door open. She's wrapped in a blanket. Sits in the rocking chair, but with her knees under her. I'm standing up, at this point, thinking. I've got my mug in my hands, having just refilled it, so it's steaming.

She glances this way—it's far enough I can't really make out her exact expression, but I can feel her longing for coffee from here.

I head back inside and make a fresh batch. I carry the pour-over in one hand and my mug in the other. Head over across the grass between the cabins. I can feel her tensing as I approach. I stop at the base of her steps.

"Uh, hi." I clear my throat. "Wondered if you might like some coffee."

Her eyes are green, a deep, dark shade of jade.

They search me. "I…yeah, actually, that would be amazing." She seems embarrassed. "I don't…I have stuff to make coffee but I…every time I make coffee, it tastes like dirt."

I lift the Chemex. "Well, grab yourself a mug." I set a foot on the lower step. "Mind if I come up?"

She hesitated. "I…yeah, sure. Yes. Please. I'll be right back."

Rising, she floats inside with the blanket trailing behind her like a superhero cape. Returns momentarily with a big ceramic mug, intentionally lopsided to mold against the hands. She offers me the mug, giving me something that might be the wayward ghost of a smile—tiny, faint, hesitant.

I hold the reusable copper filter in place and fill her up. I then dig in the pocket of my flannel shirt for packets of stevia and a spoon; in the story, she fixed her coffee black, with a little natural sweetener.

She takes the packet and spoon with a quizzical grin. "Thanks?" A question, by the tone of her voice. As in, how do you know how I like my coffee?

I shrug. "I drink mine black," I say. "I had sweetener but not milk or cream. So."

It's not like I could come out and tell her, *you know how I know how you take your coffee? Your dead husband wrote a story that seems to be about you and me getting together.*

And also, it's true. I don't have milk or cream at

the cabin, just packets of stevia, mainly because I was thinking about trying to make a cake or something and couldn't find bags of it at the local supermarket, only a small box of individual packets.

She pours stevia into her coffee, stirs, sips. Her eyes slide closed, and she groans. "Oh my god, so good. Thank you." A single small hand slips out from under the blanket; the other clutches the coffee without letting go of the blanket, keeping it pinned under her chin. "Nadia."

I take her hand. It's tiny, warm, delicate. "Nathan."

"Well, Nathan. Thank you for the coffee." Her eyes go to the sun peeking up over the top of the trees. "It's very beautiful here."

I turn and lean my elbows on the top rail, mug clutched in both hands. "Sure is." I inhale deeply. "Peaceful."

"Have you been here long?"

I shrug. "Couple weeks."

A long silence. I don't know how to fill it.

"How long are you staying?" she asks, breaking it, finally.

"Um. Open-ended."

"Same here."

I have a thousand questions, and none of them is anything I can ask.

"These cabins look like they were built by the same person."

"They were," I say. "Local fella named Roger Klupinsky."

"They're beautiful."

"Sure are. He was a real craftsman." I knock on the beam, reach out and tap the join where the upright meets the overhang of the roof. "These joins are seamless. The floors, too. Everything is just this amazing craftsmanship you don't see anymore."

"Sounds like you say that with professional knowledge."

I nod. "I'm a carpenter."

"Houses?"

I shake my head. "Movie sets, things like that. I also do some carvings on the side, and that's what I've been doing mostly, lately. Taking time away from work."

"What do you carve?"

I glance at her. "I got a couple over in my cabin. I can show you some?"

She nods, smiles. "Sure."

"Be right back."

I leave my coffee balanced on the railing, amble over to my cabin. I've got four completed, and I grab them all. Bring them back to her cabin. I line them up on the floor near her feet, step back and sit on the top step.

She leans down; relinquishing her grip on the blanket finally, and takes one. "This is...remarkable."

It's a raccoon, small enough to sit on her palm. I tried to capture it sitting up on its hind legs, its front paws clasped in front of it the way they do, looking like it's praying.

"It's so cute! So lifelike."

The next one, then. It's a dragonfly done true to scale, and this one I went all out and painted, so the body is iridescent blue, with a bulbous thorax which goes thin and narrow behind the wings, with delicate veins in the wings. It's my best piece to date.

"It looks like it could take off any moment."

"Spent several days on that one. Usually, I can do a carving in an afternoon. But that one? The wings took forever."

"I bet. They're so detailed."

Third is not an animal at all but a representation of the episcopal church in town, a picturesque small-town place, white clapboards and a red roof, a spire with a bell.

"Why a church?" she asks.

"Um. Well, that's the church that's in town here. St. Paul's. It just looks like the kind of church you'd see in a movie about a small town."

I don't tell her that Lisa was obsessed with little churches like that, that she would plan entire vacations around which churches she wanted to visit, or that we'd been married in one just like it, that her funeral had been in the same church we'd gotten married in.

Maybe there's something in the carving, but she handles it somewhat more reverently than the others. Doesn't say anything else, just stares down at it for a while, and then sets it down to lift up the last one I brought over. It's a dollhouse-sized rocking chair, a couple inches tall. I'd carved a tiny cat curled up on the seat of the rocking chair.

"Story behind that one," I say. "Came out onto my porch with my coffee a few mornings ago, and there was a cat sleepin' on it. Never seen it before. I looked at it, it looked at me, and then it just sorta hopped down and walked off around the lake, and I haven't seen it since."

"The amount of detail you get into such small things is remarkable."

"Well, it takes patience, is all. And a steady hand, I guess. Carving or whittling or whatever you want to call it, it's kinda meditative for me."

She nods. "I can see how it would be."

"You do anything like that?"

She shrugs. "No, not really. I used to be into watercolors, but I sort of…lost the habit of doing it. What with life and all, you know how it is."

"Well. No better place to try it again, right?" I gesture at the lake. "Lots to paint out here, I'd say."

"You're right about that. Maybe I will."

I refill her coffee, and then there's an awkward silence.

"I, um." I clear my throat again. "It was nice having coffee with you, Nadia. Nice to meet you."

"Thank you again for the coffee," she says. "I'll have to learn to make proper coffee one of these days, I guess."

I shrug. "I'm up early out of long habit." I hesitate. "You ever want some, just come on over."

She nods. "I'll keep that in mind."

I wave, a strange, awkward half lift of one hand. "Well. See you 'round, I guess."

"Yeah."

What do you get when you take two people who have lost the most important person in their lives and have since lost the ability to socialize normally? A lot of awkward pauses and even more awkward conversation.

I head home, carve for a while. Think about fishing, decide against it.

Should I have told her I knew her husband? How would that conversation go?

I don't know what's right, what's wrong, what's neither.

Dinnertime. I'm attempting to make a whole chicken in the oven, following a recipe I found online at the library and printed out.

Lisa always used to make fun of me for my

cooking. I was always trying stuff, but I'd get it wrong at least half the time. Forget an ingredient, or do tablespoons instead of teaspoons, or put the oven at the wrong temperature, or leave it in too long. Once in a while, maybe every other attempt, I'll get it right and it'll actually be pretty damned good. But when I get it wrong? Boy howdy, do I get it *real* wrong.

This is the latter.

I turn around from carving, and the oven is billowing thick clouds of black smoke. I shove oven mitts onto my hands, yank the oven open, and grab the pan with my chicken on it—it's all but on fire. It's filling the cabin with smoke, so I carry it outside, cursing loudly all the way, and toss the pan and the blackened chicken onto the gravel drive.

I hear a snicker. "Looks like you, um, left it in too long."

I sigh. "Seems like it." I nudge the still-smoking carcass with the toe of my boot, and bits of char flake off. "Way too long."

I hear her feet on the steps, and she comes to gaze down at the poor burnt chicken with me.

"You should have set a timer."

"I was watching the clock," I protest. And then sigh. "But I guess a timer woulda been smart, huh?"

She hesitates. "Um, I made some pasta. Nothing fancy. But I have plenty. Since your dinner is, uh, inedible, to say the least."

"It was gonna be good, too. Olive oil all over it, bunch of seasoning." I sigh. "Well, I'll have to try again."

"Lower temperature next time," she says. "Olive oil has a low smoke point. Burns easily." A laugh. "I learned that the hard way."

I snort. "Looks like I just did, too." I glance at her. "I wouldn't want to impose."

She waves. "It's the least I can do for saving my life this morning. I'm not sure what I'd have done without drinkable coffee." She indicates the chicken. "Whenever I make coffee, it turns out like that. My— I've been taught a million times. It's easy, I know it is. But somehow, it just always turns out tasting like ass."

I smile at that. "Well, you know, making *good* coffee is an art form. It's not just hot water and ground-up coffee beans. It's a whole complex chemical process. There's nitrogens that need to escape for a certain amount of time, and the water needs to be clean and fresh and filtered and just off a boil, and the beans should be ground right before you brew, and they should be nice and granular—" I break off, because she's blinking at me with a wry grin. "Sorry. My—um…I've been told I get lecture-y about coffee. I worked at a roaster when I was in trade school. Sorta got bit by the coffee bug."

I notice we've both made the same slip-up.

"I'll trade you your fancy coffee with the fancy

glass thing for a big old pot of spaghetti." Her expression goes dark, sober. "I...it'll be nice to share it. To not eat it alone."

"Eating alone sucks."

"Amen to that," is all she says, and somehow we don't need to elaborate.

"Let me clean this mess up, and myself," I say. "Should I bring anything? Don't want to mooch."

A shrug. "Nah. Unless you have garlic bread over there. The only bread I have isn't really right for it, and I haven't been into town to shop yet." She gestured at the cabin. "It was, uhh, stocked, already, with pretty much everything I need. But you know how it is, there's always something missing."

She's rambling.

"I actually do have some. It's store-bought, the kind from the freezer aisle."

Her eyes light up. "Ooh, I love that stuff. I know it's terrible for you, but it's *so* good."

"Well, my oven's already on. I'll fix it up and be over in a few minutes."

"Okay." She turns away, hesitates. "Nathan, um, I don't want you to—"

I hold up my hands. "Just a neighborly meal, is all."

A nod, her thick black hair falling in front of her eyes; she brushes it back with one hand, tucks it behind the delicate shell of her ear. She's not been taking care of herself—I don't know her from Adam, but I can tell that much. I wouldn't go so far as to say she's gaunt, exactly, but it wouldn't be a totally inaccurate description. Beautiful, though. Her eyes, that deep shade of green, the olive complexion of her skin, the inky sheaf of hair cascading down around her thin shoulders... she hunches a little, as if to ward off a blow from the world. But the ghost of the woman she was, the woman she should be, is there within her.

I don't know her, but I want to make her smile, just to leaven the sadness carved into the lines on her forehead, at the corners of her mouth.

She turns to walk away, and I remember the last time I talked to Adrian, he told me he first fell in love with Nadia because of her ass.

I catch myself looking, but her sweater, a long, gray, thick-knit cardigan, hangs over it. Probably for the best.

I look away, out at the water, and I wonder what the hell I'm doing. How does this work?

All I know is, it's nice to have someone to talk to. I've been here utterly alone but for occasional trips into town, and after two weeks of total solitude, I'm going a little cabin crazy.

So maybe that's all this is. Innocent. A little companionship.

Still, however, I find myself reading more of the book while I'm waiting for the garlic bread to bake.

Red wine, that's the ticket. More from her POV. *It's indulgent, and goes with just about everything. Ice cream and red wine, popcorn and red wine, chocolate and red wine. Never mind those fancy chef pairings, red goes perfectly well with fish. And steak, of course. And obviously pasta. The redder and richer the better. Give me a nice dry cab sav, and I'm happy. Well, maybe not anymore, not HAPPY, per se. But you know what I mean.*

At the supermarket, they have a little wine section, but whoever is in charge of it is a real wine aficionado. They've labeled the wines with tags telling of origin and pairing ideas and tasting notes, and some kind of points system that I don't understand—best of all, they're always on sale. So I'd grabbed a few bottles to have on hand, and just to try something different: what's this one? Josh. Nice label, cursive script, fancy-looking. Why not?

Childhood memories, and more recent ones from life with Lisa, waft through my soul at the smell of the store-bought, freezer-section garlic bread heating in the oven. It's the kind that comes in foil packaging and bakes up crispy and flaky on the outside and smooshy and moist on the inside; my mother used to make this stuff every Sunday, with a giant pot of spaghetti and homemade marinara, a recipe passed down through several generations of women on my mother's side— the recipe is written down somewhere at home, on a yellowing notecard in my great-grandmother's handwriting; Mom, lacking daughters, taught Lisa the art of the marinara, and she always used to make this same garlic bread with it, always on Sunday.

I wonder what day it is. I haven't looked at a clock or calendar in days. Maybe I could just pretend it's Sunday. I could probably make that sauce from memory, honestly. I watched Grandma do it until she died, and then Mom until *she* died, and finally, Lisa, until she too died. Damned if I'll teach any other woman in my life how to make that sauce.

I find a big ceramic bowl, line the bottom of it with paper towel, arrange the bread, now cut into neat little rectangles, in the bowl. Cover it with a hand towel, the way Mom used to. Grab the bottle of Josh, the bowl of bread, and head across the lawn between my cabin and hers.

She's on her porch, and she's brought out a small table, likely something that sat beside a couch. There's a large black stockpot with a glass lid on the table, a pair of plates stacked, a pair of forks. One of those big fork-spoon pasta-serving things. A small plastic jar of parmesan cheese, the ubiquitous kind with the green label.

"Eating on the porch, huh?" I say.

She nods. "It's a beautiful evening."

No need to point out that, it's also a neat way to avoid the idea of *not* inviting me inside. I understand.

I set the bowl of bread on the table, lift the bottle

of wine, and extend it to her. "I, uh, brought this. Figured you can't have spaghetti without wine, right? I dunno a damn thing about wine, so I hope this is all right."

She takes the bottle and examines the label; her expression is...not stunned, but more suspicious. "You know how I like my coffee, and now you know my favorite brand of wine."

I shrug. "Coincidence. The selection at the market in town here is pretty, uh, limited, to say the least. What they do have seems to be pretty good, but, uh, like I said, I don't know shit about wine, so I just picked that 'cause the label looked cool."

She stares at the bottle in something like consternation. "I'll get an opener and some glasses. Thank you, Nathan. It was very thoughtful of you."

I just wave. "I bought it thinking I'd try something new. But I'll never end up opening it for just me."

"What do you drink, when it is just you?"

"Whiskey, usually. Or scotch. Beer, occasionally."

Seems like she's about to say something, but doesn't. Instead, she just slips inside, leaving the door half-open, returning with a corkscrew and a pair of wine goblets. She hesitates.

"Um, here." She hands me the bottle and the corkscrew. "You do this, I'll dish up."

I just nod, and open the bottle. I don't have much

practice opening wine, so it takes a while and the cork is a mess by the time I'm done. I pour us each a half glass, by which time Nadia has plated us each a pile of spaghetti. I move aside the towel covering the bread, and we each take a few pieces.

There's another awkward silence. We both feel like we should say something. Grace, maybe? I don't know. I don't know what the hell I'm doing.

I lift my wineglass in a toast. "To new friends and cabins by the lake."

She echoes my toast; we clink, and dig in.

There's very little talking. She eats like a machine, steadily, with gusto. I find myself wondering when the last time she had a meal like this was—a long time, judging by the sharpness of her cheekbones, the hollows in her cheeks, the bags under her eyes.

She finishes her first plate, goes for more, and then pauses. "I, um. I guess I'm hungry."

I just laugh. "Hey, a woman who can eat like she enjoys it is a good thing, in my book. Don't be lookin' to me for judgment on that score."

She sighs, seeming relieved. "I guess I just don't want to seem—"

"Seem however you are. If you're hungry, eat. That's it."

She smiles. "Thank you."

I just wave, because there's nothing for her to

be thankful for. I take seconds myself; offer her more bread, more wine. By the time we both put our forks down and sit back, the pasta is nearly gone, and most of the bread. We're savoring the last few sips of wine, along with the sunset.

I don't know what to say. How to start a conversation. It's been so long, and I'm out of practice.

The food gone, the last sips of wine finally gone, I can feel Nadia getting restless.

I stand up. "Thank you for dinner," I say.

She stands up too. "Thank you for the wine and the bread."

Silence.

"I should, um…" she starts.

"Nadia, listen." I have no clue what I'm about to say. Something dumb, probably. "Don't be polite. Just say what you mean."

"I don't want to be rude."

"I'd rather rude honesty than anything else."

A nod. "In that case, I think it would be best if we say good night, now."

I grab my bowl; there are two pieces left. I laugh, and take one. "Here. No point leaving one piece left." She grins and takes it. "Now, I'll say good night. See you around."

I don't look back, just take my bowl and the empty bottle and she goes inside.

Again, I wonder if I should tell her I knew

Adrian. That Adrian gave me his last book. But how do you start that conversation? When's the right moment? In his letter to me, he specifically said she wasn't ready yet.

Damn you, Adrian. I don't know what the fuck I'm doing. You should've picked someone else.

I don't even know what this is. Other than two fucked-up, broken people living next door to each other.

Twenty-Six

Watercolors & John Denver

FOR THE FIRST TIME I CAN REMEMBER SINCE ADRIAN DIED, I manage to sleep. Maybe it was the full belly, for once. Maybe it was the wine. Maybe it was…well, I can't even say conversation because I didn't really talk with Nathan all that much. It was just a shared meal between friends. But I have to admit that it did something to soothe the yawning gape of loneliness in me.

So, I fall asleep quickly, and I sleep in. It's…well, there are no clocks in the cabin, on purpose I think, so I have no clue what time it is. Midmorning, judging by the sunlight streaming in the windows. I get out of bed slowly, lazily. Change into, well, not pajamas, but loungewear, you might call it. Cozy, soft leggings, a T-shirt, and a zip-up hoodie. Barefoot. I stare at the coffeemaker on the counter in the kitchen, which seems to mock me.

Adrian used to find it hysterical that I was so bad at making coffee. I've never understood it myself, but

I've long since accepted it as a fact and learned to live with it. Mainly because I always had Adrian to make it for me, or coffee shops.

Now, out here, I just have to learn, I guess. Finally.

I attempt it—remembering Adrian's formula. Two scoops of grinds per ounce of water. Not too coarse, not too fine. Add water. Turn it on.

Simple.

Only, I must have over-ground it or miscounted, because when it finishes brewing, twenty minutes later, it's so thick you could cut it with a knife, so black and so strong you could strip paint with it.

Dammit.

Exasperated, I go out onto the porch, half wondering if I could somehow persuade Nathan to make me some without having to come right out and ask.

I find, sitting on the porch in front of my door, a large green thermos, like my dad used to take hunting on the weekends. There's no note, but it's full of Nathan's amazing coffee.

Anyone can make coffee, but there is, as he said, an art to making *good* coffee. And this? It's the best coffee I've ever had. I've had Italian espresso pulled by master baristas in world-famous coffeehouses, and this is just…magnificent. Bold, but not overpowering. I add a little sweetener, stir it up, sit on the porch and sip.

His truck is gone.

I refuse to let myself wonder where he is—it's no business of mine.

I leave my coffee to cool—it always drove Adrian nuts that I like to let my coffee cool off of scalding. I head up to the loft and peruse the books; I choose a Lee Child thriller. Something different—I usually read romances or something similar, easy beach sort of reads. My job is stressful enough that I don't want to be stressed by my pleasure reading.

But now, everything is different. So maybe it's time to change things up a bit.

I sit on the front porch and dive into the world of Jack Reacher, and find myself enjoying it way more than I thought I would. And just like that, hours have passed, and my stomach is rumbling.

I'm feeling too lazy to prepare anything involved, so I make a smorgasbord of snacks, and keep reading.

The sun shifts, and now it's beating directly onto the porch, and I get hot. Sweaty. The inside of the cabin would be cooler, but I've spent nearly every minute of the past year inside, and I just...I want to be outside.

The water looks cool, inviting. Why not?

I change into a bathing suit, a plain one-piece that I tend to wear for real swimming rather just lounging on the beach. I don't think any of my bikinis would fit at the moment anyway—the one-piece is all but hanging off me as it is. My ass is flat as a post, and my tits, never large on my best day, have shrunk to mosquito bites. But, I'm not here to impress anyone.

I'm thankful there's no full-length mirror here. I don't think I'd be very pleased with my reflection. I need to eat, get back to a healthy weight.

I bring a towel and head to the dock. The water ripples, reflects the sunlight like a million diamonds in the sun. When was the last time I went swimming? A hotel pool with Adrian, in NYC for a signing, a year before I found out about his diagnosis.

I push that thought away.

I dive in—don't give myself time to think about it, to anticipate the cool of the water. Which turns out to be *cold*. I surface, shrieking and spluttering, pushing my hair back. Refreshing, though, once I have a moment to acclimate. I stroke across the water away from shore, and then turn on my back and float. The sounds of the world are muffled, and the sun is hot on my face and the parts of me that aren't covered in water. I splash in circles, open my eyes to reorient myself, make sure I've not floated too far away from shore. I know I'm still pretty weak, and if I were to accidentally float toward the middle of the lake, I could be in trouble.

Eventually, I start to feel a little cold, so I roll back to my belly and breaststroke back to shore. When I get there, I see Nathan's truck, but not him, not at first. It's not until I climb onto the deck and wrap up in my towel that I see him. The tree line of the forest starts a good twenty yards behind the cabins, and he's off just inside the trees, skinning a deer. He pauses, glances my way, sees me and waves. I wave back, but head inside.

Adrian tried hunting once, when we were first dating. A friend from college invited him, so he went. He hated it. Said it was cold and early and boring, and when he did finally manage to get a shot off at a deer, he both missed and felt horrible for shooting at it. Said he'd have felt even worse actually killing the thing, and when his friend made his shot and brought down a buck, he felt nauseated. Which was only worsened when his friend cleaned the carcass right there.

He never went hunting again.

My dad used to hunt a lot, when I was little, so the sight is fairly familiar to me. I'd wake up late on a Saturday morning and I'd see Dad out under the big old oak tree behind the house, a deer hanging by its hooves. We'd have venison steaks that night, Dad's specialty. He'd freeze most of the rest of the meat, and then in the winter, when things were tight and lean, he'd break out back straps and steaks and ground venison and whatever else.

Then he passed away when I was a teenager, and I'd wake up on Saturday mornings for weeks and months afterward expecting to see him out there with a deer, and I'd remember all over again with crushing sorrow that I'd never see it again.

All this flits through me in an instant, from seeing Nathan out under the tall pines in the cool shadows, his hands pinked with blood as he expertly skins and cleans.

I hurry inside, feeling nauseous. Not from the sight of the blood—I'm an ICU nurse. From an inundation of sorrow.

Missing Dad took years to get past. You stop thinking about him, forget his face, the sound of his voice. The feel of his stubble on my cheek as he gave me a peck. You feel guilty for forgetting, but the forgetting is often easier than the missing, and then you feel guilty for sort of *wanting* to forget.

So, I know how grief works. But this, with Adrian, it's different.

I didn't have him long enough.

We were just getting started.

I didn't have long enough to accept that he was dying.

I find myself on the floor of the bathroom, in my wet bathing suit, my towel rucked under me, not crying just...drowning.

I can't wallow in it anymore.

So, I force myself to take a long, hot shower. To actually style my hair. Put on a little makeup, just a touch, to conceal the hollows in my cheeks and the bags under my eyes. Get dressed in jeans and a sweater. I'm not sure where I'm going, but I get in my car and go anyway.

I end up exploring the little town, perusing touristy gift shops and the library, the general store. I walk around and smile at the locals who smile back and say hello and ask me how I am and even manage to sound like they actually care about the answer. They know I'm new, and they're all curious, but no one asks me anything.

There's a little cafe, a place that serves breakfast all day and specializes in chicken-fried steak with this incredible—and incredibly unhealthy, I'm sure—gravy that's so thick you can stand a spoon up in it, and flaky, buttery biscuits. My nutrition has been whole foods, organic, artificial sweetener-free, all that stuff for years. I got into it while I was studying for my RN, having gained way more than the freshman fifteen and having not ever lost any of it. And then it became a way of life, and Adrian converted to it when we got married because it was just easier than trying to keep two separate kinds of food. But now? I just can't bring myself to care. Maybe at some point I will, but right now, I just want to eat food that I didn't make, and enjoy it. And hell, I need the calories anyway. I haven't—and don't dare—stepped on a scale, but I know I have to weigh less now than I did in junior high.

There's a lot of staring by locals, a lot of open curiosity, but everyone is polite enough to keep it at merely open curiosity.

I look like hell, I know I do.

I probably have a look that just screams "shattered widow." Something tragic in my countenance, probably. No matter. It's why I'm here, right? To get rid of it. And I'm going to do it with chicken-fried steak and gravy and biscuits and red wine, and when I get home, a whole bar of chocolate as I lie out on the dock watching the stars.

He's on his porch when I get home from dinner in town. I wave, he waves, and that's it.

Part of me wants to go over there and talk to him, just to hear my own voice. But I don't.

I stay inside reading—I finish the Lee Child thriller and start a biography of Einstein, more reading that's out of the ordinary for me. Horizons? Expanding. The biography isn't as enrapturing as the novel, but I plug away at it gamely until I look up and realize it's dark and I'm more into it than I thought I would be.

I take my bar of chocolate out to the dock, along with a blanket. Spread the blanket out on the dock and lie down, stare up at the stars. I don't recognize pretty much any of the constellations but the Big Dipper. I make up my own, trying to trace lines from star to star in patterns.

I hear the other dock creak under Nathan's tread. I stay where I am. But I do wonder what he's doing out here, at whatever time of night it is.

I hear the feet of a chair thunk onto the boards. A moment of silence. A few hesitant strums of an acoustic guitar. A chord, tried a few times, the strings buzzing inexpertly. A muttered curse, a sigh. He tries the chord again, and this time gets it. Tries a change to a different chord, fumbles it, tries again, gets it. He plays like someone who used to play a lot, but fell out of practice. I slip a sliver of chocolate into my mouth and let it melt as I listen. He's warmed up, refamiliarized himself with the instrument, and it sounds like old skills are returning. He now seems to be working on remembering a particular song, a handful of chords tried a few different ways, a low rough hum from his voice.

I recognize it, when he remembers how to play it all the way through. "59th Street Bridge Song (Feeling Groovy)" by Simon and Garfunkel. Not what I'd have expected him to play. I would have assumed Johnny Cash, or maybe some early Metallica, or Journey. Instead, he plays Simon and Garfunkel. I hear him murmuring the words, playing and singing for himself. I don't think he even realizes I'm here—I'd be a dark lump on the dock, even from up close, and he's a ways away.

It doesn't feel so lonely out here, now. It was solitude at first, and I'm not really even sure when it became loneliness. When he came out, maybe. But now that he's over there, and I can hear his voice and his guitar, I'm not as lonely.

He moves without pause into "The Boxer" and I hum along under my breath.

Dad used to love this song. He'd sit on the screened-in back porch on summer evenings, with the cicadas singing and the heat oppressive and he'd be shirtless, hairy and a little overweight, and he'd have his old Yamaha on his belly and his feet would be propped up on a battered blue milk crate, and he'd play every song he knew, with a beer sweating on the floor beside him.

God, why is everything reminding me of my father, all of a sudden?

I swear to God, if Nathan plays—

Yeah, there it is. "Cat's in the Cradle" by Harry Chapin.

It's like they have the same damn playlist, him and Dad.

Then, Nathan surprises me even more. Freestyle. He just strums, picks, and hums, nothing I recognize. It's a slow, sad melody, and it seems half remembered and half improvised.

There's a long silence, then, the last notes quavering across the lake.

"What was that last one you played?" I ask, just loud enough to be sure he hears me.

"Didn't know you were there," he says.

"Just stargazing. And eating chocolate."

"It's, uh…a little thing I used to play. For…well, uh. For someone who's now gone."

I recognize that hesitation. Where you don't want to even mention it, because it brings on the "I'm sorry for your loss" and the pitying eyes and the questions they don't know how to ask.

"It's a beautiful piece of music," I say. A pause. "I wasn't intending to eavesdrop, Nathan."

"I know. I just haven't played in, oh god, years. Lost the habit. Life gets busy, and somehow it's the things you really love doing that get left on the wayside, you know?"

"Like me and watercolors."

"That's right—you said you painted."

"I mean, sort of. It was just for me. I started doing it in high school as a way to cope with…loss, and stress, and things like that. Then, like you said, life happened." I sigh, something not quite a laugh. "I wasn't very good."

"Neither am I. I started playing for similar reasons. My dad…those were all his favorite songs. I learned them as a way to…connect with him, I guess."

"You are good, though."

"I was once told I sound like a chainsaw at the bottom of a well when I sing."

I snicker at that. "That's not nice. And untrue."

I mean, his voice isn't *good*. It's rough, deep, and dark. Smoky. He can carry a tune well enough. But there's something raw and real in the way he sang, how he sounded.

"I wouldn't mind if you played another one," I

say. "My dad…he used to play most of the same songs when I was a kid."

"Thus the watercolors," he says.

"Thus the watercolors," I agree, but I don't know if it was loud enough for him to hear.

"Uh, how about…" A few idle strums. "Ah. Betcha you know this one."

Three chords in, and I know it.

"Thank God I'm a Country Boy." John Denver.

God, this one. Dad would hum this one while he puttered in the garage or flipped the venison steaks, and it was always the last one he played before he put the guitar away. It was his anthem, I think.

I laugh out loud. "Good god, did we have the same father, or what?"

He pauses. "Well, I grew up in the backwoods of Louisiana. You?"

"Atlanta girl, born and raised." I laugh again, and it feels good to laugh. "When I say Atlanta, though, I'm being generous. Backwoods would be a polite term for where I grew up."

He picks up the melody again, and when he starts singing, I can't help but sing with him. If you'd asked me ten seconds ago if I knew the lyrics to this song, I'd have laughed in your face—I haven't heard it since Dad died. But yet, with the melody on that guitar, his rough-hewn voice singing the words, damn if I don't sing every one.

Is it weird that it feels better to miss Daddy than Adrian? The old hurt is more palatable. It's a nice break from the raging, gaping wound of missing my husband.

The music fades, and I sigh. Eventually, I stand up; wrap my blanket around my shoulders. "I'm heading in," I say. "Good night, Nathan."

"'Night."

When I wake up the next morning, he's put the thermos on my porch again—I'd returned it yesterday. This time, there's a brown paper bag with it—a blank sketchbook with thick paper suitable for watercolors, a couple different palates of watercolors, as if he had no idea what's good or not, so he just got the most expensive they had and the cheapest, and a clutch of different sizes and kinds of brushes. Because it wouldn't fit in the bag, he'd set the easel on the deck beside the bag.

The easel smells...fresh, like newly sawn wood. It almost looks like he *made* it. Being a carpenter, it shouldn't surprise me that he'd make one instead of buying it, but the gesture touches me.

I immediately take the easel, sketchbook, a mug of water, and the paints out to the dock and set up. I'm frustrated at first because I've lost the knack of it, but after a few false starts, I start to feel it coming back... like Nathan and the guitar.

Before I know it, I've been painting for several hours. The completed painting is...not my best, but it's recognizably the lake from my dock. I'm proud of it, maybe inordinately so. Winslow Homer, I'm not, but I feel good for having done it.

The expulsion of creativity is as much an antitoxin to the poison of misery and despair and sorrow as the peace of the lake has been, as sleeping in has been, as eating well has been. As much as that dinner on my porch with Nathan.

I gingerly tear the page from the book; Nathan is out on the lake, fishing. I heard him motor out early this morning, and he's been on the far side of the lake ever since. I wedge the painting in his door, between door and doorpost.

I wouldn't say I'm alive, yet. But...maybe, just maybe, I'm feeling the first glimmers of renewal. Like a seed germinating deep in the thick black wet soil.

I'm not okay. I'm very, very far from anything like okay. I think about Adrian just about once every other breath. I still wake up in the middle of the night and reach for him and tear up and clutch my pillow and scream into it when he's not there.

But...I laughed, last night. I painted, today.

It's improvement, if infinitesimal. But still, better is better.

Twenty-Seven

One Little Thing At A Time

I HAVEN'T SEEN NADIA FOR DAYS. I WAKE UP EARLY, AND she sleeps in. But we have a system—I make her coffee and put it in my old hunting thermos and leave it on her porch. She returns it sometime later in the morning. I made her an easel and got her some watercolor stuff, and now she's out there most of the day, painting. On the dock, in the yard, under the trees, facing the cabins. She left me one, the first one she did, as a kind of thank-you. It's good. Like me and guitar, I'd say don't quit your day job, but it's damn good.

It's hard to read Adrian's story. I put it off, sometimes for days at a time.

More from the heroine's POV:

Sometimes, I wish he would just…push a little. Nudge me out of my shell. Because as much as I like it in my shell, and as much as I'd get a little spiky and snotty if he DID nudge, part of me wants to be drawn out of myself. I think he's afraid of hurting me. Of scaring me. Of getting too close too fast even for his own liking.

Just a little, at first, I'd tell him, if he asked. A walk, maybe. Take me fishing, because while it's boring as hell, it's something different, something to do besides try and pretend I'm cool, I'm fine, this is fine. I dunno. I just know he's there and I'm here, and we keep sort of slipping off of each other, not quite connecting, because my hurt is deep and my shell is thick, and so is his. I think we're also like two soap bubbles floating through the air, bouncing off each other, connecting for a moment, separating.

I read a bit more, another chapter, but I keep thinking about that part. Don't push, just nudge a little.

All right. Let's give it a whirl. I'm bored and lonely again, and I'd like to talk to her.

It's early afternoon. She just quit painting and has packed up and gone inside. It's a gorgeous day, one of those days that's on the verge between late summer and not quite fall. Cool at night, but still warm during the day. I stuff a sweater in my backpack, a couple bottles of water, my hunting compass, and a package of jerky.

Before I can reconsider, I head over and knock on her door.

She opens the door enough to frame her body. "Hi. What's up?"

"I was thinking I'd go for a little hike in the woods.

Nothing strenuous, just…walk around the lake a bit. And I thought maybe you'd like to come along."

I'm tempted to overexplain, to ramble, so I chew on the inside of my cheek to keep my mouth shut.

She just stares at me, thinking. "I…"

"If you don't want to, I get it."

She huffs. "No, I…I do. Actually. I could use the exercise." She's wearing short cloth shorts with ragged, rolled-up hems and a baggy T-shirt—painting clothes. "Let me just put on some jeans."

I nod and turn away. She closes the door—a few minutes later she exits the cabin wearing faded blue jeans, a more form-fitting T-shirt, hiking boots, with a sweatshirt tied around her waist.

I indicate the shoreline heading away from my cabin, to the right of hers. "Done some exploring around my cabin, but haven't seen much on this side."

"I've barely left the cabin except for the dock and town a few times."

"I was the same way, first couple weeks up here. I still only venture out when I feel the need, and I don't often feel the need."

We follow the shoreline, walking side by side, me nearer the water. Not too close. No risk of accidental hand touch. We walk in silence for quite a while, and then she finally glances at me.

"So who's gonna go first?" she asks, a wry grin on her face.

I laugh. "I guess I will, since you came up with the icebreaker."

I lift a branch up and out of the way, and she ducks under it; here, the shoreline grazes the tree line, so the pine tree branches hang out over the water, forcing us further into the trees.

"My wife died in a car accident three and a half years ago." I rarely come right out and say it like that. "And it hurts as much now as it did a month afterward." I pause. "But maybe that's just because I never really dealt with it."

She trips on a root, and I catch her by the arm. "Thanks," she says, recovering. "My husband died. A year ago on the day I arrived." She pauses, crouches to run her finger in some deep tracks in the dirt. "Bear, I think."

I glance at it. "Yeah, I'd say so. Big one, too."

"For me, some days, it hurts more now than it did then," she says, straightening and brushes her hands together. "As if it's…fermented, somehow."

I nod. "I get that."

We're on the far side of the lake, now, and we move through the trees to the water's edge—we can see the cabins, windows gleaming in the late afternoon sun. The docks, dark fingers out into the water. Just the two of them, side-by-side, alone out there.

Behind us, a hill rises, the crown obscured by trees.

"Want to see what's at the top?" I ask.

She shrugs. "Sure. Probably just more trees, though," she says, laughing.

"We can go back, if you're bored, or tired."

She shakes her head. "Sometimes, boredom is good, and so is being tired. But anyway, I'm not bored. I've just never been an outdoorsy kind of girl. Much to my dad's annoyance, since he was a fisherman and hunter and hiker and camper and all that. I just never liked it. Bugs, dirt, wild animals, weird noises, and did I mention bugs." She pauses as we wind around a dense cluster of trees, the grade steep up here. "This is nice, though. I'm enjoying it."

"I grew up doing this." I wave a hand at the woods. "My dad was in Vietnam, and came back having trouble being indoors. Mom left, and left me with him, and since he always wanted to be out in the woods, the woods is basically where I grew up. Once, when I was, oh, fourteen, fifteen, Dad packed us some big old bags and our rifles and told me to say goodbye to the house for a while. And he meant it. We drove up to Montana near the Yellowstone, out there where it's *real* wild, and spent a good six months living like Jeremiah Johnson." I laugh. "Minus the fights with natives, obviously."

She eyes me incredulously. "Really?"

"Oh yeah. It was the only place he was at peace. And I didn't have anywhere else to go and no one else to go to, so I went with him." I sigh. "He taught me woodworking. If he wasn't in the woods, he was in his shop out back, working the lathe and the saw. He made furniture. Tables, chairs, bookcases, bureaus. I could make a bookshelf before I could shave."

"Wow." She gestures behind us, where the cabins would be. "So, that's not really even roughing it for you."

I cackle. "I mean, those cabins are really well finished. So no. But in comparison to how I grew up? Sometimes, we wouldn't even bring tents. We'd make shelter out of branches and moss and shit. Find a cave. Sleep in the hollow of a fallen tree."

"My husband and I went camping once, like with a tent. It was terrible and we hated it and we never did it again."

I hold another branch out of the way as we top the rise. "It's not for everyone. But it can be fun. I don't think I'd do any survivalist camping anymore, but being way, way out there, where there ain't anybody for fuckin' miles, and everything you need to survive is on your back? Makes you feel…confident, I guess. Comfortable in your skin, because you're this little fragile ol' thing in a great big world that's been here before us and will be here after us, and suddenly your dumb little idiosyncrasies and the shit you're self-conscious about…it all just doesn't matter as much. Getting to the next campsite, making the next kill so you can eat, that's all that matters." I wave in the direction of the cabins. "And I guess living in the cabin is a version of that. Lessens the intensity of focus. Lets you sort of… just live with yourself, in a way you can't in the city, doing the day-to-day grind. But maybe that's just me. And I'm still figuring it out as I go along myself."

"No, I think you're right." She turns in place, taking in the vista; the crown of the hill is high enough and bare of trees enough to provide an amazing view of the lake. "I don't think I ever realized how much stress I was under. Just in general. Add in the grief and trauma of losing Adrian…?" She trails off, shaking her head, as if the rest of the statement is self-evident. Which, to me, it is.

"It's a killing kind of stress," I say. "Your body may not die right away, but your…your spirit does. Your soul. Your mind. Your heart. It all dies. And eventually, your body will give out too."

"What's the answer, though?" She leans her shoulder against the nearest tree, staring out at the lake and the now-distant cabins. "We're lucky, Nathan. Not everyone who loses someone can just…up and move to a cabin on a lake in the middle of nowhere and not work."

"No shit. I didn't even know I needed this." I hesitate. "It kinda…fell into my lap."

"Same here."

We're quiet awhile, just absorbing the vista.

Eventually, she pushes off the tree. "Well. Onward around the lake?"

"I'm ready."

Conversation loosens a bit, then, as we walk. Nothing in-depth or serious, just little stories from childhood. The few times her dad tried to get her to go hunting with him went comically wrong, and made for good stories. And I, of course, have a wealth of crazy but true stories from growing up with an antiestablishment survivalist father: bear hunts, being chased by wolves, making an igloo in a blizzard so we didn't die of exposure.

We both keep it light, innocent, nonpersonal.

It is nearing sunset when we reach the cabins. I pause on the bottom step, glance at Nadia. "I put a roast in the crockpot this morning. Just about the only thing I get right every time." I laugh self-consciously. "Care for some?"

She's hungry, but hesitant. "I, um."

"I can bring a table and another chair out onto the porch."

"Okay, then." Her face illuminates with a grin. "I can provide the wine this time."

And so we find ourselves on my porch, sharing roast beef, red wine, and a loaf of bread she bought from the little bakery in town. We don't talk much, which seems to be the usual. When we're done eating, I move with my glass of wine to the railing, watching the last of the sunset mingle and fade into dull crimson-orange becoming umber and purple.

"I enjoyed this," I say. "Thank you."

"For what?"

I shrug. "I dunno. Walking with me. Talking."

She's in my rocking chair, feet curled under her, hands pulled into her sweatshirt sleeves so only her fingertips show, wrapped around her goblet. I can feel her chewing on how to say what she's thinking. "I'm sorry if I'm...standoffish."

"Nah." I sigh, with a little huffed chuckle lost in it somewhere. "I've been standoffish and prickly for years. I mean, I've never been a super sociable Chatty Cathy typa guy. Dad didn't talk much, so I never got the habit. But then after Lisa died, I'd go days, weeks without saying much of anything but monosyllabic answers to direct questions, and sometimes not even that."

"If you grew up in the wilderness, how'd you go to school?"

I snort. "Good question. Answer is, I didn't. Dad was older, see. Right on the edge of draft age eligibility. He'd been an adjunct professor before he got drafted. So, he homeschooled me, but that's a generous term for it. Taught me to read, write, do math. Enough that I wouldn't come across as this illiterate, uneducated bumpkin, which I was. He had old copies of things like Herodotus and *the Illiad* and Mark Twain, and he'd carry them with him on our treks, and I learned to read on those. For those stretches of months we spent at home, he'd check out books from the library, books on science and history and biographies and stuff like that, and that'd be my education in that subject. Most of what he taught me was woodworking and wood-craft, and survivalism. Book learning was basically just to keep me from being a complete outcast when I left home. I was anyway. I left home at seventeen, apprenticed myself to a carpenter, and he set me on track into trade school, and I only got halfway through before a friend's dad noticed the quality of my work and hired me on at his construction company, and things went from there."

"You had a really unusual upbringing."

"Yeah. I guess I did."

"Where's your dad now? Passed on?"

I shrug. "I dunno. After I left home, he vanished. Went off into the woods somewhere and never came back."

Silence.

"I've talked and thought more about my child-hood these last few weeks than I have in years," she says.

"Same."

"Why, do you think that is?"

"Easier than the hard stuff?"

"That's what I was thinking, too." She pauses with her goblet partway to her mouth, making her words echo. "The hard stuff is just so fucking...*hard.*"

"Maybe the past is another way for us to keep trying to avoid the hard stuff, though."

"Yeah, I'm worried you're right there, too." She finishes her wine, stands up. "I'm going to go. I did really enjoy today, so thank you."

"See you 'round."

She pauses on the top step, next to me, gazing sideways at me. As if considering saying something. I meet her gaze, and wait. In this light, her eyes are more emerald than jade. She's filling out, her cheekbones less sharp, the hollows in her cheek less pronounced. Her clothes don't hang off her quite as noticeably.

"Maybe..." she starts. Stops. Clears her throat. "Maybe knock on the door, tomorrow. With coffee."

I smile. "Will do." I raise an eyebrow. "I'm an early bird, I gotta warn you. Probably be around six thirty."

"It's okay." A grin. "Maybe I'll get up in time to make pancakes or something."

"I'd like that," I say.

My heart squeezes. Pancakes are my favorite thing in the world to eat. I don't know how to say that, though. There's just so much layered over the topic of something so simple as breakfast food.

She seems to notice, or maybe I'm inventing that. She just nods. Heads down the steps, one last sidelong, hesitant, shy smile at me. "Good night."

"Night."

I discovered, somewhat by accident, that she was crazy about mimosas. We'd gone ice-skating, and afterward stopped at a little hole-in-the-wall cafe. It was early, between breakfast and lunch, and the place wasn't serving liquor yet. But they DID have mimosas, and when I suggested we get mimosas, god, the way her eyes lit up. She got wasted on mimosas, and I had to all but carry her home, and I think that's when I really, truly fell in love with her. They made her goofy. Wine made her sleepy and serious. Whiskey made her cranky. Beer upset her stomach and she claimed it all tasted like ox piss. Why specifically ox piss, I could never get her to say. Tequila she flat out refused to drink, saying she'd learned her lesson the hard way, and wouldn't elaborate. But mimosas? Silly, a little wild, and so funny.

I shut the book, considering.

It's still fairly early, yet. Not even ten. I bet the supermarket is still open a bit longer, I could snag a bottle or two of champagne and some orange juice.

I grab my wallet and keys and head out—I catch the supermarket five minutes before close, much to the annoyance of the sullen teenager behind the register. Two bottles of medium-expense champagne, two cartons of orange juice.

Rash, probably, bringing mimosas to breakfast. Shit, she may not even wake up tomorrow. And if I bring mimosas and she DOES love them like Adrian's book is hinting, what do I say? Another coincidence?

She needs to cut loose, though. She's wound up tighter than a spring coil.

I want more time with her.

I like talking to her.

I like telling her things about me. I like knowing things about her.

It may not mean anything. It may not *become* anything but friendship. I'm too scared of what that would look like, feel like. And I'm terrified of what that would be like with her specifically. I just...don't know how to do that.

But I can do this. One little thing at a time, and just take it as it comes.

Twenty-Eight

Lie Just A Little Longer

I WAKE UP AT FIVE FORTY-FIVE, ON MY OWN, WITHOUT AN alarm.

I have no idea what's possessing me, but I go with it. Give in to impulse.

Heading out to the kitchen, I rifle through the cabinets until I find the box of pancake mix. Preheat the cast iron griddle I find in another cabinet, mix the ingredients and whisk until it's smooth. I hear his door open as I'm ladling the first four palm-sized circles of batter onto the griddle, and the cabin is filled with the sizzling of the batter in the oil and the scent of pancakes. While they wait to be flipped, I open my door, right as he's tromping up the steps; he has a brown paper bag under one arm and has his glass pour-over thing, full of coffee, in the other hand.

His nose lifts, and he sniffs, and his face lights up. "Hell yeah. I love pancakes."

I grin. "Me too. I didn't learn how to make them until college, though. My college roommate and still best friend, Tess, taught me. All throughout college, every Saturday, we'd wake up early and make a shit-load of pancakes. Half the dorm showed up, usually."

He hesitates on the threshold, and for some reason, I don't invite him in. "I, uh, figured I'd up the ante, a little, if you're making pancakes."

He sets the pour-over on the stump-table by my rocking chair, and reaches into the paper bag, pulls out a bottle of champagne. My heart does a flip, and then hammers when he produces, next, a carton of orange juice.

Mimosas.

It feels too direct. Like he *knows* things about me he shouldn't. I mean, it's just mimosas. It's a pretty common morning thing for a lot of people. He can't know the joyful memories I have of mimosas.

Paris, with Adrian, sleeping in late and waking up to sip mimosas on the balcony with the Eiffel in the distance.

Weekend brunches in college with Adrian, Tess and Clint, Elmore and Tanya, and Kyle and Tanner, and we'd all crowd around a too-small table in our favorite brunch haunt and eat piles of fruit and pancakes and waffles and omelets from a chef station, and we'd get absolutely clobbered on mimosas and laugh ourselves stupid.

That trip to Germany with Adrian when we were promoting *Pocketful of Posies*. The hotel's room service had been middling at best, but their mimosas came in giant goblets with fresh-squeezed orange juice and were stupid cheap, and we'd spend half the morning still buzzed from mimosas with breakfast.

"Uh. Pancakes need flipping," Nathan says, shaking me from my reverie.

Crap. I smell them, and they're about to burn. I fly over to the stove and flip them as fast as I can, and most of them are fine, but one of them is charred to inedibility.

"Sorry," I say.

"No worries. I don't mind them a little crispy."

I snicker and tilt the burnt pancake so he can see it. "I think this may be a little bit beyond merely crispy, Nathan."

His eyes widen. "Oh. Well, yeah. That one, maybe."

I laugh, and plate the three that are edible, toss the ruined one in the trash, and ladle four more onto the griddle. "I'm good at this, I swear. I just got a little… distracted."

He's leaning against the doorway. "It's all good." He sets the champagne and orange juice down, lifts the coffee. "Mugs?"

I bring him mugs, and champagne flutes. Or, rather, I bring him mugs and start to bring him flutes and rethink it. Instead, I bring him regular wineglasses. "Might as well do it properly."

He pours coffee, hands me a mug. "I'm in. I haven't had a mimosa since my…" he trails off. "Well, in a long time."

"Say what you were going to say. No point in dancing around it, right?"

"Since my honeymoon," he says. He stares into his coffee. "Nine years ago."

"Used to have them all the time. I had a big circle of close friends in college. Me and Adrian, my best friend Tess and her then-boyfriend, later husband, and now ex-husband, and two other couples. We'd go to brunch every weekend and get day drunk on mimosas."

"I thought it was pancakes on the weekends."

"That was Saturdays. Sundays were for brunching."

"Oh." He grins. "You did weekends right in college, it sounds like."

I sigh. "Yeah, I guess I did. Haven't had a weekend like that in…well, in a long, long time."

I flip the pancakes, and this time they're perfect golden brown, fluffy and dense.

"When did they stop? Those weekends, I mean."

I sip the coffee while leaning on the counter beside the stove; he's still leaning against the doorway. I don't invite him in, and he doesn't seem to mind. I don't let myself examine this too closely.

"Adrian and I graduated. We all went to UNC, and after graduation, we moved back down here. Tess and Clint stayed up there a few more years, and the others I just lost track of. I started work, and Adrian was working nights at a bar and writing during the day. We'd have some good weekends, but we needed money so I started covering shifts on the weekend in addition to my normal schedule. And he'd be up early writing on Saturdays and Sundays, since those were his busiest days at the bar at night." I shrug. "I guess we let life stop us from…I don't know. From enjoying life. Sounds dumb, now that I put it that way."

"It's not dumb. It's normal."

"Shouldn't be, though." I'm on the third batch of pancakes by this time.

"No, it shouldn't." He smirks. "You know, I have no idea what day of the week it is? Literally, no clue."

I blink. "You know, now that you mention it, me neither," I say, laughing.

"So why don't we just agree it's Saturday." He uncorks the champagne with a loud *pop*, pours a short layer of orange juice at the bottom of the wineglass and then a generous amount of champagne over that. He extends one to me, and I take it. "Here's to enjoying the weekend."

I clink it against his. "Here's to the weekend."

We sip, and I'm transported back to more carefree days. I close my eyes, and I can almost hear Tess cackling at her own lewd jokes, Kyle and Tanner egging her on, Clint embarrassed by her and pretending to laugh along with us—he always was an asshole like that, he never appreciated her for who she is.

I take another sip, eyes closed, and I'm with Adrian in Paris. The last time we were happy together, before The Big C took him from me. He knew then. That's what that was for. A goodbye. Memories to die with.

I swallow hard, blink away tears. Turn away before Nathan notices, and scrape the flipper under the pancakes so they don't stick to the griddle. Clear my throat.

"Thank for this," I say, lifting the mimosa.

"I dunno, seems like I stepped in something complicated."

I shake my head. "You couldn't have known."

He doesn't answer that. I plate the last of the pancakes. Grab the syrup, plates, forks, and a stick of butter, and bring it all out to the porch. It's a glorious morning, cool but not cold, sunny and bright, the early morning light golden and clear.

Nathan is wearing perfectly tight blue jeans, a red-and-blue flannel shirt open over a gray waffle-print Henley, the sleeves pushed up to his elbows. His stubble has grown into a thick beard since I met him, and he seems content to leave it. His hair is a little too long, shaggy and feathered around his ears and the back of his neck. He could use a haircut.

I used to cut Adrian's hair. I have no formal train-ing, just some cosmetology shears from Amazon and some YouTube knowledge. But he liked me cutting his hair, liked the way I did it. Mainly because I'd do it in booty shorts and a bra so I didn't get hair on my clothes. He'd only get a professional haircut if he had to do an interview or before a big international signing or promo event.

I shake these thoughts off, settling into my rocking chair and gesturing for Nathan to go first. "Help yourself, please."

He forks four pancakes at once, cuts himself a thick slice of butter and spreads it on the steaming top pancake, and then the others under it. Liberal syrup. And then, oddly, he cuts his stack into pieces all at once, which makes me grin.

"What?" he asks, partway done chewing.

I shake my head and shrug, but I'm laughing. "Nothing."

He sighs. Sets his fork down with dramatic finality. "It's because I cut them all up first, isn't it?"

"I've just never seen a grown man do it that way."

"It's convenient, is all." He spears another forkful. "A little bit of cutting up front and I can eat them a lot faster. Which means I can get more sooner."

I cackle. "A-*ha*! The real purpose comes out."

"I'm a big guy. I eat a lot. Dad would only make pancakes for us once in a while, but when he did, he'd make a shitload, and it'd be a race to see who could eat more." He pauses, and I sense a heaviness settling on his shoulders. "Then, after I was married to Lisa, she'd get a kick out of feeding me pancakes. She'd call me to breakfast some random morning, and she'd have the first two batches done, and she'd wait till I was sitting, and then it'd be a race. Could I finish them all before she was finished making the next batch? She'd have two griddles going at once, and I'd be just, god, just gorging myself on them. She thought it was equal parts hysterical and baffling how many I could eat." He perks up, laughing. "Course, back then, I was going to the gym regularly, so I could afford the extra calories." He pats his stomach, which I wouldn't say is anything to be embarrassed about, but is probably not going to win any Instagram best six-pack awards. "I haven't touched a barbell in years, but haven't changed my eating habits all that much, least until I got here, that is. So I'm not in the shape I used to be."

"Well, we all cope in different ways."

I steal a glance at the rest of him—he *is* big. It's not that I hadn't noticed, before—he's of a size that you can't miss. Six-four, with heavy, rounded shoulders, as if the weight of muscle on his shoulders is almost too much for his frame to bear. His arms stretch the sleeves of the flannel. He doesn't have a noticeable, protruding belly, but generously speaking, it's clear he likes to eat. His hair is black, longish, with touches of gray at the temples, and streaks of gray shot through his beard near his ears and jawline. He has enormous hands. His fingers nearly meet around the width of his wineglass, which requires both of my hands to accomplish. He has scars on his hands, cuts and nicks in crisscrossing white lines. His knuckles are scarred—he's leaving out some dark periods of his life, I think. My dad's knuckles looked like Nathan's, and I know Dad had a history of getting into scuffles, before they had me.

Nathan catches my eyes on his knuckles, and flexes his fist, shakes it out. "Had some rough times, after I left home. I was angry at life, and thus at everyone. I'd hit walls as much as people, if I couldn't find anyone to pick a fight with."

"You seem very much the opposite, now."

He nods. "Get locked up for assault and battery, you start to reconsider things. Realized if I wanted to end up like Dad, all I had to do was keep going the way I was and I end up there sure as shootin'." Every once in a while, I can really hear the Louisiana in his voice. "Or, I could pick a different path. So, I quit feeling sorry for myself and quit letting my anger at a shitty hand in life make me ornery, and I found someone that'd let me work with wood. A shop teacher at a local community college. Mr. Greene." He sighs, thinks back. "He never asked me a single question. Saw me on the street one day, whittling, invited me to the college shop, and we ended up friends. He let me come as much as I wanted while the college was open, and even if he was teaching class, I could be there working on something."

"Were you homeless?" I ask.

He nods. Spears more pancakes, and suddenly I'm glad I made what I'd thought would way too many. "For a time."

"You've overcome a lot of hardship, haven't you?" I sip coffee, and then mimosa.

"I guess," he says. "But I've never really thought about it like that. It's just my life. It is what it is. Shit comes at you, you can either lay down and let it roll over you, or you can figure it out." He tosses back the last of his mimosa. "Lisa getting killed, though, that's a hardship I couldn't figure out. Getting over her was just too goddamn hard. It was so sudden, so unexpected. She was just...gone. And I ...I couldn't deal."

I nod. "I know how that feels. The not being able to deal."

He eyes me. "Yeah, I guess you do."

I hand him my wineglass. "More, please."

He snickers, and fixes us both another. The pancakes are nearly gone by now, two-thirds of them in his belly. My appetite is coming back, slowly but surely, and I find myself taking thirds, to my own surprise.

The coffee pour-over thing is empty, and he lifts it. "You want more?"

I nod. "If the question is coffee, the answer is always yes."

"Be right back. You keep eatin', I'm full."

A few minutes later, my plate is empty, my belly is

about to burst, and he's clomping up the steps with a fresh pot of coffee. There are three pancakes left, and I notice him eying them.

I stab them with my fork, fix them the way I saw him do it for himself, butter on each one, syrup. I'm not sure why, but I cut them up, too.

And then I had the plate to him.

He takes the plate slowly, as if he's confused. I am too, honestly. Why did I do that? Fixing his pancakes for him feels…intimate.

"I couldn't eat another bite," I say, by way of explanation.

He nods, again slowly, eyeing me almost warily. He eats, and the look of happiness on his face is a beautiful thing. "Damn good pancakes, Nadia. Thank you."

"As good as Lisa's?" I hear myself ask, and then immediately bite down on my tongue until I taste blood.

His fork clatters abruptly. "Don't do that," he says, with a tinge of anger in his voice.

"I'm sorry," I say. "I don't know what the hell came over me. I'm really, really sorry."

He sighs. Sets the unfinished plate on his knees. "They're different. She made hers smaller, the batter thinner. Not better, nor worse. Just…different."

"You didn't have to answer. It was a monumentally stupid question."

Why would I sabotage something as good as this? It's been comforting, friendly, no pressure. A companion in a dark time. I realize I really appreciate him, the little bit of time I've known him.

I blink back tears, stand up, and take my mimosa out toward the dock. Why sabotage a good thing? I can't figure out why the hell I'd say something like that.

I don't like the answer that bubbles up inside me. *Because it's a good thing.*

Because you like him.

"It's fine, Nadia. Don't be upset." His voice is close, directly at my left shoulder, closer than I think he's ever been to me, physically.

"I am." I sniffle. "I'm sorry. I truly don't know what came over me."

"Mouths run away from brains, sometimes. Happens to the best of us. No worries."

"It was an amazing morning, until that. I feel like I ruined it."

He bumps against me, his big, broad shoulder nudging me sideways. "Nah. We had delicious pancakes. Mimosas. Pretty damn good coffee, if I do say so myself. It's a beautiful morning. So, still amazing."

"Thank you for being understanding."

"Pain makes people stupid," he says. "Don't worry about it."

I grin at him. "It does make us dumb, doesn't it?"

"So dumb." His grin in return is warm, forgiving, kind. His eyes, deep dark brown, seem open and welcoming and full of life.

I clear my throat, put a few inches of distance between by stepping closer to the lake. "It's no excuse."

"Sure it is."

Silence.

"You, uh, wanna go for a drive?" he asks.

"A drive?"

"Sure. Just…away and back. Windows down, we can trade playlists."

I smile. "I'd really like that."

"Good." He lifts the mimosa in his hand. "Maybe we plan on going after lunch, though. I'm feeling pretty good right now, don't know about you."

"Pretty good," I say, smirking as I finish the last of mine. "But I think one more might go down real nicely."

We don't end up going for a drive.

We get to talking on the dock over one more mimosa, one more reveals that he actually bought *two* bottles of champagne, and then it's noon and we're cackling on the dock together, and I'm realizing I'm having *fun*. Real, actual *fun*. No strings, no expectations, no reminders of sad things, just conversation that goes from rabbit trail to funny story to rabbit trail to lists of favorite authors and favorite movies.

Despite having little to no formal education, I discover he's widely read, and can discuss classics like *Hamlet* and *Huckleberry Finn* and *The Three Musketeers* as easily as he can the giants of science fiction and thrillers and everything in between.

At some point, he excuses himself to his cabin and returns with a giant block of Colby cheese, a package of deli salami, a jar of pickles, and a twelve-pack of beer. I excuse myself to my cabin and come back with bars of chocolate and my iPhone and a small Bluetooth speaker that Tess, for some reason, packed into my duffel bag, and we go into music lists, playing favorites from my library and then his.

Suddenly it's sunset, and I don't know where the hours went.

I'm sleepy.

We've been into discussions of classical, and I choose my favorite Bach cello suite played by Rostropovich. The music soothes and me and lulls me.

Him, too.

Conversation fades.

I feel him beside me, listening to the slow golden curving notes of the cello.

I sink into something like slumber, wherein I'm not fully asleep, but not awake either, just floating. Lilting on the cello and the alcohol and Nathan's easeful presence and a day of sunshine and good food…

I wake up abruptly. I'm warm, covered.

My eyes open.

I'm in bed. On top of the covers, with my favorite blanket over me. I'm dressed as I was, minus my shoes.

He carried me to bed, covered me.

He was in my home.

Weird: this is home. It feels as much a home as my house back in the Atlanta suburbs.

My emotions have never felt so complicated.

They are so complicated, in fact, that it's easier to just go back to sleep and pretend everything is fine, fine, just fine.

I can lie to myself a little bit longer…can't I?

Twenty-Nine

Kintsugi Heart

SLEEP TONIGHT IS A LONG, LONG TIME IN COMING.

So long, in fact, that tonight becomes tomorrow and then it's dawn and I've been lying in my bed staring at the ceiling wrestling with those pesky motherfuckers, my emotions.

I like Nadia Bell.

A lot.

I like talking to her. I like having coffee with her. Eating food with her.

For the first time since Lisa died, I feel like life is worth living. Which makes me realize fully that I didn't really believe it to be worth living up until now. I wasn't living. I was just subsisting. Not dying. I was an automaton cycling through my programming, a clockwork golem clothed in skin and bones.

Nadia puts fire in my belly. Or, at least, a spark in my chest.

But that's problematic at best. Because…Lisa.

She's in me. She'll always be in me. She's woven

into the DNA of who I am. Missing her is like breathing. She was my true love, my one and only. I promised her till death do us part, and I fucking meant it, goddammit, I just never anticipated that particular vow would be tested. Richer or poorer, sure; I've been poor my whole damn life, and while I wouldn't mind trying rich I know it ain't gonna fix the problems inside me. In sickness and in health, yeah. Easy. I'll sit at her bedside and bring her soup and take her temperature and I'd even wipe her ass if I had to.

I didn't get that. We got to be a little less poor, a little more comfortable. There were flus and stomach bugs, and blowout fights over dumb shit after which we made up delightfully, sinfully, endlessly.

But then she died, and she's gone, and I vowed till death do us part. I vowed.

Death parted us.

I know, I know, I had that dream. But it was a stupid dream, dammit. It wasn't really her, visiting me in my sleep. This ain't *Ghost*. It was my subconscious playing idiotic games with me.

I was fine subsisting day to day, going to work and coming home alone and being celibate and drinking myself to something like sleep, waking up and doing it all over again. Repeat as needed until I go to heaven or nirvana or wherever, and I get to be with her again.

Then Adrian sent me to this cabin, and then he

sent Nadia to live next to me, and now I don't know which way is up.

Because I could…I could imagine her being something that comes before THE END.

When I threw that one red rose and that handful of black loam onto the polished cherry wood coffin, that was me writing THE END. On me, on her, on us, on my life as I knew it. It was over. The rest was just filler, details not worth remembering. There would be no after.

And then Nadia.

Coffee. Pasta. Mimosas. A hike around the lake.

A few little things. I don't know her middle name. I've never held her hand, or even thought about what she looks like naked. It's not that.

It's more. It's deeper. Both innocent and indemnifying at the same time.

It's putting the lie to THE END. It's creating a possibility of AND THEN.

And I just don't know how to reconcile the two.

I sit up in bed and twist on the bedside lamp and reach for the book.

At some point, I think you just have to jump. It's hard and scary when you're young, when your heart is new and fresh and unscarred. You're risking so much, then. Trusting the virgin vulnerability of your precious, secret heart, and you have no guarantee how it'll turn out. His POV. *You dive in, headfirst, terrified. Wonder of wonders, it turns out more amazing than you could ever expect. Joy is such an effervescent thing, isn't it? The giddy happiness of true love is the purest emotion a human can experience. That sacred falling, the majestic weaving of two lives, two souls, two personalities into a single entity…that, I believe, is the meaning of life. The big WHY.*

And then it's taken from you.

You hear those words, "I'm sorry, sir, but your wife didn't make it. We did everything we could."

And suddenly, you're not you anymore. Your face looks back at you from the mirror and your hands are the hands that have sat at the ends of your wrists all these years of your life, but you've been scooped hollow by the vicious talons of Loss. And you're not you.

You wallow. Grieve. Drown. Moving on is a joke, right? That's for people who didn't love the way you did.

But then. Oh, but then. You meet HER. And somehow, the sun might just be trying to peek out from behind the haze of storm clouds that have followed you. There just might be something like a tomorrow that doesn't include barrels of whiskey just to be able to fake a semblance of humanity.

Only, how do you get past this mountain that is grief, that is sorrow? It's insurmountable. You didn't WANT to get past it, over it, under it, around it. You wanted it to just bury you and be done.

SHE makes you think maybe you're not done. Not yet.

And what I'm coming to, what I'm realizing, is that you just have to jump.

It's so much worse than the first time. Your heart isn't whole. It's not even a kintsugi heart, a fragile pottery thing broken into pieces and repaired with seams of gold and silver. It's just dust in the corner on the floor, a few bits and pieces here and there to give you a hint of what it might once have been. You aren't just vulnerable. You're all exposed nerve endings. You think you've armored up against the assaults of the world, but that's a silly lie, easily exposed. I mean, shit, you walk down the street and some lady you've never met walks past wearing her perfume and suddenly you're fighting back sobs and hyperventilation. That one song you danced to at your wedding comes on the radio and you have to pull onto the shoulder, because you can't see and you can't breathe. Armor? Ha.

Now, jumping is a thing of bravery. Before, it was bravado. They're not the same. Before, you felt invincible. Jumping was a risk, but calculated. You stood to gain so much, after all, right? The love of a good woman is worth any risk. That's what you thought, then.

Now, you know better.

Now, you know it can be taken away.

Tennyson can go to hell, right? "'Tis better to have loved and lost than never to have loved at all." Go to hell. You don't know shit, Alfred.

But…she makes you wonder. It won't be the same. You won't forget. It's not replacing. It's different. New. Strange and hard to figure out and there's no words in any language to express how scary it is. But...

Maybe.

The problem is, you can't inch your way into these waters. There's no acclimating yourself to the depths, the unfamiliar currents and swirling cold.

It's dark down there, in the unknown.

Hic sunt dracones.

You just have to fucking jump. You may hit bottom and be broken further. There's no guarantee. There may be nothing but an endless fall down a well of infinite depth.

Or...or there could be new life. Happiness in a strange, unfamiliar guise. Hands which do not yet know yours. Eyes which have not plumbed your depths. A kiss unpracticed and hesitant. Secrets of your past life must be, yet again, revealed, painfully, fearfully. And now you have more secrets, more pain, more sorrow. It's all so much.

But the question which drives you onward resounds deafeningly, tolling like a bell in the tremoring depths of your little boy soul: Would it be worth it?

Is SHE worth it?

Only one way to find out:

Jump.

A knock on my door startles me. I step into gym shorts but forget a shirt. Stumble out to the door, tug it open.

Nadia. Pale pink cotton shorts with fraying,

rolled-up hems, short enough to leave a good ninety percent of her legs bare. A white ribbed tank top under a thin gray zip-up hoodie made from T-shirt material; the hoodie is unzipped, the zipper pull dangling at her hip, the edges pulled closed far enough to provide a covering over the fact that she's not wearing a bra.

She's holding her big stockpot in both hands, with the glass lid with the black handle covering it. "I made oatmeal."

I blink. Stammer. "Um, I...yeah. Oatmeal." I step backward. "Come in. I'll...shirt. Coffee. Just hold on."

She takes one step inward, over the threshold. No further.

I fumble into a shirt, trying to fill the electric kettle at the same time. Grind beans. Pretend her presence isn't flustering me.

The book is on my bed, visible from the front door at certain angles.

Fortunately, her eyes are on the table, which is covered in shavings and wood peelings and finished carvings, and my half-finished scale model of these two cabins and the curve of the lake they're on, with the stand of pines behind them—it's all made from one piece of wood, a large section of pine I found sliced up near the roadway, where a storm in the recent past knocked trees over.

Somehow, I manage coffee. Pour us some the moment it's done dripping, and bring bowls and spoons out onto my porch. It's the norm, now, it seems: break-fast on the porch.

I'm trying to not think about how much of her legs are visible. How they've gained roundness, regained what I imagine is their former and natural plushness.

Her cheeks have normalized, her waistline no longer frighteningly tiny. Her shoulders no longer look like they could snap if you touched her wrong. The shad-ows under her eyes are fading, even if the shadows *in* her eyes have not.

The edges of the hoodie bulge over breasts, where before it wouldn't have.

I turn away and stare at the sunrise over the lake. "You're up early."

She shrugs. "I fell asleep early, I guess, and stayed asleep." Her fingers touch my forearm, a brief, light moment. "Thank you for carrying me inside."

I clear my throat. "I, uh, yeah. You were sleeping so peacefully, I didn't want to wake you. Hope it's all right. That I didn't invade your privacy or anything, I mean."

"Not at all," she murmurs. "I'm grateful."

"Thanks for breakfast," I say.

She pulls off the lid, revealing thick oatmeal lib-erally sprinkled with fresh blueberries and quartered strawberries, and my nose detects a hint of honey, I think. "My grandmother's recipe. A stick to your ribs breakfast, she used to call it."

It's delicious. Wakes me up, fills me, warms me.

"I was going to head into town later this morning. Go to the library, return books and check out new ones. Probably grab lunch at one of the cafes." I glance at her over my bowl. "You wanna come with me?"

She smiles. "Absolutely! I haven't been to the library yet."

"Great. I like to take my time there. Read bits of the books I'm gonna check out. I kinda make an event of it, I guess. Just so we're on the same page. I don't just pop in, find books, leave again."

Another smile. "I haven't been to a library in ages, actually. It sounds fun."

"I mean, I dunno if fun is the right word, but I sure enjoy it."

⁂

We've been browsing separately for an hour. We cross paths now and then; she has a small stack under one arm: a biography of Amelia Earhart, a Jack Reacher novel, and something by Nora Roberts; I have an Agatha Christie mystery, a Tom Clancy novel, and two small sci-fi space operas by writers I've never heard of, chosen for the blurb, the cover, and the first few pages.

I find her, later, sitting in a corner with her books on the table beside her, reading the Nora Roberts book. I sit next to her, place my books on hers, and dig into one of the space operas.

We read quietly for...well, I'm not honestly sure.

It's quiet, only a few other older folks browsing here and there, the librarian gliding around with a cart of books to be reshelved, and there are no clocks.

It's easy to sit here with her, in the silence, reading.

It's not until I hear her stomach growl that I glance at the windows and see that, judging by the movement of the shaft of sunlight, we've been here reading for several hours.

"You wanna go get lunch?" I ask, in a whisper.

She nods. "Yeah, I'm hungry."

I smirk. "I heard."

She gives me a droll eye roll. I take our whole stack of books, carry them to the check-out. This is when she realizes she doesn't have a library card here.

"It's fine, I'll check them out for you," I tell her. "No worries."

"But..." she starts, and then trails off, appearing to reconsider her protestation. "Okay, thank you."

Lunch is cheeseburgers and beer at the bar, with ESPN running highlights of college football. The books are in my truck. The bill arrives, and Nadia frowns.

"I don't have my purse," she says, her frown deepening. "I didn't even think about it. It's been so long since I've even needed it."

"Nadia," I say, tossing my card onto the tray. "It's fine."

She shakes her head, and seems unduly upset. "It's not. You shouldn't pay for me."

"It's like forty dollars. No big deal."

"It's…" She lets out a breath. "It's not about the money. It's about the principle of the thing."

I nudge the tray toward the bartender as he passes by with a pair of beers for a couple of local old guys. Then I glance at her, toying with the leather stitching on my wallet. "Doesn't make this a date, if that's what you're worried about."

She blushes, rolls a shoulder in a vague, unsure gesture. "I…I don't mean anything against you, Nathan." A deep, delicate pause. "I…I enjoy spending time with you." Another pause. "It's just…I don't know if I'm…"

"It can be just two friends having lunch, Nadia. I get it." I try to catch her eyes. "If anyone gets where you are on this, it's me. Okay?"

She seems to be struggling with what she's feeling and how to express any of it. Boy, do I get that, too. "I'm really confused, Nathan."

"Like I said, I get it."

"Are you confused, too?" she asks, looking at me, finally.

I nod slowly. "Yeah, I guess I am."

"Or you mean you've *have been* confused like I am now, so you get it?"

"No, I'm pretty damn confused right now." I'm the one wrestling with what to say, now. "I like you, Nadia. You're easy to be around. Easy to talk to. I don't have to…explain things that most other folks just won't ever understand. I like that, around you, it's… it's easier to not think about…all the heavy shit." I lick my lips and wish the pint glass in front of me wasn't empty. "But I feel guilty about not thinking about it…"

Harsh, thick, acid pause.

"About her," I finish."

She tilts her head back, sniffles at the ceiling, and the sniff is not quite but almost a laugh. "Yeah," she murmurs, wiping under her eyes with her two middle fingers. "What you said."

"You want to head back?" I ask, after a minute.

"Yeah," she says. "I'm sorry."

"Don't be."

We drive back, and it's silent between us. I let it be, that silence. Sometimes you just can't talk your way out of awkward silences. Sometimes, the awkward silences are important.

When we get back to the cabins, she stops halfway between my cabin and hers. Her blue jeans fit her just right, and she fills out the plain white V-neck T-shirt in a way I've not noticed, until now.

"Nathan?"

I kick at the grass. "Yeah."

"I'm sorry I freaked out."

"Don't apologize to me, Nadia. I told you, more than anyone else, I get it. No apology is ever necessary."

"Can I apologize in advance for the fact that I think I need some space for a few days? To…think?"

"No," I say. "You can't apologize for that." I leaven it with a smile. "I'll still bring you coffee. I'll just leave it on the porch like I used to."

"I can make my own," she protests.

I snicker. "No, you can't."

"Nathan."

"Kidding. I mean, you can't make coffee for shit, but I'm just teasing. And it's fine. Take whatever time you need." I let out a slow breath. "I'll be around."

"I know you will," she says. "I just need to—"

I hold up a hand. "Explanations are as unnecessary as apologies." I take the burden of ending the exchange on myself. "I'll see you when you feel talking again. No worries."

She wants to say more, but I go inside, because it'd just go around in circles.

Shit, I think I need to think, myself.

Thirty

Heart Work

HE BRINGS ME COFFEE IN THE MORNING. I LEAVE HIM offerings of food in return—I'm relearning how to cook. I used to be good at it, used to love it. I used to cook on the weekends, when I wasn't working. Every once in a while, Adrian would get a hankering for something in particular, and I'd oblige. But now, I'm cooking for me.

I make biscuits, the way Mom used to make them, light and flaky and buttery. Beef stew, with thick chunks of meat and big wedges of potato and slices of carrot. Chili, as taught to me by my college friend Tanner, who learned Tex-Mex chili from county fair cook-off winners. I even figure out the trick to my aunt's bread, which took a whole day of try, try, try again until I got it just right. I bake pies and cakes, *pain au chocolat* from an internet recipe, which is nowhere near as good as it was in Paris, of course.

I make some for me, and some for him.

I told him I needed to think, but really, I'm just scared.

I like him.

I like his coffee. I like his big, rough, strong presence. I like the occasional Louisiana twang in his voice. I like how he's so smart despite having never been to real school. I like that I can sit on my beanbag chair late at night, reading, and hear him on his porch playing his guitar. I hear him playing Ed Sheeran and Harry Styles and Alan Jackson and Tim McGraw and songs I don't know. I hear him play that one tune he wrote, for his wife I assume. He plays it a lot, and seems to be adding to it, perfecting and polishing it. I like that he can sit in silence with me and not need to fill it. I like his eyes, big and deep and brown. I like his hands, which are the size of dinner plates just about, scarred and weathered and lined like a map of the world carved into old hickory.

I hate that I like these things. That I've noticed them.

That they're lessening the pierce of sorrow.

I hate that it's easier to wake up, now, and that it seems to be, in some ways, directly attributable to him. But it's not, not entirely. I'm sleeping, and eating, and relaxing, and I'm not dehydrated constantly and I'm not stressed out about work. These things help. I'm learning that waking up and missing Adrian is just part of living, not the entirety of me. I'm learning that if I read and bake and cook and paint and walk along the shore in the Georgia fall sun, that I can go hours now without missing him so bad it hurts.

I'm learning to sit through the missing him, to let it dwell in me, and that eventually, the sharpness of it will subside. Like being hungry in the middle of a long shift with no opportunity for lunch—ignore the hunger, and it fades. It'll still be there, later. But your body seems to just go, *oh, we're not eating now, huh? All right, I'll wait.*

Sorrow, with the space of weeks and months between the event and emotion, seems to function much the same. It hurts, hurts like a motherfucker. Hurts like it did the day he died, some days. But you just have to sit in it. To let it run its course. It'll fade.

You'll make it through it.

You won't actually die from how bad it hurts, even if it feels like you could, even if, in the midst of it, you almost want to.

It's all so confusing.

And I don't know what to do.

Because as a day turns into two, turns into a week and there's no more breakfast on his porch or mine and no more lazy afternoons on the dock, and his understanding presence always seeming to be right there when I needed it and comforting in a way I didn't know was possible.

I miss him.

And that hurts.

It's weird, though—it's the same verb: to miss. If you Google it, the third definition of miss has three entries: to notice the loss or absence of, to feel regret or sadness at no longer being able to enjoy the presence of, and to regret or be sad about not being able to do, have, or be or go.

I can say I miss Adrian, and that I miss Nathan, but despite meaning the same semantic thing, the two are a universe apart.

What do I do with it all?

Was this whole "I need space to think" an experiment? To see how I'd react to not being around Nathan? If it is, I'm not sure how I feel about the results.

I don't know what possesses me to do so, but I dig into my purse and pull out the letter from Adrian.

Read it, more than once.

I pause and reread a specific section several times:

There will be more for you to do, in learning to live again, but the important thing for you to hold foremost in your mind, my love, is this: I WANT you to move on. In every way. Please. When I made you promise to live, this is what I meant. Move on.

Love again, Nadia.

Yes, even that.

It hurts, I admit. You're mine.

But I'm gone, now. And it's time for you to live again. You have too much love to keep hidden inside. To keep buried under my skeleton.

Dig that up, my love. Dust it off. Try it on, and then, before you feel ready, use it again.

I want you to. I expect you to.

If we meet in heaven and you have spent the rest of your life alone, I shall be angry with you, my love.

Life is for the living. So live.

Easy for you to say, Adrian, you're not the one here left trying to do it.

How do I do that?

I'm not ready.

I'll never be ready.

But I guess that was his point, huh?

I put the letter away, back in the envelope, back into my purse.

It's late. Past dark, into the cricket-song night. His porch light is on. I'm not thinking. Not planning. I just let my feet carry me to his porch. Let my fist knock on his door.

I forget how I'm dressed until he answers. My comfiest, tightest, shortest booty shorts, which until recently hadn't fit; a sports bra, and my T-shirt fabric hoodie, only half zipped. No more protruding ribs, and I've even got something to put into a bra, finally. I'd almost forgotten how that feels.

His eyes slide down, back up, and fix on my eyes. "Hi."

I have no clue what I want to say. "Um, hi."

Not stellar as far as opening gambits go.

"You think about what you need to think about?" he asks.

I laugh. "No. I just realized I wasn't getting anywhere, so I gave up."

He lets his door swing open, revealing his table, where a bottle of whiskey sits half-empty beside a glass, along with his carving materials. "You want to come in?"

It's the first time he's asked.

"Uh, we can sit out here."

"All right." He glances at his kitchen counter, where a small wrought iron wine racks sits empty. "I don't have any wine or champagne. Just whiskey or beer."

"Would you be mad if I asked for lots of ice in the whiskey?"

"No," he laughs. "I'm not that kind of whiskey snob. I like specific stuff, and I guess it's true enough I don't drink cheap shit, but if you like it with ice, you like it with ice. No harm in that."

He removes a tumbler from a cabinet, reaches into his freezer—it's an antique, that fridge, avocado colored and half his height—for a white tray of ice. Twists, cracking ice out. Scoops four big cubes into the glass, then a fifth for good measure, and fills the glass with amber whiskey.

We sit on his porch, in the rocking chairs—it must

have been a set of four, his two and my two, because they're nearly identical, but for little differences which only highlight the individual craftsmanship that went into them. The whiskey is smoky and tastes like fire and honey. It's almost viscous on my tongue, and the ice is cold on my lips as I sip.

"What did you mean by that?" he asks.

I don't have to clarify what he's asking about.

"I think it was more just to see how I'd feel not seeing you every day." I swallow hard—the truth is thick and hard to get past my teeth. "It was getting too familiar, seeing you every day. And I don't know what to do with that."

"Ain't nothin' wrong with a widow and a widower gettin' to know each other, Nadia," he says, his voice low and rough. "Not sure a body could take things much slower than we've been."

"I know." I shake the tumbler lightly, and ice clinks. "I guess it's that I'm not sure I'm ready for there to be anything to take slowly."

"Doesn't have to be that," he says.

"But it is." I look at him. "We both know it."

"Yeah, I guess so."

"Do you want it to be that?" I ask, watching his reaction closely. "For there to be something to take slowly?"

He nods, and it's as if his head is heavy, too heavy for his neck. "Yeah, I guess I do." He sips. Stares out at the lake, which is lit only with slivers of moon behind a ripped blanket of gray fleece. "I said I like you. I meant it. Doesn't mean it's not weird, and scary. And hard. Doesn't mean I know what the hell I'm doing. But I'm not going to pretend I don't…feel what I feel. If you're not ready, I get it. I can be friends. It's all it is right now anyway, right? Coffee on the porch. A meal here and there. A walk around the lake. A drink of an evenin'." Sometimes he sounds like he's from a different millennium, an older time.

We drink whiskey over ice and listen to the crickets and the frogs, watch the last of the fireflies flitting on the fading warm evening.

"I like you too," I whisper. So quiet, I wonder if he even heard me.

He did. His eyes slide across the space, to mine. Search me.

"You always hear that the first step is the hardest," he murmurs, in his rough woodsmoke voice. "Maybe that one's true."

"Maybe it is," I agree.

I finish my whiskey.

"Coffee in the morning?" He sounds hopeful.

And that does something very complicated to my belly.

"Yeah," I say. "My porch. Six thirty."

"Could you, uh, sometime, if you feel like it, could you make that bread with the little pieces of chocolate in it? That stuff was good."

I laugh. *"Pain au chocolat."* I'm glad he picked that one—I've never made it for anyone but him. "Yeah. I can."

"I didn't mean tomorrow morning."

"I know." I consider how long it would take. "We'll have to see how early I wake up."

I walk back home, and I feel him watching me. The sensation of being watched, looked at, *seen*—I don't mind it. There's no judgment in his eyes. No pity, either. Just warmth and understanding and the depths of a soul, which some part of mine seems to recognize.

Like when you meet someone, and it feels as if you've been friends before, if you were to believe in reincarnation. Similar to that, with Nathan. Only…far more complex.

I go to bed, and I'm thinking about Nathan as I drift off. That's new.

It's over coffee, the next morning.

I've made *pain au chocolat,* he's made scrambled eggs and bacon in a huge cast iron skillet.

We're done eating. Sipping coffee and watching the sun poke salmon-colored fingers through the rim of pines over the lake.

"There's a restaurant, just outside town," Nathan says, apropos of nothing. "A nicer place, I guess. On a lake kinda like this one. Do you want to have dinner there with me, tonight?"

I swallow hard. "I...I..." I search myself, and again the truth is a viscous, multilayered thing within me. "Yes, I do." I lick my lips, run my finger around the rim of my mug. "This might be weird and stupid, but... could we drive separate?"

His smile is not mocking. "Yeah, of course."

"I just—"

He holds up a hand to halt me. "What'd I say about explanations or apologies?"

I sigh, and I'm almost smiling myself. "Fine." I take the last piece of bacon, because it's obvious he's not going to, and I munch on it. "What time?"

"Leave at six?"

"Okay. Next question: what should I wear?"

A shrug. "It ain't a formal place, I don't think. Never been there, but folks in town have told me it's nice. Whatever that means." He picks at the crumbs of pastry and bits of chocolate on the now-empty plate. "It's called The Boat Dock."

"Six o'clock then."

He nods. "Nadia, just so you know, this can be just two friends sharing a meal—"

"No explanations or apologies is your rule, Nathan. Goes for you too."

I mainly don't want to rule anything out any more than I want to label it with anything.

His smile is hesitant, like he wants to be happy, eager, excited, but doesn't want to get his hopes up, or let me see what he's really feeling. Or some confusing emotional admixture of all that and more.

Neither of us seems to know what to say next; we just agreed to what is, despite my precaution of driving separately, a date.

We're not calling it that. We're not calling it anything. But it's a man and a woman, who have tacitly agreed that there is in fact a thing which is being taken slowly, having dinner together. It's a step beyond breakfast on the porch, but a step less than inviting him in for wine by the fire.

He grabs his pour-over, his skillet. Stands up. Goes down one step, hesitates, turns. "I'm looking forward to dinner with you, Nadia."

"I'm looking forward to it, too." I stand up, too. I'm not sure why. "See you at six?"

He chuckles. "It's gonna be a long day, isn't it?"

I laugh at that. "Yeah, I think it is."

"You, uh, you ever been fishing?"

I hold up both hands. "Not if you paid me, Nathan."

"Too boring, huh?"

"Watching golf is boring. Watching C-Span is boring. Fishing is…something there isn't a word for."

"So that's a no."

"Firmly."

"See you at six."

I laugh. "Yeah, see you at six," I call after him. "If you catch anything, I'll cook it. I think I remember how."

He waves a dismissive hand. "They're all tiny, in there. Fun to catch, but not worth trying to eat."

Weird how we both seem to have trouble ending conversations.

He smiles at me over his shoulder as the conversation just kind of abruptly, awkwardly ends, because he's doing his thing and I'm doing mine and we're going to see each later. So do you say goodbye, see you later, or do you just stop talking and do what you do until it's time to see each other again? Neither of us seems to know how to navigate that.

I can't help wondering what that means, and then further wondering if maybe I know what it means, but I just don't want to admit it.

Time to go spend the rest of the day worrying about what I'm going to wear on this date-not-date.

Is it a date?

Do I want it to be a date?

I head inside and paw through my hanging clothes, dresses, skirts, blouses. And while I'm trying on outfits, I'm also trying on, experimentally, how it would feel to let myself admit that tonight with Nathan *is* a date and that I do in fact *want* it to be.

I can't quite get there.

I haven't been on a date, as in a getting-to-know-you-because-I-think-I-like-you type of way, since I met Adrian freshman year of college. Which feels like a long, long time ago. Because, *damn*, it was. I was nineteen when I met him. That's almost twenty years ago.

Makes me feel old.

I like Nathan. That's an established fact. But I hate how that feels, sounds—like I'm a sixth-grader with my first crush. *Do you like me, check yes or no.* But what other language is there for this feeling? I appreciate who he is. I enjoy spending time around him. Conversation with him is easy, natural, and lively. I feel safe around him. At no point has he ever done or said anything that makes me feel physically uncomfortable, pushed past my limits of propriety and comfort. He doesn't look at me like I'm a piece of meat.

Which, I mean, until lately, at least, there wasn't any meat on me for him to be looking at me in that way anyhow. I was emaciated. By the time I got that letter from Adrian, I was working a hundred hours a week, sleeping four or five hours a night max, and eating *maybe* a thousand calories a day, most of the time far less, and what I did eat was largely nutritionally useless, bits of fruit, some cheese, a microwavable frozen burrito from Costco, half a bagel dipped in cream cheese as I drove to work.

I'm back to normal, to some degree. I'm not even doing yoga. I'm eating, sleeping, and relaxing.

Reading. I barely have what you could call a hobby. I've read almost all the books in the loft library, which is going to start prompting more trips to the library in town, especially now that I've been there with Nathan. I've put on plenty of weight, which for the first time in my entire life is a *good* thing. I not only need to wear a bra again, I'm not cinching it to the tightest set of clasps anymore. My jeans don't hang off my hips anymore. My yoga pants are actually stretched around my legs instead of flapping loosely. My fitted T-shirts fit like they're supposed to. I can actually look in the mirror and not cringe.

Case in point, for the first time in months, if not more than a year, I strip naked and stand in front of the full-length mirror on the back of the bathroom door, and look at myself. I don't know that I feel pretty, yet, but that's likely as much a mental hang-up as it is anything to do with what I actually look like. My hair has its luster back, glossy and full of life again, although I badly need to trim my ends. My skin isn't papery thin and dry and sallow anymore, or pale. I've always been on the more svelte side, but I finally once again have something like feminine curves, and I like that.

Feeling pretty, let alone beautiful or desired, though? That's going to take a hell of a lot more than filling out my bra and underwear again. That's heart work. You have to like yourself to feel beautiful. You have to be desired by someone to feel desirable. I'm not sure I'm in a place where either is possible. I'm getting there, slowly, but I'm not there yet.

And I think…if I'm going to be brutally honest with myself, part of me doesn't *want* to get there. Liking myself enough to feel beautiful and having someone in my life that desires me so that I feel desirable again means I'll have moved on. Left Adrian behind. Forgotten him.

Let him go.

I'm not ready to do that.

I'll never be ready to do that.

So why am I going on a date with Nathan?

Because of that other part of me, which *does* want to feel beautiful and desirable, and if not cherished and loved again, at least admired and liked.

I know it's very unfair to Nathan, but I'm going into this date-not-date holding a lot back. Knowing I'm doing something that I know I'm not psychologically or emotionally prepared to allow, not in the fullness of what it is, and could or should be.

Is it another experiment, like the week without him?

Or is it an experiment of another kind, one wherein I test the waters of letting him a step or two closer, a little further in? I want to warn him, in a way:

Beware—it's dark in here, close to my heart, near my

soul. The curtains are drawn, and sheets cover the furniture. Dust inhabits the corners. Ghosts moan in the halls. Are you sure you want me to let you in?

I'm opening the door a crack, letting him peer in—maybe he'll see the wrecked abandon within me and get scared off. Or maybe I'll panic and slam the door in his face.

I don't even know anymore.

I'm going on this date-not-date, but how I'll react is a mystery to me.

Thirty-One

Too Right, Too Soon

*I*T WAS THE THIRD OR FOURTH DATE-LIKE OUTING BEFORE *anything felt like more than just friends doing friendly hang-out stuff.*

His POV. It's five thirty, and I've been ready for an hour, so I'm reading to pass the time. And maybe, possibly, hoping for some helpful hints as to what the fuck I'm supposed to do, feel, say, or be. Hints as to her.

The first date, we just talked, on the front porch of my house. Second, we went for a walk in the park, several feet between us, almost as if it was the nineteenth century and we were courting. Third date, she had me over to her house and I brought carryout from a local Chinese place and we ate on her back deck and there was no alcohol and we sat on opposite sides of the square, glass table with the hole in the middle for an umbrella she didn't have. That one felt almost like a date. It was the fourth one that crossed some sort of invisible line. I'd found this place online, a restaurant way out in the country, in the hills, surrounded by forests and two-lane highways. I figured the drive there would be as much the date as the dinner itself.

The place is called The Boat Dock. Cute, quaint, and unique. It has a very much misplaced nautical theme, considering the lake it's on is barely big enough for Jet Skis and tubing. I wouldn't call it pretensions of grandeur, exactly, but close. Big thick nautical ropes on the walls in ornate knots, which probably have complicated names and functions. Oars from ship's boats, the ten-foot-long kind meant to lock into rings on rowboats. Draft charts and maps with incomplete representations of shorelines with antiquated names for familiar places. But it's cozy, with little booths in shadowy corners, votives on the tables and single-sheet laminated menus with imported fish-and-chips and tender veal and overpriced lamb chops. Low ceilings and big windows overlooking a maze of weathered docks festooned with an excess of largely decorative ropes.

We sat outside, and there were tiki torches that gave off thick smoke smelling of citronella. In the center of the table was a small glass vase with a single bright orange Gerbera daisy.

"Those are my favorite flower," she said, in a by the way sort of comment.

I tucked that tidbit away—Gerbera daisy. Got it.

There was music playing low in the background, a playlist that seemed to waffle between accordion-heavy French-inspired instrumental melodies and old standby Frank Sinatra tunes. She flipped the menu over several times, and *then set it down decisively. She ordered chicken parmesan, and when it came, let it slip that if a restaurant had chicken parmesan, that's what she got. She'd tried a million times to make it at home, but could never get it to come out right. The breading was never crispy and golden brown enough, and the cheese never went stringy the same way, and the sauce never had the right balance between smooth and chunky. So, chicken parmesan remained a delicacy she could never get anywhere but a restaurant.*

Another tidbit.

She hated Frank Sinatra—I learned that, too, on that date. She thought he sounded smarmy, like yeah, I know I'm hot stuff and would you just listen to this voice of mine? I'm crooning, baby. Doesn't it make you swoon?

So many things to know. It's hard work getting to know a whole person from scratch. We're such complicated creatures; we humans, and women are, to me at least, a six-dimensional puzzle with no frame of reference to work from. We're so much more than the sum of our parts, more than middle names and favorite elementary school teacher and first kiss and which best friend betrayed you in high school and go-to sex position and which foods you hate and love and which musicians you love to hate and which ones make you cry because there are just so many fucking memories attached to that ONE particular song, which always seems to be playing when heavy shit goes down. For me, it's "Satellite" by DMB. It was playing when I lost my virginity, and was playing when we broke up, and it was playing on the radio when we got in the wreck and my wife died. So now I can't listen to it. I hear it, and I still love that goddamn song because it's just so good, but each note sends a hail of emotional javelins slicing into me, a montage of awkward sex and tearful yelling and the moment I knew she was dead when that thick red blood of hers dripped onto the seat belt buckle and her eyes went glassy and empty like the eyes in a stuffed deer head.

Now I have to do it all over again, with her—the NEW her. Because the other her is still there, right? Inside, in the fibers of my muscles and the dark veins of memory. And now they have to coexist. The previous her loved Ol' Blue Eyes, found his music unbearably romantic. Disliked Italian food because it was too heavy, too rich. Gotta keep it straight.

Fuck.

Damn you, Adrian Bell. Damn you. You were the one dying; so how the *HELL* did you get it so exactly right?

The bit about the song, that one song? "Found Out About You," Gin Blossoms. Lisa and I danced to it on our first date in a dive bar, and after that it was ubiquitous throughout our life together, playing on a Bluetooth speaker on the balcony rail that one hot night when the A/C went out and we had slow sticky sex on a blanket in the backyard, and in the car on the way to the O/B where we found she'd miscarried, and yes, on the radio in the bathroom of the restaurant literally moments before my phone rang with the news of her death.

So fuck that song.

Because it's still a good song.

I close the book and check the time: 5:58.

Gerbera daisies and chicken parmesan and *not* Frank Sinatra. How much is actually *her*, though? Nadia. She loves red wine the way his book said. And, actually, every detail about Nadia in the book is true of Nadia.

I check my reflection one last time, as if it's going to change. I've trimmed my beard so it's not as bushy, combed my hair so it's not as shaggy. My best jeans, cleanest Caterpillar boots, and the green-and-blue checked flannel with the pearl snap buttons, which Lisa always went nuts for.

It's just a shirt. And I look good in it. It's not a betrayal of Lisa to wear that shirt for a different woman.

It's not.

Am I asking myself, or telling myself? I'm not sure.

Instead of cologne, I use the trick Lisa invented for me: I shave little curls off of a piece of fresh cedar, and tuck those shavings into the breast pockets of the shirt, which I then button closed. Boom—fresh cedar scent, without the oils.

Clean hands, clean fingernails. Fresh breath.

It's been forever since I've done this, and my hands are a little trembly, and I wonder if I'm doing the right thing, if I'm missing something.

It's 6:02, and I head outside.

I wish I had time to run into town and buy some

daisies to give to her. And then I wonder if that would be too forward, too much too soon, giving her flowers.

I spin my truck keys around my middle finger, waiting for her.

She comes out a few minutes later. My breath catches. A deep blue shirt-dress down to her thighs, with a wide brown leather belt around her waist, her long tan legs bare between the hem and knee-high boots a similar shade of brown as her belt. The shirt-dress has several buttons plunging down her chest, and she's left most of them unbuttoned. Is she wearing makeup? I can't tell. Which means if she is, it's skillfully enough applied that I'm not supposed to know. Her eyes look bright green, more emerald than jade today. Her lips are plump and red.

"You look…" I hunt for an appropriate but accurate word, and settle for lame but true. "Beautiful."

She grins, teasing. "You had to think about that one, Nathan."

"Only because there's a lot of words I could use." I smile at her. "Gorgeous. Breathtaking. Stunning."

She blushes, ducks her head. "Thanks." Her head lifts, and her eyes flick over my shoulders, my hair. "You look great, too. I really like that shirt."

"Thanks." I slap my hand awkwardly on my thigh. "Well, shall we?"

"Sure. I'll follow you."

I hesitate. "You sure you don't want to change your mind about driving separate? I'm fine either way."

She makes a face. "Yeah, I'd just be more comfortable this way."

"Okay. Well, it's not far, and not hard to find. We're just heading out right on the highway at the end of the drive, and then left at the next intersection, maybe five miles south, and the restaurant is on the right another few miles from there."

She frowns but laughs. "I'll follow you. Just don't lose me."

I eye her sporty little red convertible. "I don't think we need to worry about that, with you driving that."

She rolls her eyes. "I'm no speed demon. Adrian hated riding with me because I always drive obsessively at exactly the speed limit."

"Lisa hated riding with me for the opposite reason—I'm a five over at minimum kind of guy."

A moment of silence as we each realize we've just referenced our dead spouses moments before leaving on a date…

But it's not a date, because we're driving separately, and I anticipate her fighting me on the bill.

She sighs. "Okay well that was a conversation killer."

"It's fine. How about we have a rule that we will not feel bad, embarrassed, or awkward if we happen to make a comment like that. It's part of our lives, part of who we are, and there's no point dancing around it."

She nods, tries a small smile. "I think that's good.

And actually, that's one of the first times that I've mentioned him that hasn't left me feeling like I'm going to break down in hysterics. So there's that."

"'Baby steps to the elevator, Bob.'"

She snickers. "I want, I *want*, I need, I *need*."

We laugh at the shared reference, and then I pull open my truck door. "Ready?"

"As I'll ever be," she says, and without giving me time to process what that might mean, heads for her car.

I don't have to wonder too hard what she means, though, because I get it. You're never ready. You can't be.

It's a bit farther than I thought it would be, getting to the restaurant—closer to thirty minutes than fifteen. When we get there, the parking lot is speckled with vehicles, mostly luxury vehicles that were cream of the crop a few years ago and are now aging a bit, but still very nice. A few trucks like mine, and couple dusty little sensible sedans. Not full, not waitlist busy, but a decent crowd for…whatever day of the week this is.

It's bigger than I expected, too, a long, low building spreading out around the curving end bank of a long, thin lake glittering in the red-gold sunset. Waist-high wood posts connected by thick nautical ropes line a wood plank leading to the front door. The building is white with blue shutters and a slate-gray roof, lots of tall, narrow windows running around back. I open the door for her, and she pauses as she passes me.

"You smell good," she murmurs.

I'm tempted to reveal my secret, but she moves the rest of the way in, and then the hostess is greeting us, asking if we have a reservation.

"Yeah. Two, for Fischer, at six forty-five."

Nadia glances up at me. "You made reservations?"

"This morning, after we said we'd go. I just didn't want to get all the way here and have to wait an hour for a table."

"Oh. Probably smart." She looks like she's feeling as unsure about this as I am.

The place is swanky. I'd expected a cute little place, nice but not super upscale. This is…more than that.

Low ceilings, heavy wood beams. Lots of pillars, high-back booths with a handful of tea lights and a single flower in the middle. All exactly as in the book. Which, in the description, sounded cozy. The over-all effect, now that I'm here, is far more intimate and romantic.

The hostess leads us to a table at the back of the restaurant, overlooking the lake and the docks. The walls along the back slide open and accordion against the far corners so the whole rear of the building is open to the warm early fall evening. Our table is small, the walls at our backs tall. The only light except for the sun-set is from the tea lights, which are scattered in an art-fully haphazard way around the small vase of bubbled blue glass, which contains a single lavender Gerbera daisy. White linen napkins rolled around the silverware.

The table is rough old wood—actually old, not fake-old; as a carpenter, I can tell the difference. French-inspired, semi-nautical music plays low in the background.

She's looking around, taking it all in. And looking, to my perhaps unpracticed eye, a little green around the gills, so to speak. As if this is more than she expected, more than she was ready for.

The waitress is young, effervescent, and efficient. Some instinctual part of me takes over when she asks if we'd like to start with some wine, and I don't even need to look over the rest of the wine menu when I see Joseph Carr, and I order us a bottle—she likes J-name red wines, I think. She eyes me as I order for us, apprehensive and reticent. The wine comes, and we've exchanged a half dozen words. I order us a charcuterie appetizer, and her eyes light up. She loves cheese. She dips the crumbly white goat cheese in the fresh honey which comes complete with bits of honeycomb, and there's fancy little white almonds dusted with salt and parmesan and oil, and pitted olives, candied walnuts, thin slices of pastrami and other fancy meats with names I can't pronounce, all piled in artsy coils.

The wine loosens our tongues, and the charcuterie helps. It's the kind of conversation that flows naturally, easily, but if you'd asked me five minutes later what we were talking about, I wouldn't have known. Just… talking.

Then our server returns for our dinner order,

and Nadia is still perusing the menu, but somehow I know what she wants. Maybe it's the wine, maybe it's nerves. Lisa used to love it when I ordered for us—took the pressure off, she said. I think she just liked being surprised, liked knowing I knew her well enough to get her what she would want.

"I'll have the flank steak, medium, with truffle fries and the veggies of the day," I hear myself say. "She'll have the chicken parmesan, with a house salad, ranch dressing."

Her mouth flaps, open, closed, open. "Um. Can I have a side of the truffle fries with the chicken parm?" I think she added it just to go against me ordering for her.

When the server is gone, notepad tucked into her black half-apron, Nadia leans forward. "Why did you order for me? How did you know I like chicken parm?"

"I—" I swallow. I have no clue how to answer.

"Is that coincidence too?" She scratches at the table with a fingernail, following the deep, aged grooves of the grain. "Sometimes it seems like you just *know* things about me, Nathan. It's weird."

"I'm sorry," I say. "I overstepped."

"It's just...I *love* chicken parmesan." She laughs, a light tinkle. "Like, weirdly *love*. You don't even know how many times I've tried to make it for myself, and it's never quite right. If I get one thing right, another is off."

Almost verbatim from the book.

"A good guess," I say, but my voice is weak, low, rough.

"How do you *guess* that someone likes chicken parm?"

"You like cheese, and it's the cheesiest thing on the menu." True.

She fingers the petals of the lavender daisy. "This flower, too. My favorite kind of flower. They're always such different, beautiful colors. I've wanted for years to uproot the beds in front of my house and replant it with all different colors of Gerberas, but I've never gotten around to it."

"I had nothing to do with the flower," I say, trying to make it sound like a joke. "That *is* a coincidence."

She sits back, sighing. "You've never been here before?"

I shake my head. "Nope. First time. Heard about it in town." Also true—several people in town recommended it as a point of local pride.

"It's lovely. Very...intimate." She's not sure if she meant that as a positive.

There's a Sinatra song playing. "My Funny Valentine."

Her nose wrinkles. "I know his voice is super amazing, and I always *want* to like him, but for some reason Frank Sinatra always sounds smarmy to me."

You really knew her, didn't you, Adrian?

"Smarmy, huh?"

"Yeah, like he's just absolutely *sure* he can charm the pants off you by singing a couple lines."

"I can see what you mean. Never thought about it that way, but now you say it, I can hear it."

The song ends, and there's a silence in the restaurant, the kind of unusual hush when it's just the ambient noise of quiet conversation and silverware clinking and clattering, when the music has stopped unexpectedly. I didn't even notice it, but there's a big black grand piano in the front corner, opposite the entrance to the kitchen, and there's tall silver candlesticks with white candles on the closed lid, yellow flames flickering. A middle-aged man sits down on the bench, wearing a trim gray pinstripe suit, no tie, collar unbuttoned. There's no sheet music. He just sits there a moment, head cocked to one side, as if listening to the piano, or to music in the air only he can hear. And then a gentle tinkle rises, his right hand tickling the ivory keys. It's a light, merry little tune, almost an accidental ditty. He's just playing around. Teasing the music to life, within himself, within the piano. Gradually, his other hand joins, and the melody becomes more complex, an improvisational masterwork that ranges from light and joyous to deep and thoughtful.

"He's really good," Nadia says. "My friend from college, Kyle, is a pianist. He was offered a scholarship to some fancy East Coast conservatory, but he turned it down to study sociology at UNC, mainly so he could be with Tanner. There was an old upright in the lounge of my dorm, and we'd hang out there and do homework, and he'd always be at that out-of-tune piano, playing these wildly difficult jazz pieces, just half-assing them while talking to us, this improvisational stuff only a small handful of people in the world can play."

"He didn't do anything with it?" I ask.

"What, with piano?" She shrugs. "I don't think so. He graduated with a degree in sociology and he and Tanner moved to LA. I think he just loved playing. He probably found a little jazz bar to play in, something like that." Her eyes flick over me. "I have a question. You don't have to answer it."

I nod. "Okay."

"It sounds like you had a complicated relationship with your dad. Like, you lived out in the wilderness and didn't go to school. Basically, you didn't have a childhood. And I can see how you might end up feeling a little bitter about that. But yet, you said you learned to play the guitar to connect with him."

I sit back, sigh. "Yeah, you had it right—it's complicated. I don't know if bitter is the right word. He was a combat veteran. He rarely talked about it, but he'd have these awful nightmares. He'd wake up screaming, thrashing, yelling names. Again, I don't know for sure, but I think he was a POW, too. It would explain why he couldn't be indoors for more than a few hours at a time. I think I understood this about him from a very young age, that he had…demons, I guess, that he was wrestling with. Not something for a kid to have to know about his dad, but…" I shrug. "So, no, I didn't have a normal childhood. I spent more time learning how to track a rabbit or a deer than doing algebra or chemistry, more time learning how to build a shelter with nothing but a hatchet than reading, like, Nathaniel Hawthorne."

"Wait, when you say track a rabbit…"

I laugh. "I mean, like, track it. Find its footprints and figure out where it went, where it is, and how to kill it."

"You can't track a rabbit. They barely even leave footprints."

"But they're predictable. You snare them, more than you'd actually hunt them."

"What does that mean?"

"Figure out where it's likely to routinely go, and set a trap. They walk through it, trigger the snare, and it catches them. The most effective ones break their necks pretty much instantly."

"Poor little rabbit."

"Yeah, but poor you when you haven't eaten meat in a week because the deer are hiding and a rabbit is all you can get."

"And that was your childhood."

"Yup."

"You seem so…normal."

I laugh. "Thanks, I think?" I sigh. "But as regards

my dad, and the guitar. I knew I had to go my own way. He expected it. He was just mainly trying to get me close to adulthood so I could figure my life out. So, as soon as I felt ready, I knew it was time to leave. My dad was difficult and weird. My childhood was difficult and weird. But my dad loved me. He just had his own way of showing it. So when I left, I missed him. I don't hate him. He didn't abuse me. He never yelled at me, never hit me. He taught me a lot. He taught me how to craft things from wood, how to take pride in what my hands can do. How to see what the wood wants to be and help it come out." I swallow hard; I haven't talked about Dad like this in a long, long time. "I missed him. I missed his voice, those songs he'd play. He always packed that guitar with us, wherever we went. We'd sit in the shelter by the fire and he'd play. Teach me a few chords, and we'd sing songs together, whatever he could figure out by ear. So yeah, once I was on my own, I really missed him, and picked up a cheap old guitar from a pawn shop and learned how to play all his favorite songs, because it made me feel…closer to him, I guess. Like maybe we were playing the same song at the same time. Him out in the woods somewhere, me in my shitty sub-level one-room roach- and rat-infested apartment."

She blinks hard. "That's really sweet, Nathan."

"You asked."

"Thank you for telling me."

Our food comes, and we take a few minutes in

silence to dig in. By unspoken agreement, we save the rest of the wine for after. The food is really, really good. The piano player is teasing out a romantic rendition of a pop song I recognize but can't name. The sun is setting, and it's probably the most gorgeous one yet.

We finish eating and I let her give me some folded twenties toward dinner, and I put it on my card. We take our wine out onto the dock and walk along—it extends around the shore quite a ways, and there are benches every few yards.

We find one not far from the restaurant, and we sit. Too far away from each other, at first. I slide closer; extend my arm across the back, my wineglass resting on my thigh. She sits upright, prim, not quite in the shelter of my arm, but not shying away either.

Several loons paddle in a gaggle, creating complicated V ripples in the sun-stained lake. Geese honk overhead.

There's nothing to say for a moment. We just sit, and somehow, inch by impossible inch, Nadia seems to slouch closer and closer to me. Until she's nearly against me. My heart is beating, hard. I want to curl my arm, let it drape around her. Maybe she feels it, maybe I let it slump lower a little, I don't know.

She looks at me, and in this light her eyes seem lit from within, star-shine jewels of iridescent green. Smoothed by olive skin, her high cheekbones now seem elegant and exotic. Her hair is the purply gloss black of a raven's wing in the summer sun, long and thick and shimmering, loose and twisted to fall over one shoulder. Her lips are plump, red, damp.

God, she's beautiful.

My eyes must show my thoughts.

"Nathan, I…" she murmurs, and her voice catches.

She shoots to her feet, pauses, staring at the last sip of wine in her glass. Shakes her head, and sets the glass on the arm of the bench.

"I…I have to go." She swallows, refusing to look at me. "I need to go. I'm sorry."

And she's gone, speed walking around the side of the building to her little red convertible, the black top forward and closed. She's in, the engine starting with a smooth purr, and then she's squealing out of the parking lot too fast. She had two glasses of wine spaced out over a meal and more than an hour, so that's not an issue.

I lean forward, elbows on my knees. Sigh harshly, head in my hands.

What went wrong?

Maybe, though, it's more of a question of what went right: too right, too soon.

That's a cruel joke, if that's what it is.

Thirty-Two

Learn me, Find You

I CAN'T BREATHE PROPERLY. MY LUNGS WON'T OPEN ALL the way. My hands shake, and I grip the steering wheel until my knuckles hurt.

I don't know how I get back to the cabin. I don't remember the drive, and I'm not sure how I even know the way back. But here I am, skidding to a stop beside the cabin. I'm on the porch before I realize I didn't even turn the car off. I go back, press the button to shut off the motor, close the car door, and barely make inside before I start sobbing. Not even sure why. I'm up against the door of the cabin, the wood pressing against my forehead. Hand on the knob. Shaking. Sobbing.

Why am I so upset?

It's too much to figure out.

I hear his truck, the rattle-thrum of the diesel engine coming to an idle and then silencing. Door opening, closing. I hear his boots clomp slowly up my steps, across the porch, stopping outside the door.

No, no, no. I can't deal with you, Nathan. It's too much. You're too much.

"Nadia."

He's on the other side of the door. I feel him. I can almost see him, hands braced high and wide, gripping the frame with his huge rough hands. Forehead to the wood, eyes closed.

"Nadia?"

"I can't."

"Can you let me in, Nadia?"

"I can't do this with you, Nathan."

"I can't *not* do this." His voice is so rough, a ragged rumble. Vulnerable.

"Nathan, god, please. Just leave me alone."

"I can't." I hear him inhale deeply, hold his breath, let it out in a rush. "You tried, remember?"

I don't know what to say.

I hear him humming something. A song. I don't recognize it, at first. And then the hum becomes singing: "…I knew you were trouble when you walked in…"

He's singing Taylor Swift. Starts with the chorus, his voice like stones tumbling in a well, and he sings it through, I don't know why. He knows the whole song, start to finish.

I could sing it with him, but I don't have a voice.

Once he's sung the song, there's silence, and it feels deafening. Hearing it sang *a cappella*, I realize despite the peppy melody, it's a sad, depressing song and I wonder why he sang that one. Stuck in his head, maybe. How does he even know that song?

He's right on the other side. I can hear him breathing.

"I can't walk away from this, Nadia. And I don't think you can either."

"Just...please, just give me tonight. I need to...to think."

"I'll bring coffee."

"Okay."

He's still there.

"Nathan?"

"Hmmm."

"I just don't know how to do this with you."

"I know."

"Just...just give me tonight to figure myself out, okay?"

"I'll be at your door in the morning. Six thirty."

"Thank you, Nathan."

Still silence.

Then I hear a scuff of a boot on wood. Hesitant, reluctant. The porch creaks, and I hear his heavy sigh. Slow tread, as if still hoping I'll change my mind at the last minute and open the door for him.

After a while, I hear his cabin door thunk closed.

I turn my back to the door, slide down to sit against it.

It was just too much. The candle, the flower on the table. My favorite color, lavender. The sunset on the lake, loons swimming, fluting to each other. My favorite food.

How did he know?

Something isn't adding up.

Or it's adding up too well. My favorite wine, my favorite flower, my favorite dinner.

The champagne thing.

So many things.

He just *knows* me.

He knows me too well.

It scares me. Because I feel comfortable with him.

That was a date. It was utterly romantic, perfect. Incredible. I've rarely felt so...seen. Known. So intimate. I felt myself falling.

I felt myself toppling toward him. If we'd finished the date, we'd have sat on the dock looking at the stars and I'd have kissed him.

Invited him in.

Kissed him by the fire.

Kissing is as far as my brain goes, as far as I can allow thoughts to progress, but the full reality is there under the surface.

It's happening. In some ways, it's already happened.

Love again, Nadia.

Tears trickle.

How can I, Adrian? You were my love. You were my present and my future, my past, my everything. You WERE. Now you're gone but my heart doesn't totally realize it. Can't quite accept it. I've learned to exist as a human without you by my side, but *living* again, without you?

To hold another's hand. To let him into my heart, into my world. To put my body at his mercy. How do I do that again?

I don't know what to do with myself. I'm not sleepy. I don't want to drink. Can't think clearly enough to read; I have no focus, no mental or emotional direction. I'm a ship without a keel or rudder, becalmed, just floating, spinning with the currents.

I never turned on a light, and I realize I'm sitting alone in the darkness, lost in my thoughts.

Wondering what would have happened if I'd stayed at the restaurant. If I'd opened the door for him.

Everything; nothing. The impossible—the inevitable?

I am drowning again. I was doing better, but one date, and I'm lost again. Did I really think by simply driving separately and paying for my own part of the meal that it would be less of a date? Less romantic, less intimate. Less meaningful.

I enjoyed it. It was beyond mere companionship, when I've been so lonely. Even with Nathan to talk to and hang out with, there's a loneliness in holding your heart aloof. In keeping people out. I've kept even Tess out, to a degree. Kept her from seeing how destroyed I am. She knew, but I wasn't showing her. With Nathan, I've kept the shell of ice around my secret heart, and that date melted it. That armor of uncaring cold melted in the candlelight and sunset warmth, in the glow of his smile and easy conversation, in the delicate complexity of good wine and the savory satisfaction of good food.

Now that secret, broken heart of mine is bare, unarmored, exposed. And I am absolutely terrified.

I make it to my bed, fall in fully clothed and lie there, unsleeping, staring at the ceiling for hours. Maybe I should just leave. Go home. But something in me shies away from that. I went a week not seeing Nathan and I honestly hated it. I kept the depth of feelings buried under the ice, but it was lonely and not as fun and I missed him.

Now that I've had that date with him, it'd be even worse. I miss him right now, I hate that I've hurt him, made him sad, made him feel rejected.

I could feel it on the other side of the door.

I feel it from here.

I have to talk to him.

I don't know what I'll say, but…I have to see him.

I'm out the door before I realize I'm even on my feet. The weather has turned—a strong wind blows, whipping my hair and bending the trees, stirring the lake into frothing waves. There's rain on the wind, drops here and there portending a downpour.

His lights are off, but I see a flicker of orange, smell smoke on the air; he's lit a fire in the fireplace.

I don't knock. I just open the door and walk in, like I have every right to, like he's expecting me. He's sitting on the floor in front of the fireplace, bare feet presented to the flames, wearing only his jeans. Bare chest, spackled with dark curly hairs, some silver here and there. Heavy chest muscles, heavy shoulders. Broad arms. Huge, leathery hands.

He has a book in his hands.

"Nadia," he murmurs. Stands up. "Hi."

I swallow. Not sure what I'm doing here. "Nathan, I…"

My eyes go to his hands. To the book held open by a big thumb. I can read the spine.

Redemption's Song.

By Adrian Bell.

I know every book he ever wrote, including the half-begun, abandoned projects, the deleted chapters, the partly finished short stories and unpublished novellas and experimental sci-fi outline. That is not one of his books.

Yet there it is.

In Nathan's hand.

"What is that?" I ask, my voice a hoarse whisper.

"Um…" He's flummoxed. "I, it's—" A sigh. "His last book."

"Why do you have it?"

"That's kind of hard to explain."

"Try."

"He…" Nathan trails off, licks his lips. "Shit."

"Nathan, why do you have a book written by my dead husband that I've never heard of?"

"This is the only copy." He slips a receipt out from between the last two pages, sticks it in his place and closes the book. Crosses the floor between us in a few long strides. "Here."

He hands it to me. Turns away, goes back to the fireplace and grips the mantle as if it's all that's holding him upright. The fire plays on his bare chest. I never really realized exactly how big Nathan is until now. Easily twice my size, and then some. So much power in him, but he's so gentle.

Right now, all that power seems taut, the wires pulled tight. As if he's barely containing everything boiling inside.

I hold the book in my hands. The cover is something I can tell he did himself, with public domain images and some design software. It's matte, and the colors are all pastels, an out-of-focus flower made into abstract art. Just something to use on the cover, since no one but Nathan, apparently, would ever see it. The title on top in an all-caps script, his name on the bottom in a sans serif font. I open the cover, and there are two individually folded packets of paper, letters, from a very familiar yellow legal pad.

"Might as well read those too," he mutters. "Get it all out there." A sigh. "Read the longer one first."

Nathan,

Out of the blue, I know. On purpose.

You're still mourning Lisa. I could see it on you, hear it in your voice, when we sat down to drinks that last time. And yeah, buddy, I knew then that I was dying. I was in denial still, to a point, but I knew. I was picking your brain, that day. I hope I didn't cause you pain with my questions, but I needed to hear the answers from someone who knew.

I was coming to grips with understanding that I'd be leaving Nadia behind. How could I prepare her for it? What would it be like, for her, after I'm gone? Will she be okay?

The letter blurs as tears haze my vision. I blink them away, try to settle my nerves. "You knew him."

"Yeah."

"How?" I'm still processing, so I'm numb, yet.

"I was set construction foreman for *Love, Me.* We would meet downtown for drinks now and then. Talk westerns and whiskey, mainly."

I sniffle a laugh. "He loved old Western movies. *Rooster Cogburn, The Good, the Bad, and the Ugly.*"

"Yeah." A sigh from him. "I wasn't a secret best friend or anything. We weren't even really drinking buddies. Friends, that's all. We'd get together once in a while, in the years since the movie, drink some whiskey and talk some shit."

I nod. Go back to the letter.

Read it through, make a sound that's half sob, half laugh at the signature: The Ghost of Adrian Bell. What an asshole. There's a single slip of a note, explaining the cabin, and a lockbox in town.

"He bought both cabins and gave one to you, one to me."

He nods, facing the fire, nods as if his head is too heavy for his neck.

"And I assume the other letter and the book were in the lockbox?"

"Yeah."

I read the second letter.

I wrote it for you. And for Nadia...it's about moving on. About finding love after loss...

You're here for her.

Don't show it to her. Not yet. She's not ready.

I'm not crying, but my eyes sting, feel damp and salty. My throat burns, feels tight, constricted. I float across the floor to the large easy chair by the fire, sit, and start reading on page one.

Nathan just stands by the fire, staring into the flames. Waiting.

By the end of the first chapter, I understand. "He set us up."

Nathan just nods heavily again.

"You knew."

Another nod.

"Why didn't you *tell* me?" My voice is tight, hard, sharp.

He turns, a hurt, confused, angry frown on his face. "What was I supposed to say? When am I supposed to bring that information out, Nadia? First day we meet, I say, 'oh, by the way, I knew your dead husband. He gave me a secret book about you, and he wants us to...'" he trails off, shaking his head.

"Wants us to fall for each other," I finish for him. "But all this time, he was feeding you information about me, in this." I shake the book. "It explains so much. How you knew about Josh wine, and my thing for champagne, and chicken parmesan, and...how I can't make my own fucking coffee. He's showing you how to make me fall for you." I stand up, and I don't know if I'm more angry or confused. "And you know the craziest fucking part? It was totally working."

I walk out. Leave his door open, and the book upside down on the chair, still open.

It's drizzling. I don't care. I'm heading for my cabin, and then Nathan is in front of me.

"Nadia, wait." His hands are on my arms, gentle but *so* strong. "Please, wait."

"Is this part in the book, Nathan?" I stare up at him; raindrops freckle his cheeks, bead in his eyelashes, on his beard. "Is this part of the...the script?"

"No." He sighs. "We're off-book, now, as they say in show business."

"I think that means something different. Like, you've memorized your lines to the point that you can extemporize, improvise, just play the role without having to think about the lines you're supposed to say."

"Right."

"So are we off-book?" I pull out of his hands. "What's my line, here, Nathan?"

"I don't know. It wasn't supposed to go this way."

"How was it supposed to go? I fall for you, we make love by the firelight, and maybe in a few years you tell me the truth? That my dead husband gave you pointers from beyond the grave on how to woo me? Or were you not going to tell me? Were you just going to keep that little tidbit to yourself?"

"I don't know, Nadia. I don't fucking *know*. I wanted to tell you. I didn't know how, or when. When was it right? When was it going to...god, I don't know. When was it going to go any different than this?" He turns in a circle, wipes his wet face with a palm, and then returns to towering over me, turmoil written in the lines on his face. "I didn't ask for this, Nadia. I was doing just fine on my own."

"Oh really? Were you? I read the letter he wrote you, and he makes it sound like you weren't."

It's raining harder, now. "Maybe not. I was exactly where you are, or were when you first got here. I'd quit sleeping except for a few hours. I was drinking all the time and barely eating. I'd take job after job, anything to keep working, to keep myself out of the house. I dropped to nearly one-sixty, and I'm sitting at two-thirty right now. Maybe less since I'm eating more healthily than I was before I came here."

He stares at me, his eyes hooded, his emotions so mixed up it's hard to read them all. "I got past that to a degree, on my own, but...I was no more over her or past my grief or okay than you. And she died almost four years ago. My point is, I had no idea he was going to do this. No clue. I had no idea how anything was going to work. What he wanted. Why do this? What did he expect? I was just fumbling my way through, Nadia. Everything I've said is the real, raw, God's honest truth. Everything was legit, and heartfelt."

I shake my head. "Is that supposed to make me feel better?" I choke on my own rush of words. "That book...why didn't he write it for *me*? Why did *you* get his last book? Why couldn't he send me out here to heal, but alone? Why did he think he had to set me up? Feeding a perfect stranger intimate details about who I am? What the fuck am I supposed to do with this, Nathan?"

"Knowing things on paper doesn't make the discovery of them through experience any less real." He reaches for me, but I dance out of reach. "I'm not okay with this either. It's scary and hard. I don't know what I'm doing. I'm feeling things I don't understand, and I don't know what to do with it."

"You're *feeling* things, are you?" I sound as bitter as I feel.

He flinches. "Hey, that's not fair." He thumps his chest. "Look me in the eyes and tell me you think I've faked anything."

"I didn't mean it like that."

"Then how did you mean it? You think, what? That I'm only in this to...get something out of you? Get in your pants? You can't honestly tell me you think that either."

I can't, not on either score.

I close my eyes. Just breathe. But it doesn't help. It's all wrong. I was falling for him—exactly as Adrian planned.

I feel so betrayed—but more by Adrian than by Nathan. And that sucks, because I can't yell at Adrian, I can't storm out on him.

I push past Nathan, inside my cabin. Grab my purse and head for my car.

"Where are you going?" Nathan asks, following me.

I get behind the wheel. Close the door, nearly

catching his fingers in the process. He stands beside the car, and now it's pouring. He's soaked. His hair is pasted to his head. He seems heedless of it.

"I can't let you go, Nadia."

I put my finger on the start button. But I can't push it.

My hand shakes; I want to drive away. I want to forget him. Forget these weeks at the cabin. How long have I been here? Two months? I've lost track, if I was ever keeping track. But I can't. I can't start the car. I can't drive away.

"Don't go, Nadia." His big hand on the window, fingers splayed. "It was all real. All me."

"I know." I choke out the words. "It feels like a betrayal, though."

"I'm sorry. I should have told you, I just…I didn't know how."

I look up and out the window at him. The wind is blowing the rain in sideways sheets, and he stands with feet braced wide against it, oblivious. Shirtless and enormous, all craggy rough features and deep dark eyes. His hand drops from the window, and now he sways, like a punch-drunk fighter.

"Don't go," he says again.

My finger curls into my palm, away from the start button. My hand rests on my knee. I can't.

I keep seeing him—us—at the restaurant, on the bench. His bulk beside me was a bulwark against the world, against my own grief. I was just sitting there, with him. Close. His arm around me, almost intimate, almost holding me. And for a moment, I'd felt...okay.

With him.

And that was what made me panic. That feeling of being okay. It felt like I was betraying Adrian by not clutching my grief to my chest and hoarding it and stockpiling it and counting it like Scrooge McDuck with his vault of gold coins. I was swimming in my grief, like a shark through waters. Gathering it and pouring it over myself. Pain, pain, pain, hard and jagged—armfuls of shale, clattering as I gathered and flung the pieces over my head like mourning ashes.

I pull the lever and push at the door. He tugs it open and reaches in, takes my hand. Folds my hand into his—my hand is a fragile dove held in the cage of his fingers. Pulls me to my feet. Holds my hand in his against his chest. Rain is cold, driving in sharp splinters on my scalp. The wind is aggressive and hungry, a bully, shoving at me. He turns us, and now the wind is at his back and I'm sheltered in the lee of his body.

"I didn't fall for the Nadia version of you in the book." His forefinger touches my cheekbone, ginger, tentative; he traces across my temple, tucking a wet tendril of hair behind my ear. "I fell for *you*. For the you I've gotten to know over coffee in the morning. Over sunsets on the lake. That day we drank champagne and beer and talked all day and you fell asleep beside me."

I swallow hard. Cold raindrops mingle on my cheek with hot tears. "You don't know me. You know the me he told you about in the book."

"You like your bacon crispy, almost burnt. That's not in there. You always thought you liked your coffee black and sweet, but you're starting to prefer it just plain black. You like reading biographies. You miss your father and you're angry at him for abandoning you when you needed him most, and you feel guilty for feeling that way because he didn't really abandon you. And Adrian dying only reinforces that. You're angry at the world for taking the men you love away from you. You feel safe with me, and that's a big deal because you weren't sure you'd survive after he died, or if you even wanted to. You've never said it in so many words, but I think you were suicidal, at some point. I know I was. There was no one around to care if I lived or died, and it felt like it'd be easier and simpler to just…die. But something always stopped me. I don't know what. And I think you know exactly how that feels. And none of that is in the book."

It's all tears, now, and we're both so wet we might as well have just jumped in the lake.

"My mom gave up," I whisper. I don't know if he can even hear me over the wind and rain. "After Dad's heart attack. She tried. But…she just kind of wasted away. It felt like losing her too, only slower."

"Is she still alive?"

"Sort of." I close my eyes. "She had a stroke several years ago. She's paralyzed on one side, lost a lot of cognitive function. She doesn't know me, can't talk, just sits staring out the window, missing Dad." I ache. "I visit her, and she just sits there, doesn't even seem like she sees me. I feel like a shitty person and a terrible daughter, but I don't visit her very often. It hurts, and she's…"

"You're alone."

That breaks me. I sob, shake, and the only thing I can do is nod and let my forehead fall against his chest. Despite the ragged sheets of wind and sharp little pellets of rain, he's warm, billowing heat, as if he has a furnace inside.

"I'm so lonely," I whisper. His chest hair is tickly and soft against my cheek. His hand settles hesitantly on my back where my shoulder blades meet. "I have Tess, my best friend. I'm grateful for her. So grateful. She's done *everything* for me. I'd be dead, literally, if not for her. But…"

"It's not the same."

"He wasn't just my husband, he was my best friend and…he…he knew me inside out. He knew everything. He *saw* me, all of me, all there is. And now he's gone and everyone is gone and I'm so fucking *lonely*."

My other hand lifts, curls to nestle against his hot hard chest, and then claws in desperately, the vicious abandon of sorrow and grief and confusion and hurt and betrayal and need and desire and relief and...love, all coiling and braiding, boiling and twining, exploding and bursting and raging.

Nathan bends and scoops me up, cradles me against him with his arm under my knees and the other around my shoulders, and he carries me to his cabin and kicks closed the door—open all this time. He settles on the floor with his back to the easy chair, close to the fire. Reaches out with one long arm and snags a blanket off the couch, wraps it around his shoulders clutching the edges like a cape or cloak and closes his arms around me and now the fire beats in hot waves and his body heat and the blanket all conspire to warm me, and it's not until I feel warmth that I realize how cold I was, how chilled to the bone.

My hair is wet, in draggled limp chunks and curls. Steam rises off me, off of his jeans. I'm curled on his lap, resting against his chest.

"It's not fair that I don't have a book on you," I murmur.

"The book on me is...me. Ask me anything."

I shake my head. I can't think of anything to ask. And then something occurs to me. "Why do you even like me? I must be miserable company."

A gentle laugh, a shake and a huff. "Because I'm just as miserable company. We get each other. We don't have to pretend."

I tilt my head to look up at him. "Why did he pick you?"

He exhales slowly, through his teeth. "I can only guess."

"Try to guess, then."

"Why don't you try to guess why me? You know him better than I do."

"You said it, I think—because you know what it's like to be where I am. You're the only person who could understand well enough to be around me in a way that would ease me out of my shell." I feel the rightness of it as I say it; I rest my head against his chest again, close my eyes and let my thoughts flow. "And…I think in some ways, because you're nothing like him."

He nods. "Yeah, I can see that."

"I mean, in a lot of ways, you're total opposites. It makes it easier to…I don't know—to be around you, because nothing about you reminds me of him or makes me think of him. You're totally you."

"I didn't like feeling like I was lying to you, Nadia. So many times I'd sit there, those silences we have sometimes, and I'd be trying to figure out how to tell you, and it always just sounded…I don't know, crazy. Like, unless I showed you everything, would you even have believed me? And…he *told* me not to tell you. Or, not to show you the book because he felt like you weren't ready yet, but…I guess that seems like the same thing. Amounts to it, in my mind."

"I'm angry at him," I say. "For so much."

"Tell me."

"For leaving me. He promised me he would never leave. Before I knew he was sick, I knew something was wrong, and he promised me he wouldn't leave. And he left. He left me. He *left* me. And now this. Setting me up with you, giving *you* the book, when I would have killed for another word from him, for anything from him. I'm mad at him for trying to force me to move on. He sent me here, let me wallow in my grief for a whole year and then sent me here. And I thought it was a coincidence you were here, but it was *him* all along. He schemed this whole thing. To make me move on."

"And you don't want to move on."

I shake my head. "No, I don't." I feel my wet dress sticking to my chest and thighs. "Moving on feels like betraying him. And I guess part of me now is thinking, like, he did this on purpose, because he knew me so fucking well that he'd have known I would be angry at his meddling in my life even after he's dead, and he'd know that that might push me away from him. From the not wanting to move on." I laugh bitterly. "It's so complicated."

"But it's not all that complicated, if you boil it all down." He shrugs.

"Boil it down for me, then."

He touches my chin, and I look up at him.

"You're left with a few simple things. One, you'll never forget him. You can't and won't ever replace him, who he is to you, what he meant to you, what you had together. Two, he's gone. The brutal truth is, he's dead and you're alive. The memory of him isn't *him*, and I know you know that on a brain level, but on a more visceral level, you're not there yet. You still think you can hold on to him by refusing to let go. Three, you're young still, and you have a long life ahead of you to fill however you want. He wanted you to fill your life with happiness. I'm guessing he wrote you a letter too. No, I don't want to read it— it's yours. But I can guess that he said something along those lines. Because he did know you, and he knew you'd resist."

"That feels like more than three things."

"More simply put, then: you'll never totally forget him or replace him, you can't and won't and shouldn't. He's dead, and nothing is going to change that. You have a life to live, and only you can choose what to do with it."

"Easy, right?" Sarcasm drips from the two little words.

"No." No elaboration, just the answer, because we both get it.

Silence. I look up at him, and his eyes drill into me. Search me. He's unrushed. Patient. Still and gentle and strong.

"What do you want?" I whisper it to him. "With me, I mean."

"More." Soft, and his usually rough voice is almost smooth, but that's just because he's nearly whispering. He's admitting something at great cost: risk, vulnerability. I could and might reject him—again.

The fire crackles, the only sound. Except my hammering heart.

His hand cradles my face, his palm like sandpaper and leather. He's waiting. For me to get up, to tell him again that I can't, that I don't know, but I do know and something inside me, a tender just-germinated seed of something tiny knows that I *can*. And that I want to.

I'm warm, wrapped in the blanket and in his arms.

I shift to sit more upright, so my face is closer to his. Look at him, and tell him yes with my eyes even though my voice is caught in the hammering trap of my throat. My hands rest on his chest.

He angles his head to one side. Closes in. "I'm gonna kiss you, Nadia."

And then he does.

It's soft and slow. The beard is unfamiliar and ticklish, brushing rough against my upper lip and somehow soft at the same time, and his lips are warm and dry, and they feel cracked against mine and taste of rainwater. It is an unhurried first kiss. Gentle and questing at first, waiting for the pull-away. But it doesn't come because I don't want to pull away. I'm okay, here, in his arms, in the shelter of the blanket and his body and the cabin and the forest and the weeks and months of time to ache and hurt and question and rage.

It's all right to kiss Nathan.

I'm giving myself permission.

He pulls away, first. Only a little. Enough for his lips to move, a barely vocalized question, his eyes too close to mine so they seem more like one cyclopean eye. "Okay?"

I nod. My fingers trail up from his chest to his shoulder, feeling the thick hard layer of muscle over dense bone, and then further up the side of his neck, and I momentarily feel his pulse drumming fast under my fingertips—he's nervous too—and then I tangle my fingers in his beard.

"Kiss me again," I whisper.

He shakes his head. Brushes at my damp hair. "Nope."

I frown, pull away further. "No?"

A smirk, small and sly. "*You* kiss *me*."

I weave my fingers into his beard; pull him back to my lips. "Fine."

And now I kiss him, I lift up and I curl my other hand around the back of his head in the soft feathery damp weight of his hair and I let feelings for him well up inside me. Let them rise. Let them exist. They've been buried inside, deep down, locked in a cupboard. Growing, until the hinges were creaking and fit to burst.

He's good.

He's kind.

He's patient.

He understands my bad days, my ugly moods, my morose silences, my simmering anger. He doesn't judge me for them or let them hurt him because they're not about him.

He's handsome.

He has gentle, creative hands that can tease artful life out of dead wood.

I kiss him, slowly, and let the things I feel escape, all of their complicated whirring wings like a twisting murmuration of starlings whispering and fluttering out of their too-small cupboard and let them escape and let their song begin to rise.

And I think of the title of Adrian's last book, the one he didn't give to me: *Redemption's Song*.

I get it, Adrian. I hear your song.

I'll always love Adrian. I won't forget him. I'll always have days where I miss him. I'll hear a song and think of him. I'll pass by a restaurant downtown where we had dinner after a movie, and I'll see his ghost and mine walking hand in hand in the sweltering Atlanta evening and for moment I know I'll almost hear his voice telling me how he'd rewrite the movie, which is why he usually only read nonfiction in his spare time.

But those moments will pass.

He'll still be gone, and I'll still be here, alive, on

earth, with a future I still have to fill with memories, with life. I can't live in the past: he's not there any more than he's here. I'll have the memories, the time with him. His love.

He's loving me from beyond the grave.

He was telling me how much he loved me—he has been, through this whole thing. The cabin is his love letter to me. Each item was his voice and his hands, caressing me. Reminding me that he loved me that I was his and he was mine and he knows me. But the cabin was also him telling me that I still have to remember to live.

That I have to go on without him.

That I *can* go on without him.

He chose Nathan for me. God, only Adrian could do that. Would do that.

"Lost you," Nathan murmurs, and I realize I've pulled away.

"I'm sorry."

"Don't be sorry. You can share it, if you want."

I shake my head. Smile at him. "No, I was just… talking to him." I sigh. "Hearing him. Hearing what he's been saying all this time, and finally understanding it."

He lets me sink back down and cradles me against his chest again. Doesn't pressure me to talk. Doesn't try to get me to kiss him again.

"You're too patient," I say.

"This is what we make of it. There's no rush for anything."

"So if I say I'm probably going to have to keep taking it slow…?"

"Didn't I already tell you no apologizing or explaining is necessary?"

"Sometimes it is, though." I take his hand where it rests heavily on my shoulders, and press mine to it, palm to palm, fingers to fingers. "I still don't know how we do this. What it looks like. I'm still scared. But I want to try."

He curls his fingers between mine. Brushes a thumb over my lips. "One step at a time." He gently pinches my chin, tipping my lips to his, kisses me again, lightly, quickly. "It's okay to be scared."

"Are you?"

"Hell yeah." He rests his forehead on mine. "I've got you, Nadia."

It's a comfort, hearing him say that.

I kiss him again, testing the feel of it, the taste of him. It's as natural and easy as breathing, but still somehow unfamiliar. His lips are his own, unique and different and I have no memories of the feel and taste of his mouth. His hands on my shoulders and arms and back and cheek are new, different, rough, strong, intentionally gentle. His body and bulk are big, and that's foreign, too. It's all new. I have to learn him. I have to let him learn me.

The fire crackles, and its light is dull and orange and casts long shadows on the ceiling and walls.

I kiss him, and then we pull away and just sit together and breathe. And then he kisses me, and this time I let desire pull at me a little.

I twist in place, throw my leg over his hips and sit straddling him, facing him, and he lets the blanket drop and his bare broad anvil-hard chest is under my hands and his dinner-plate palms and thick strong fingers toy with my hair and trace the arch of my cheekbones and the curve of my spine, and I feel my shirt-dress riding up my thighs and the belt digging into my diaphragm and the undersides of my breasts.

I'm fully in my body. A weird thing to feel, as if I'm reinhabiting myself, reanimating my skin and muscles and nerve endings and hormones, as if until now I was a fading spark of consciousness riding along in a clockwork robot of me.

I feel his lips on mine, feel his tongue beginning to think about questing out, and I meet him halfway, and now his tongue and mine tangle, dance. This kiss isn't so slow, isn't so soft. His hands span my back, low.

I pull away, breathing hard. "Wow. That was…"

"Intense?"

"Yeah." I drape against him, press my nose into his neck and breathe, wrap my arms around him; I'm trying these things on to see how they feel, and I like them. "I'm the one who said I had to take it slow, but that didn't feel slow to me."

"It can be what we want it to be."

"Could we just…kiss? For now?"

He stands up with me, effortlessly, and I have to cling with arms and legs as he moves to the couch. Leans back against it, still holding me. "The floor was hurting my butt." He grins. "Now we can just kiss as long as you want."

He knows what I'm asking, and doesn't need me to ask it any more explicitly. I don't trust myself, given the sudden rush of heat within me, the way I delved into the expanses of his kiss.

Safeguard me, I'm asking.

I will, he's answering.

Thirty-Three

If I Kiss You

TAKING IT SLOW MEANS KISSING ON THE COUCH BY firelight until dawn. Ignore the ache of needing and wanting more burning inside, because what I want and what I need are not the same thing. Taking it slow means falling asleep on the couch, fully clothed. Waking up and having coffee, this time inside.

It means days like that, coffee and breakfast together, sometimes in my cabin, sometimes in hers. Talking all night, kissing like teenagers who've just discovered the art. But nothing more. Holding hands, touching faces. Learning lines and curves, learning bodies. Learning where the edge is, that line where the gunpowder of desire meets the spark of need. Skirting it.

Some nights, we sit up in the loft of her cabin, on the beanbag chair, my knees splayed wide with her back nestled to my front. Both of us reading, sometimes sharing thoughts, mostly not.

There's as much silence as there is talk.

Taking it slow means the days grow shorter and the winds off the lake colder, and the pine trees sway and the lake produces wavelets and now making a fire in the evening is a necessity, because there's no other heat source for these cabins. Taking it slow means kissing and kissing, knowing at some point we'll cross into more, but still content to explore this space first.

It's growing at ease with each other.

We become more and more comfortable in her cabin than mine. I sleep on the couch, sometimes.

We have not ventured into her bedroom.

I shower at my place, she at hers.

I've seen no more of her body than when I first met her.

She has days where she needs space, and I go fishing or work on carving in my cabin. Sometimes I'm the one who needs that space, and she gives it to me. And we understand.

Is it weeks? Months? I don't know. Time just sort of slips by, unnoticed, here at these cabins on the lake.

I never finished Adrian's book: we're off-book, now. I will, at some point. Now, I'm following the script as we write it.

It's fully fall, and being outside means thick sweaters and wool socks. It's been a day where Nadia needs space, and I can tell this time it's not because she's missing him, but because she's thinking. It's the gloaming, silvery-purple autumn evening.

I find her on the dock; I can almost feel her out here, waiting to talk to me.

I sit in the chair beside hers. Wait for her.

"It's like you knew I was going to come looking for you," she says.

"I did."

"Are you getting impatient?" she asks, eventually.

"With what?"

"Me. Us." She turns in her chair to look at me. "Holding back."

"I'm not holding back."

"Nathan." Her eyes are scolding, but her smile is understanding. "The truth, please, always."

I sigh, think. "It's not that I'm holding back. We're taking our time exploring what it means for us to...be together. And I'm okay with that." I reach out and take her hand. "Yeah, I'm a man, with a man's desires and needs, and yeah, it's been a hell of a long time. But I'll wait. And I'm not waiting for *you*, I'm waiting for *us*."

She rubs one of my knuckles with her thumb. "Thank you for being so patient. For understanding."

"It's as much for me as it is you, Nadia. I want this between us to be...right, and good. I'm not ready to rush into anything either. It's new, for both of us."

"But you're still taking your cues from me as to... how far things go."

"Yeah." I shrug. "I've had more time, I guess. I know I'm as ready as I can be to be intimate with someone again. It's a big step, and it's not something I take lightly. I'm not gonna rush into that just because my dumb growly male hormones are being pushy. It means more to me than just something physical."

"You are holding back what your dumb growly male hormones want, then."

"Of course."

She stands up, still holding my hand. "Let's go in. I'm hungry." On the way up the steps to her cabin, she glances up at me. "Nathan?"

I pause with my hand on the doorknob. "Yeah."

"You're spinning it to be about you, but really, it's for me."

"Yeah, maybe a little."

"Or a lot." She lifts up and kisses me, a slant-wise kiss across my lips. "And I just wanted to say thank you." She touches my lips. "Don't say anything else. I just want you to know that I see it, and I'm thankful."

We go in, and we have a quiet dinner which we make together, something neither of us has ever done before. There's burgers fried in a cast iron skillet, puffy whole grain buns, a tossed salad, a bottle of wine.

We're on the couch, and lately, this is where we kiss, and then eventually she goes to bed and I sleep here, on the couch. Better than alone, in my cabin, far away from her. And I think she likes having me near. It's a nice couch, comfortable. But I think I've also been sensing her coming to a shift.

She has something on her mind, something she's still chewing on, and I wait her out.

"So…" she trails off, starts again. "I've tried to come up with the best way to say this, but can't make it sound any better. So here goes."

I touch her cheek with my thumb. "Whatever it is, just say it."

"I'm ready for the next step, but I want you to lead us there. I know you've been waiting for me, and like you said earlier, I think I'm as ready as I can be."

"There's no rush, Nadia."

"I know." She smiles, takes my hand. "I'm not rushing. I don't feel rushed. I feel ready, even though I know some part of me will never quite be all the way ready. And I want more. I'm getting impatient with just kissing you." Another thoughtful pause. "You make me feel beautiful, and seen, and appreciated, and safe. And I want the next step."

"What did you mean by wanting me to lead us there? I mean, I guess I know what you mean, but… explain it anyway."

A shrug. "Just…stop holding back your dumb growly male hormones."

I nod. "I can do that."

We just sit beside each other for a while. She's waiting for me, now.

I think she was expecting me to turn half feral or something. Instead, I cup her face and I kiss her. I leave it slow, like the first kiss. Gentle. Exploring her mouth, stoking her desire.

Her hand slides up around my neck and she turns toward me, I bury my hand in her hair. Still familiar territory. Nadia slides her thigh over my legs and straddles me, and except that once, that first kiss, she's never done that. I like her weight on me, her softness against me, in my arms. I cradle her face in both hands and hold her close, kiss her until we're breathless, and then we trade breaths and breathe each other.

Now, I let myself explore. I let the ravening beast I've kept so tightly chained inside me off the leash, a little. Let my hands drift down her arms, to her hips. She lifts, sitting on her knees, and her hands are in my hair and knotted, tugging, and *god* I like that.

I don't anticipate anything she does, because I've never done any of this with her, and not with anyone in, now, over four years. The anniversary came and went, and that was one of my quiet, solitary days out on the fishing boat, catching nothing but a day of memory and mourning, and it still hurt as it always will, but there was more to life now and it was okay to put it away again, to look to shore and see Nadia standing on the dock, waiting as I row in.

I let my hands fill themselves with her curves, coursing over the bell of her hips and pausing there, and then rounding over the swell of her backside and she moans as I clutch her butt, and her hands dig into my shoulders.

She settles to sit on me. Pulls away enough to meet my eyes. "This feels good."

"Yeah, it does." I hold her gaze. "More?"

She unbuttons the four buttons of my wool sweater. "Yes." A pause, her fingers going into the open V, touching my chest over the thin cotton of my plain white T-shirt. "More, please."

I stand up, and her legs latch around my waist, and I walk with her to her bedroom. Stop just inside, assessing her reaction. Her reaction is to reach over my shoulder and swing the door shut behind us.

Then, she slides down to stand in front of me. Pushes up the hem of my sweater, lifts up on her toes to pull it off over my head and my arms, which I raise for her. She takes my shirt with it, and I think she likes me in nothing but my jeans.

She's wearing a cashmere sweater the same lavender as the daisy on the table at our first and only date. Under it, light wash blue jeans, low-ankle black boots. She's watching me, waiting for me again.

"Quid pro quo," she whispers.

I curl my fingers in the hem of her sweater, and she lifts her arms. I peel it off her, and the cashmere is downy, impossibly soft. She's wearing only a black bra underneath. She spills out over the top of the lacy cups. I swallow hard at the vision of her.

"You're so beautiful, Nadia," I murmur.

Her smile is giddy, pleased. Her hands roam my bare chest.

I lean down to kiss her, but she touches my lips with one finger, stopping me. "Not yet. I like this step of the process. If I kiss you, I'll close my eyes, and I might miss something. I don't want to miss anything."

I sing a few bars of "I Don't Want to Miss a Thing" by Aerosmith, and she smiles, laughs. "I love how you always have a song for the moment." She said it, and we both realize it. Her eyes are wide, searching. "I don't take it back."

"Good. I wouldn't want you to."

She bites her lower lip. "Nathan?"

"Yeah."

"Kiss me after all?" she breathes. "I'm nervous to go any further, but I want to. Kissing you makes me feel bold."

I put my hands on her lower back, warm flesh under my eager palms, and she makes a sound in her throat as my lips meet hers and my hands caress her lower back, over her bra strap and across her shoulders. Her breasts press soft against my chest, and I feel everything inside me rising, expanding, wanting, needing.

She feels it, the hardness of my need standing rigid between our bodies, and she murmurs again, pressing more closely to me. Hips to hips. Chest to chest.

I feather my hands in her hair and brush it back, and I kiss her more deeply, and I hold her back in my hands, and then I grip the straps of bra in my fingers, pause for her to stop me. She doesn't; she kisses me harder and creates space between our bodies for her hands. I feel my heart crashing in my chest like I've sprinted a mile. I unhook the clasps, and she breaks the kiss, and I scrape the bra down her arms. She lets it fall to the floor between us.

Reaching for me, for my jeans, she's got her eyes dropped, on me, but also out of nerves.

I catch her hand. "Nadia, wait." I let her go. "I want to look at you."

She stands up straight, but crosses her arms over her chest. "Nathan…"

I pull gently at her hands. "Don't." I give her my eyes. "You're so beautiful, Nadia. Please, let me see you."

She lowers her arms, and her eyes fix on mine, nerves and need singing contrasting songs in her gaze.

I devour her body with my eyes. Lush, firm, full breasts. Small areolae, plump nipples standing on end. She stands boldly, now, seeing the adoration and the desire in my eyes, and it strengthens her.

"So fucking beautiful," I murmur.

I run my palm up her stomach, pause at her diaphragm—I can feel her heart slamming. I cup her breast, and her eyes slide closed soaking up the sensation of being touched. Of having her body enjoyed, treasured. I take my time, and she lets me. Cup and caress, pinch and rub. And then she gasps, once, sharply, as I roll her nipple in my fingers, and she dances backward. A smile grows on her face, a sharp, hungry smile, a needful, eager smile. She stands just out of reach, chin lifted, eyes on me, on the evidence of my desire for her bulging against my zipper. She unbuttons her jeans, lowers the zipper. Hesitates, and then inhales and holds her breath and locks her lower lip in her teeth, eyes wide and on mine, now. She lowers her jeans past her hips, but they catch at her thighs, and she does a little shimmy to loosen them past her thighs, and the shimmy sends her breasts shaking and swaying in a way that is nearly my undoing. I groan, and my hands ache to be filled with the softness of her curves.

Now she's in a pair of underwear, black lace to match the bra. She swallows hard. I reach for her again, but she shakes her head. "Wait. Not yet."

"Nadia…"

She hooks her thumbs in the waistband, swallows again and inhales shakily, and then does that same lush, lust-inducing, heart-stopping shimmy again and the black lace joins denim and underwire on the floor of her bedroom. I didn't think I could feel desire any more painfully, but at the sight of Nadia, naked, for me, I do. I groan, rub my palm over my mouth.

"God…*damn*, Nadia."

She seems to melt at my words. "You look at me like…like I'm the most beautiful thing there is."

"Because you are."

She steps forward, closer. Eyes on mine. "I hope—I hope you see the same thing in my eyes."

"I do," I whisper. Waiting. "Sure do."

She frees the button of my fly, tugs down the zipper. I press out of the opening, straining against the imprisoning fabric of my underwear. She lowers both jean and underwear in the same motion, shoving them down to my knees so I can toe them off and kick them aside.

My turn to take over. I step into her, and the bed hits her knees, and she sits, abruptly. I follow her, and wrap one arm around her, under her, cradling her head as I lay her down on the bed. One knee on the mattress beside her, and then she scoots toward the head end and I go with her.

"I want to make you feel good," I murmur.

"I already do feel good," she says. Her hand slides from my shoulders down my back, to my butt, where she pauses to spend a while.

"Not what I meant."

Her eyes glitter in the darkness; the only light is from the full moon through her window, and it bathes her with liquid silver light. "Take me there," she whispers. "Show me what you mean."

And so, I do.

Thirty-Four

A Song Of Us

AT FIRST, NATHAN JUST KISSES ME. BUT THIS KISS IS meant to distract, to incite, and god, does he do that. His tongue whips my need into a frenzy, and I realize how very, very long it's been since I felt anything good, anything this good, and I only dare approach that thought before just flinging myself headlong into simply *feeling*.

His mouth on mine

His body heavy and big and hard above me. His skin under my hands—I touch his broad shoulders and thick arms, his wide back and taut butt, his hairy, strong thighs. The hard weight of his sex is there, hanging and bobbing between us, but I wait. I want to hold him, stroke him, feel him, but I wait. Not quite yet.

He braces himself on an elbow and a hip, beside me more than above me, now, and his kiss seems to slow, as if settling in for the long haul. His hand caresses my breasts, his touch deft and greedy and soft.

My breasts feel heavy, taut, my nipples sensitive, and his touch draws fire in my belly. And then, the fire in my belly hardens and descends lower, to the delicacy of my folds, the apex of my thighs. His touch moves there. I'm trembling, afraid and eager at once, and I'm grateful he takes his time. He doesn't just plunge right to touching, but explores me first, and never stops kissing me. He touches along my thigh, over the top, everywhere. And when he does touch me at last, it's gentle and slow and light, tracing the seam. I hold on to his neck and his shoulder, angled toward him, one thigh flung aside, opening myself to his touch. I'm greedy for it even as I tremble in anticipation, more than a little fear, as a million what-ifs crash through my mind.

Doubts are silenced when he slips a fingertip through me, and then finds the nexus of my need. I moan, and then he follows the trail of my whimpers and lifted hips to discover what moves me, what draws groans from me. He learns me, becomes a student of me. I can feel him memorizing my whimpers, absorbing the knowledge of where and how his touch makes me shift under him, lift, pulse against him.

Despite my desire, my nerves dull the sharpness, and it takes a while. He is patient, pulling back when I need it, racing ahead when I'm ready. He knows my rhythms, somehow. His touch circles, and I'm on the edge. Teetering, unable to topple over.

I'm becoming frustrated. I *want* to.

He slides a finger into me, gathers wetness. Pauses, there, just like that. "Nadia."

I open my eyes. "Hmm?"

"Relax."

"I can't. I'm so worked up, and I'm getting frustrated because I can't just…"

He finishes my sentence for me with a kiss. "Just breathe." I take a breath. "Now look at me."

I meet his eyes. "This is us. You and me. Nothing else. No pressure. All the time in the world. If you're not ready, it's okay."

I shake my head, and reach for him. "I *want* to. But I think I'm just so keyed up from anticipation, that I just…"

His eyes go heavy-lidded as I gather him in my hand, for the first time. So much of him, more than I was even expecting, and given the overall size of the man, I was expecting a lot. So hard, but the flesh sheathing his hardness is silken, almost delicate, thin, with a tracery of veins. I look where I'm touching, and watch as my hand slides down his length, and he groans.

"Go easy," he murmurs. "Been…a while. Might not take as long as I'd like if you do that too much."

I smile, and keep doing what I want: touching him. "Your rule, remember? No explanations, no apologies." Both hands, then, because the size of him requires two. "We have all the time in the world. If it's quick the first time, then we'll have all night and all day and as long as we want."

His fingers resume their exploration. "You're so soft, so wet."

"Nathan?" I swallow hard, tasting a bold question on my lips. "Could you...would you use your mouth? On me? Please?"

He smiles, a heated, pleased smirk. "I *love* that you asked."

"I was kinda scared to. But I need it. If you want to, that is. If you don't, that's fine, I just—"

Once again, his mouth on mine silences me. "I want to."

I close my eyes as his mouth teases downward, kissing my shoulder, my breastbone, licking my nipples to hard peaks, and then kissing downward, over my belly, and I involuntarily draw my stomach in as he touches his lips to my seam. A flick of his tongue, and I gasp, and my feet draw up to the backs of my thighs and my knees angle away, and his tongue delves into me, and then drags luxuriously upward, and then there's an explosion of sensations all at once, as his tongue and lips find the nadir of my desire and makes my sex sing, and his fingers are everywhere, in me and twisting my nipples and cupping my breast and it's all so much all at once and I'm crying out, maybe just flat-out crying, sobbing or screaming I don't even know or care, I'm just a far-flung spark of a mind hurtling through the space of an endless climax.

He keeps me there and refuses to relent, and the waveform of climax dips to a brief trough of between, and then he does something else and I'm riding another crest and his hair is soft on my belly and his beard scratchy against my inner thighs and his tongue is clever and his fingers strong and gentle. I can't take any more, I'll explode if there's more—but there is, and I fling through that as well, and each time I think I've reached as far as I can go, that I've come as hard as I can come, he finds a way to push me past that edge.

And then I just need him.

I pull at his jaw, tug at his beard, and he ascends my body, wiping his lips with his hands. A million thoughts rifle through my head, but none of them make it past my lips. I roll away from him, to my bedside drawer. Pull out a new, unopened box, hand it to him.

"I guessed at the size," I whisper. "I thought I was being generous, but I think they may even be too small."

"Nah. They're perfect." He opens the box, pulls one out.

This feels so weird, so foreign. In my previous life, we never used these. And again, that's as close to that line of thought as I can go. Just that this, too, is uniquely ours, Nathan's and mine.

I watch him rip open the square foil packet, and my nerves flutter in my throat.

He sets the foil aside, and is about to roll it on; I take it from him. Use my hand on him for a moment, just touching. And then I sheathe him in latex, and there's a pause, him on his side, me on mine, facing each other, as we silently debate what's next: whose going on top?

He pulls me to him. Rolls to his back. Yes, this. Our first time should be like this. I look down at him as I straddle him, like our first kiss when I straddled him—I never told him, but that moment, when I sat on him and kissed him, I had a vision of this, us like this, and I knew then it would like this. And that's why I stopped, because I wasn't there yet.

I am, now.

I reach between my thighs and find him. Grasp him, touch him to me. Hesitate. His eyes rake my body, then fix on my eyes, and we're both shaking, trembling, panting, neither of us ready and knowing we never will be.

I sink onto him. My groan is involuntary, torn from me as he fills me and overfills me and tears fill my eyes, tears of wonder and ecstasy and even a pinch of pain at the size of him that I'm so unused to, like nothing I've ever felt; I shy away from that thought at first, but then I embrace it. This is Nathan, and it's okay. It's okay that it's new and strange and different and that it's overwhelming.

He brushes a thumb under my eye, a smile on his lips, encouraging, loving. His hand rests on my waist, on my hip. Then he grips both hips and helps me settle more fully on him, and he's in me and I'm surrounding him enveloping him falling forward onto him and clinging to his neck and groaning, waiting for myself to get used to him.

He's stone still. Waiting. Shaking all over, stomach hard with tension.

Shaking with the need to move.

I'm wild with ecstatic glory, and he fills me and presses into me and scrapes against me such that I need only to move, to feel more, to fall higher. He isn't moving—he won't, I know it. He knows he's big, that if he moves too fast, too hard, he could hurt me, and so he cedes control to me, even as I know everything inside him is driving him to take me, to take his release. His hands caress me, all over.

Finally, I feel the need to move exploding inside me. I press my palms flat on his chest and lift up, and his eyes meet mine, and I don't look away as I begin to move. Lift up, pause, sink down. Gasp and moan on the downstroke, the filling thrust. A groan isn't enough, though. It's a song inside me, and the note I need to sing is loud, wild, enthralled, lost, gloried. So I lift up and sink down and let my voice go, give in to need, to nature, to what we are becoming together in this moment. He growls counterpoint to my long-drawn hoarse ragged cry, and the cry becomes a constant wail as I move faster, needing more, more. His big hard strong hands are not so gentle now and I relish the power in them as he grips my hips with rough dominance, tugging me downward, and the more I demand of him the more he gives me, and the tug of his hands becomes forceful and my bottom slaps against his thighs and there's only us, and his lips are against my ear as we move in orchestral unison.

"Nadia," he whispers, growls, grunts.

"Nathan, oh god, Nathan, Nathan."

I think deep in the darkest corner of my soul, my hesitation at allowing this moment with Nathan to come was that I'd forget, that my lips would utter a different name. But that's impossible. I am fully present, fully alive and fully aware of where I am, when I am, and whom I'm with.

Nathan.

I feel him reaching climax, and our rhythm goes slow and gentle and delicate and purposeful, and I press up so I can look down at him, and my arms press against my breasts as if offering them to him and he takes the offering, his mouth loving on them, and then his eyes tell me he's there and his voice goes rough and it's him, now him in control, lifting me and bringing me down, pushing up, thrusting up as I drive down, and I watch him through it, watch his face lose whatever composure he had left as he fills me, as he detonates and I collapse forward on him, cradle his face to my breasts and let him pump wildly into me through the mad starburst of his orgasm, and there's more and more and more, until he slows to half thrusts and then to stillness.

I just lie on him, filled with him.

It feels like this was always us, always meant to be.

From the moment I saw him sitting on the porch of his cabin, reading, I think I knew.

My head on his shoulder, his hand on my butt.

"Be right back," he says, wiggling out from under me.

I watch him go, clean up, watch him return, and I move the covers back and get under them. Lift them up for him. Lift myself as he sidles in beside me, and I resume my place against his side, tucked into him, head on the pillow of his strong arm.

I feel him working up to something. "Don't say it," I whisper.

"Okay. But it's true."

"I know."

"Nathan?"

"Yeah."

"Thank you."

A wry laugh. "For what? I should be thanking you. I think you just changed my world."

I snort. "Who changed whose world is up for debate I think, because mine feels pretty damn well rocked." I lift up to look at his eyes. "Thank you for waiting. Thank you for being patient. Thank you for taking the time to…to know that you love me, before making love to me."

His arm tightens around me. "I do."

"I thought you were gonna say it for a second."

He chuckles. "I would. But for some reason, you told me not to."

"Because I want to say it first."

Another laugh. "Okay, honey."

"Honey?"

"No?"

"No, I like it. Just…seeing how it feels. And I like it. It's good."

"You're sweet as honey, so I figured it fits."

I laugh, patting his chest. "You're silly, you big sweet man."

We float together in a long glowing silence. Doze, maybe.

It emerges from me unbidden, abrupt, a raw whisper into the afterglow silence.

"I love you, Nathan."

His chest rises and falls, harsh. A ragged breath escapes him. I reach up and brush a droplet of overwhelmed emotion from his cheek.

"Sorry, I just—"

"Try that again," I interrupt. "This time, no apologizing."

A not-quite, almost laugh. Another heavy sigh, this one long, an attempt to control.

"Nathan." I brush my fingers over his cheek again, and again they come away damp. "Feel it. Don't control it. And most of all, let me see it."

He swallows hard—I hear it. "I never—" he pauses, clears his throat. "I never thought I'd hear that again. Or feel this way again."

My eyes begin to sting. "I know. Me either."

"I thought maybe I was…broken. Like I'd been wrecked beyond repair." He's breathing hard. "And then I met you, and…and you fixed me. One day a time." He clears his throat. "And so I guess, to hear you say that just…I dunno. It's a lot. Kinda overwhelming. Or, a lot overwhelming. I don't cry much, and it seems kinda silly to cry after something so amazing." Another sigh, another clearing of his throat. "I just never thought I'd hear that again."

I lean up on my elbow, wipe at his cheeks. Kiss them, one and the other. "Thank you for giving me this, Nathan."

He peers at me with a half-open eye, still embarrassed of his tears in the way men have. "Giving you what?"

"You. Fully, just…you. It's brave of you."

I touch my forehead to his. Kiss him. Just to taste him, the salt on his lips. But then something births in the kiss and becomes more.

I find him ready.

"Already?" I ask, surprised and pleased. It hasn't been very long.

He laughs, nods.

We fall into the new rhythms of us that feel old and perfect as well as new and wild. Sheathed, he rolls over me. This time it's him, his arms pillars beside my face, his body blocking out all the world, and I lift and lock my legs around him and accept him into me and this time it's long and slow, even as we find our mutual explosion together, in unison, he loves me slowly and deliberately and drives each thrust with his eyes devouring mine.

In the moment right after we've come together, still stroking gently into me, arms braced, panting, sweating, he dips his lips to mine. "I love you, Nadia."

His moment, not just a return of mine.

And the next time we lose ourselves in each other, later that night, instead of crying out or calling on god, we chant each other's name, a song of us.

Into the dawn we slumber and we delight in each other.

※

I wake up, and he's not in bed beside me. But I smell coffee, and I smile.

He comes back, naked, with two steaming mugs of coffee. "Six thirty," he says. "Figured it'd be nice to have it together in bed."

"How do you know it's six thirty?" I ask. "There are no clocks."

A shrug. "We've had coffee together at six thirty just about every day since we met. I just know, now."

"Oh."

We drink our coffee together, in what is now *our* cabin.

And I wonder, do we ever have to leave? Or can we just...stay here? Can this be life?

I look at Nathan, and I know the answer.

Epilogue

The Art To Living

"MR. CRENSHAW, PLEASE—IT'S FOR YOUR OWN good. You won't even feel a thing, I promise. Just sit still."

"How in th'damn-hell is you gonna know what's best for me, little girl? I ain't had a shot or a pill or a stitch in m'whole damn life, and I ain't about-ta start now."

"I know that you stepped on a rusty nail, barefoot, never saw anyone for it, and that you've never, by your own admission, had a tetanus shot."

"So? I'm fine."

I sigh. "You have a fever of a hundred and one—"

"I worked through worse fevers than this afore."

"You are having trouble swallowing, I can tell, and I'd render a guess that, even if you'd never admit to it, you're experiencing jaw pain. You have elevated blood pressure and heart rate. Soon, you'll be experiencing seizures, or at least, involuntary spasming or jerking." I speak over his protestations of so what.

"This is what we in the medical profession call lock-jaw, Mr. Crenshaw, and it is, if left untreated, *lethal.*"

That quiets him.

"And by lethal, I do not mean quickly or painlessly. I mean, you will experience spasms that could fracture your spine and leave you paralyzed. You could experience lasting brain damage. Your jaw, as the name suggests, will lock up and render you unable to eat, which means you'll survive on a feeding tube, for as long as you do survive, which won't be long. With a tetanus shot and antibiotics—meaning *allowing me to treat you*—we can mitigate quite a lot of this. There is no cure for tetanus, but we can manage the symptoms."

Mr. Crenshaw, clad in dirty denim overalls, bare chested under them, with a filthy, ragged red International Harvester hat on his graying, thinning hair, barefoot, burly and overweight and recalcitrant and tougher than shoe leather and roofing nails, lets out a gusty sigh. "Fine. I'd rather die than have a feedin' tube shoved down my throat, let alone be paralyzed and have to have my ornery old wife wipe my ass. But if it wasn't life or death, I wouldn't be here."

"You wouldn't be here at all if you'd gotten a tetanus shot. This is entirely preventable." I say this as I swab his arm, prepare the shot.

He snorts. "Don't you start in on the vaccination rant, lady. I done heard it all."

I snort back at him. "Well, next time you come in with an entirely preventable illness, I'll remind you of that."

"Took me an hour to get here," he says, grumbling. "And this is the closest place to my land where there's anything like doctors. And you ain't even a doctor."

"I'm a physician's assistant, which as far as your needs are concerned, they *are* the same thing." I stick the needle in while he's formulating his response, slowly plunging the medicine into him. "If someone were to come to you, would you get vaccinated?"

He sighs. "Mebbe. But what, you're gonna get in your little red city slicker car and drive out to my homestead? I'm fifteen minutes in a four-by-four to the closest electrical grid. Your little car wouldn't make it a quarter of the way to where I am, lady."

My car being the only one outside the clinic, it's obvious it's mine, I suppose. And for someone like Mr. Crenshaw, it says everything he thinks he needs to know about me.

"You'd be surprised the kinds of roads my little Audi can handle. It has world-class all-wheel drive, as a matter of fact."

A snort. "There's ruts your car could disappear into, and that's just my driveway."

"My husband has a pickup, if you must know." I smile at him. "I already have a handful of clients for whom I do house calls. Once a quarter, meaning every three months, I will come to where you live with antibiotics and vaccines and painkillers—a veritable pharmacy, as well as a whole medical kit. And I'll treat you, and your whole family."

"And charge a mint for it too, I bet."

"I've been known to accept value in trade." I widen my grin. "Eggs, sides of ham, quarters of beef, bushels of fruit and vegetables, things like that."

He blinks. "Bullshit."

"Not a word of it, Mr. Crenshaw. I'm taking night classes to get my MD, at which point the name on the outside of this facility, and on the side of my husband's truck, will be 'Nadia Fischer, MD, Country Medicine,' which means I'll be practicing medicine the way it has been done out in the country for... well, a long time."

"Why in th'damn-hell would you do a fool thing like that? Ain't gonna make no damn money that-a way."

"Because it's a need which I can fill, and I don't need money. I'm...independently wealthy, Mr. Crenshaw. I do this because I love practicing medicine. And more than that, I love being a doctor—even if I don't yet have the official MD after my name yet—to the kind, wonderful folks who live out here, where I live. I do it because I can, and because I want to. I accept value in trade because my clients may not have much by way of money, but they do have pride, and they make a living off the land. And while I may not need money, I *do* need to eat."

He eyes me, and I can see his estimation of me rising. "Guess mebbe when I assumed you was a stuck-up city girl, I was wrong."

"I guess maybe that's true." I pat his shoulder. "Now, sit tight. I need to calculate the dosage for your antibiotics, and get them mixed up. You are very lucky, Mr. Crenshaw, that your wife coerced you into coming out here when she did, or you would have been too far gone for me to be able to do you any good, and then you *would* be doomed to a lengthy and expensive stay in the hospital."

He eyes me. "Well, I guess I'd be the fool to not take you up on the offer of visits. My wife has been fighting the arthritis for a while now, and it ain't gettin' no better." His eyes go to my belly. "But, you be careful on those roads, missy. I may be a cranky old country boy with no education and less sense, but I know bouncin' around back roads like that ain't good for th'unborn."

I rub my belly, six months rounded. "Thank you for the concern, Mr. Crenshaw. I'll be careful."

Mr. Crenshaw writes out a misspelled I-O-U for several pounds of bacon and pork belly as value in trade for my services, along with a detailed map of how to get to his property.

The rest of the day is slow. The baby kicks, hard, and often, but I'm grateful for it, even when it hurts; being over forty, it's a minor miracle that I could conceive.

There's a young man skipping school who comes in for stitches after crashing his four-wheeler, and an elderly woman with a respiratory infection. There is, technically, a doctor in attendance—Dr. Oscar Gutiérrez—but he's older than dirt and prone to long naps in his office, and he's perfectly content to let me do things my way. And once I have my MD, which I'm trying to finish before I have the baby, he'll officially retire and the community practice will be mine.

At closing time, I rouse Dr. Gutiérrez and send him home, and then head home myself.

Nathan is in his workshop, of course; the cabin which was his home when he first arrived at this little lakeside paradise of ours has been transformed into his workshop. Better lighting, more ventilation, less furniture. The bedroom is now an office, the kitchen is still a kitchen with the same antique appliances, but the rest is open-plan, with a workbench and all his tools. He's a craftsman, now, an artisan. He has a little shop in town where he sells his handmade bookshelves, dining room sets, sideboards, end tables, desks, and anything else he takes his fancy to craft, as well as his now-trademark and locally famous wildlife carvings. Which are, I'm proud to say, garnering attention beyond our little community. There's even been talk of a few places in Atlanta giving him shelf-space.

Mainly, he just likes working with wood. Making things. Letting the wood tell him what it wants to be and helping it become that. He loves doing it, and he's amazing at it. And the beautiful fact is, he's doing well enough at it that he can almost entirely support us with his woodworking business.

Which, of course, we don't need. He had quite a bit saved from his career as a Hollywood set builder, as well as a few real estate investments a friend once convinced him to buy into which have panned out profitably. And I have the massive windfall Adrian left me, which I've invested so we'll be comfortable for the rest of our lives.

More importantly, we can focus on doing what we love, and raising this baby.

I stand in the open doorway of Nathan's workshop, watching him. He's oblivious, for the moment, absorbed in his latest piece. It's a rolltop desk, modeled after an antique one he found on the side of the road on one of my house calls a few weeks ago. He made one copy of the desk, and it sold so fast he's planning on making a few of them.

I love watching him work. His gaze is soft, sort of distant, as if he's listening to a voice only he can hear. No two pieces he makes are ever alike; each one receives a unique thumbprint of artistry, a touch here and here, which makes it beautifully and uniquely itself. This one, for example, is getting an elaborate system of cubbyholes and hidden drawers which the previous one lacked.

Eventually, he notices me, sets his tools down and hurries over to me. "How long have you been standing there, honey?"

I lift up on my toes to kiss him. "Oh, not long, just a minute or two." At that moment, the baby does a cartwheel, which I assume will be followed by an extensive program of calisthenics and gymnastics; I press Nathan's palm to my belly over the movement. "Here, feel."

His eyes close, and a smile of blissful joy lights up his features. He sinks to his knees, cupping my belly with both hands. "Hi, little one. You dancin' for mama?" He kisses my belly with delicacy and gentility, as if I'm made of porcelain and starlight.

"Doing the conga, more like," I say, with a wince and a chuckle. "Or maybe an Olympics floor routine." I hiss as he or she twists, rolls, and then seems to kick and punch me in at least four different places. "*Hoooo*, wow. It has to a boy, because he's as strong as his daddy."

He keeps his hands on my belly, feeling. "Nope. Girl. She's strong like her mama."

"Guess we'll find out in a couple months, won't we?" I feather my fingers in his hair as he holds my belly in his big hands, and sings some tune to him or her, under his breath so I can't quite make out what it is. "I have that ultrasound down at the clinic next week, don't forget."

"Won't miss it for the world."

Being over forty, I'm considered high risk, so I've gotten regular ultrasounds through my pregnancy. An unnecessary precaution, so far. The baby is huge, strong and healthy—so much so my doctor is planning on inducing me a couple weeks early, because the baby is looking to be big enough that if I were to go to term it'd be risky for me to try to deliver naturally, which is my plan.

He stands up. Grins at me. "I've got something for you."

I tilt my head. "You do? What is it?"

He strides across the workshop, brings over a wooden box. He made the box himself, obviously. It's oak, polished and stained to a glossy shine. There are no fasteners or metal, only cleverly joined wood. The top lifts off, and within is a bedding of straw, cradling a carving.

It's us, I can see, before I've even lifted the carving out. Carefully, I withdraw the carving from its bedding. I know what it is immediately: a representation of our wedding photo, framed and standing on our mantle: Him and me, on our dock, at sunset. He's wearing a tux, I'm in an ivory mermaid dress, my hair long and loose and curled into wide spirals. We're facing each other, hands joined at our waists, about to kiss. Our bodies form a heart, framing the setting sun.

Nathan has captured this photo in white pine, in extraordinary detail, in figurines some six inches tall. Individual fingers, even eyelashes, tendrils of hair, his beard, the planks of the dock under our feet. It's unpainted, just polished and stained, and the more beautiful for it.

My eyes start to sting. "Nathan, my god...it's incredible." I blink the happy tears away. "But...why? I mean, why today?"

He smiles, an amused smirk. "You mean you don't know?"

I frown. "It's not our anniversary, I know that. I may have pregnancy brain, but I know our anniversary."

"Not our wedding anniversary, no."

"It's not my birthday."

"Nope."

I huff. "Are you really going to make me guess?"

He tugs on a lock of my hair. "One more guess, sweetheart. Then I'll tell you."

"It's not the day we found out I was pregnant." I hold up a finger to forestall him telling me—I have an inkling, and it's forming into knowledge. "Oh! I know: the day we met."

"Bingo." He places the carving back into its nest

of straw, and leads me out onto the porch of his workshop. The same rocking chair sits there still. "I was sitting here, reading. You pulled up in that car, and I saw you for the first time. It was three years ago, today."

"We didn't actually meet the first day I arrived though, you know." I'm teasing him. "It was the next day."

"Don't split hairs with me, woman. Today is the three-year anniversary of the day I first brought you coffee. You were on your porch, and you were wrapped up in your favorite blanket."

"And seriously jonesing for coffee," I tease. "I fell in love with you for a lot of reasons, but I think that cup of coffee was the first step."

"I know the date, because I'm thankful more and more every day for having met you. You've changed my life in so many ways that I can't even begin to list them all. And I guess I just wanted to make you something to memorialize the day you first began saving my life."

I laugh, but it's a wet, choked sound. "Stop, Nathan. I already married you, you big sentimental goon. You don't have to try and make me more in love than I already am."

"But I'm going to. Or try, at least. Every day."

I cling to him, nuzzle kisses just under his beard. "Have you thought about names?"

"Yeah. It's a girl, and her name is Leanne Belle Fischer. B-E-L-L-E. Leanne for Lisa's middle name, and Belle in honor of Adrian."

"And if it's a boy?"

"It's not. But, if it is by some chance, Robert Thompson Fischer."

Robert, for Adrian's middle name, and Thompson, for Lisa's maiden name.

"Perfect." I look up at him. "You're really certain it's a girl?"

"I know it." He smiles down at me. "She'll have my hair and your eyes." He traces a finger over my temple. "You like the names? I've been thinking on 'em for a while."

"I love the names. They're exactly perfect." I try the girl name out loud. "Leanne Belle Fischer."

"We can talk about it more if you're not sure."

I shake my head. "No." I kiss his cheekbone, and then his lips. "Nathan, Nadia, and Leanne Fischer."

I took his name. He told me I could keep Bell if I wanted, but I knew part of moving on and starting a new life was taking his name when I said, "I do." I knew it's what he would have wanted. Adrian, I mean.

There are still days where I miss him. I wrap the blanket he bought me around my shoulders and I sit on the dock, and I remember him, and I let myself miss him, let myself think about him. Nathan recognizes it, and gives me that space. He has his days, too.

I see it in him, and I give him that space. He usually goes for a hike in the woods, spends the day out there by himself, and when he comes back his eyes are clear and his lips once more hold that smile that so lightens my heart.

Our wedding was just him, me, Tess, and a justice of the peace, out here on the dock. And by justice of the peace, I mean the county sheriff, with whom Nathan is good friends. We had a small ceremony, just the essentials of I love you and I vow and I do, and then we went into town and spent the evening with our adopted community, celebrating.

What else could you ask for?

Nothing, I think.

※

"One...two...three...four...five...six...seven...eight...nine...*ten!*" He's holding my hand, counting out the seconds as I push.

When he gets to ten, I gasp for breath and let myself cry a little, moan, whimper, and his hand is there, in mine, letting me squeeze it until I'm sure I'll break it.

He wipes sweat off my forehead, kisses me. "You're doing great, honey. Just a little more."

"I can see the crown!" the doctor says, from down between my legs. "All right, here comes a contraction. Ready, mama? Push!"

Nathan counts, and I push, teeth gritted and clenched, straining. Even through the epidural, the pressure is immense. Nathan gets to ten and I start to relax, catch my breath.

"Push again for me, mama! Don't stop now; you've almost got it! I've got the head; one more good push and you're done. Come on, push for me, now!"

I suck in my breath and set my teeth, tuck my chin to my chest and bear down as hard as I can, eyes clenched shut and sweat pouring down my face. Nathan is just holding my hand, now, squeezing back and watching.

Suddenly, abruptly, impossibly, the pressure is gone.

"Great job, mama!" The doctor, the resident OB/GYN rather than my personal doctor, is an older man, thin, lean, with small, nimble hands and a soothing presence. "Baby is out, I just have to…" A pause. "There we go."

I can't see, my eyes are blurry, and I'm dizzy from pushing, and I feel Nathan beside me, but he seems stunned. There's a gasp, a tiny sound. And then a cry, thin and wavering and very, very angry.

"Come here, dad," the doctor says. "Cut the cord for me, right there, between my fingers. Great. We'll just clip it off…"

And then I see him bringing me a naked messy bundle, howling with outrage and indignation and shock, and I have my baby in my arms. Wriggling, slimy, and so, so beautiful. Pink flesh, a thick crown of jet-black hair, just like Nathan's and mine.

"It's a girl," Nathan murmurs in my ear, choked up, awed. "It's Leanne."

I'm crying, but now I can see more clearly, and she's beautiful and perfect, ten fingers and ten toes and a loud voice. My gown has slipped, and she's against the bare skin of my chest, little tiny hands waving, pawing at me and the air. Nathan's huge finger touches her hand, and for some reason the sight of his huge finger bigger than her whole hand just makes me sob.

"Mom, can dad hold her before we get her cleaned up?"

He crouches, and I extend the precious delicate bundle up to him, and he has never been so gentle as when he cradles her in his arms, and he stares down at her with tears in his eyes, a big strong manly man not afraid to cry with joy and being overwhelmed in a roomful of strangers.

I'm not done—I feel another contraction, and there's another flurry of activity as I deliver the after-birth and placenta, and the baby is being measured and weighed and tested and cleaned and I'm *so* exhausted—so thrilled, overwhelmed, joyful, grateful, but just bone tired. It was twelve hours of labor, getting to a dilation of six, and halfway effaced but not progressing past that for hours and hours, and then all of a sudden I was fully dilated and effaced and it was baby time.

And now, here comes the nurse with the cart, and our little baby burrito in that blue and pink and white blanket and the little beanie hat. She's warm, mewling quietly as the nurse settles her into my arms. Nathan watches as the nurse helps me get Leanne cradled in position, and her little mouth searches, and then she finds my nipple and latches on, and her suckling is strong, insistent.

"So beautiful," Nathan whispers, watching. "You did so good, honey. I'm so proud of you. She's beautiful. *You're* beautiful, and I'm amazed by how strong you are."

His hand is on my shoulder, and I reach up with my free hand, the baby cradled against my chest with the other. Hold his hand. "She looks like you," I say.

I'm a mother. A mommy. I'm overwhelmed, and so happy.

"Thank you," I whisper.

I'm not sure if I'm talking to God, or Adrian, or Nathan, or even to Leanne for making me a mommy, but I'm thankful.

The art to living is hard to learn, there's grief and loss and sorrow and pain, but there's also joy and fulfillment and meaning, and you can't have one without the other. The pain makes joy more potent, I think. It doesn't mean you seek the pain or want it or like it, but when you find the joy after the pain has healed, you understand more fully that the dawn of redemption only comes after the long night of sorrow has passed.

I found mine. The sorrow was long and the pain deep, so much that there were days I wasn't sure I'd find any more tomorrows, that I wasn't sure there'd be any more joy. But yet, here I am.

Full of joy, overflowing with hope for the future. Grateful for the now. It doesn't make the sorrow of loss hurt any less, but I know now that you can survive it. And maybe, if you can hold on a little longer, if you can try to trade hope for despair, you'll find something beyond the sorrow.

You won't forget.

There's no replacing those whom you've lost, those who have been taken too soon. But you can still live. And if they're anything like my dear, beloved, departed Adrian, they'd *want* you to live on, to find hope, to seek new meaning and new joy.

That, I believe, is the Art to Living.

THE END

A NOTE FROM JASINDA AND JACK

A few things, before you go.

First: no, neither of us are dying! Just forestalling any worries you may have about this being in some way autobiographical.

Second: if you've read anything else by us, you know music is an integral part of our process. Sometimes it features heavily in the story, sometimes it's just in the background, part of the writing process. This one is a bit unique, in that regard. There are songs in it, meant to provide a kind of soundtrack, but the music which inspired us and provided the melody and rhythm of our writing is a band of extraordinarily talented young people: The Hunts.

They don't know we're acknowledging them in this; we don't know them nor they us, except insofar as we love their music. We're not sponsored or sponsoring or affiliated or anything, we're just putting it out there that we listened to them A LOT as we wrote this story, and want more people to listen to and love their music.

Lastly: Thank you, thank you, thank you. We know this story is different for us. We know it's heavy at times. But, in this difficult and quicksilver era of our cultural history, we felt it appropriate to dig in and tell a story which moves us, which inspires us, which challenges us, and which might change us.

We hope you love this story, that it touches you and perhaps makes you cling more tightly to your loved ones. Hold them close, and tell them how much they mean to you. Love is all.

In the words of Lin Manuel-Miranda: "Love is love is love is love is love is love is love is love, cannot be killed or swept aside. Now fill the world with music, love, and pride." This story is our attempt to fill the world with music, love, and pride.

Also by
JASINDA WILDER

Visit me at my website: **www.jasindawilder.com**
Email me: **jasindawilder@gmail.com**

If you enjoyed this book, you can help others enjoy it as well by recommending it to friends and family, or by mentioning it in reading and discussion groups and online forums. You can also review it on the site from which you purchased it. But, whether you recommend it to anyone else or not, thank you *so much* for taking the time to read my book! Your support means the world to me!

My other titles:

Preacher's Son:
Unbound
Unleashed
Unbroken

Delilah's Diary:
A Sexy Journey
La Vita Sexy
A Sexy Surrender

Big Girls Do It:
Boxed Set
Married
On Christmas
Pregnant

Rock Stars Do It:
Harder
Dirty
Forever

From the world of *Big Girls* and *Rock Stars*:
Big Love Abroad

Biker Billionaire:
Wild Ride

The Falling Series:
Falling Into You
Falling Into Us
Falling Under
Falling Away
Falling For Colton

The Ever Trilogy:
Forever & Always
After Forever
Saving Forever

The world of *Wounded:*
Wounded
Captured

The world of *Stripped:*
Stripped
Trashed

The world of *Alpha:*
Alpha
Beta
Omega
Harris: Alpha One Security Book 1
Thresh: Alpha One Security Book 2
Duke Alpha One Security Book 3
Puck: Alpha One Security Book 4
Lear: Alpha One Security Book 5
Anselm: Alpha One Security Book 6

The Houri Legends:
Jack and Djinn
Djinn and Tonic

The Madame X Series:
Madame X
Exposed
Exiled

Dad Bod Contracting:
Hammered
Drilled
Nailed
Screwed

Fifty States of Love:
Pregnant in Pennsylvania
Cowboy in Colorado
Married in Michigan

Goode Girls
For a Goode Time Call...
Not So Goode
Goode to Be Bad
A Real Good Time
Goode Vibrations

Standalone titles:
Yours

Non-Fiction titles:
You Can Do It
You Can Do It: Strength
You Can Do It: Fasting

Jack Wilder Titles:
The Missionary

JJ Wilder Titles:
Ark

To be informed of new releases, special offers, and other Jasinda news, sign up for Jasinda's email newsletter.

Made in the USA
Las Vegas, NV
08 September 2021

29867739R00246